ck."

"I sa_____'re doing," Liliana said.

He gave another shrug, seemingly indifferent except she sensed undercurrents beneath. Dangerous ones.

"I'm here. I'm alive. Consider your obligation fulfilled."

"I'd like to make sure you're okay. Are you hungry?"

Some emotion finally cracked the stern lines of his face. A hint of a smile and glitter in eyes that had gone to slate gray. He took a long stride toward her, until bare inches separated them. Laying a hand at her waist, he bracketed her side with it, sending her insides quivering.

Jesse glanced down at Liliana, sensing the tremor in her body.

She was as aware of him as he was of her. At his touch, her gaze had gone wide, revealing eyes that were nearly black with desire. When she moistened her lips, the last of his restraint disappeared.

He bent his head, whispered against her lips. "I'm hungry, but not for food."

Praise For
SINS OF THE FLESH

"Caridad Piñeiro never disappoints, and her new series looks to be a winner in every possible way. No author is better at crafting novels which explore the paranormal than Caridad Piñeiro. *Sins of the Flesh* expertly intertwines suspense and passion to create a spellbinding story of the paranormal."

—SingleTitles.com

more...

Also by Caridad Piñeiro

Sins of the Flesh

STRONGER THAN SIN

CARIDAD PIÑEIRO

FOREVER

NEW YORK   BOSTON

Copyright © 2010 by Caridad Piñeiro Scordato
All rights reserved. Except as permitted under the U.S. Copyright Act of 1976, no part of this publication may be reproduced, distributed, or transmitted in any form or by any means, or stored in a database or retrieval system, without the prior written permission of the publisher.

Forever
Hachette Book Group
237 Park Avenue
New York, NY 10017
Visit our website at www.HachetteBookGroup.com.

Forever is an imprint of Grand Central Publishing.
The Forever name and logo is a trademark of Hachette Book Group, Inc.

Printed in the United States of America

First Printing: November 2010

10 9 8 7 6 5 4 3 2 1

ATTENTION CORPORATIONS AND ORGANIZATIONS:
MOST HACHETTE BOOK GROUP books are available at quantity discounts with bulk purchase for educational, business, or sales promotional use. For information, please call or write:

Special Markets Department, Hachette Book Group
237 Park Avenue, New York, NY 10017
Telephone: 1-800-222-6747 Fax: 1-800-477-5925

Stronger Than Sin is my twenty-fifth published novel and, because of that, very special because of how hard it is to hit that milestone. It takes a great deal of personal sacrifice on the part of a writer, but it also takes a lot of support from so many. I'm dedicating this novel to my husband, Bob, and my daughter, Samantha, who have been there for every joy and disappointment in my writing career. I'd also like to thank all the rest of my family who has been there for me, as well as my mom, who never got to see this dream come to fruition. I couldn't have done it without the many valuable lessons my mom gave me and that helped make this dream possible. Finally, to all my friends who have stood by and cheered me on and offered commiseration when things didn't work out quite as they should. My thanks to one and all who have helped make this milestone possible.

STRONGER
THAN SIN

PROLOGUE

Meadowlands, New Jersey
Mid-November 2008

Slant right on two," Jesse Bradford said, clapped his hands, and led his offense out of the huddle.

Squaring up behind the center, he watched as the other team's defense adjusted, linebackers, safeties, and linemen shifting positions in answer to his team's formation. Glancing back and forth, he realized he was going to have to call an audible if they were going to have any chance of breaking through the defense for the last few yards to the goal line.

He changed the play and barked out the new count. From the periphery of his eye, he noted his wide receivers responding, as well as his linemen. The defense swung into action, attempting to compensate for his team's actions.

With a final call, the center snapped the ball solidly into Jesse's hands. He took the two or three steps back and turned in the direction of the fullback coming up from behind him.

Faking a handoff, his fullback plowed ahead of him toward the left, further opening the hole at the line of scrimmage created by his tackles and guards. His wide receivers raced for the end zone, pulling the linebackers away from the line. Seeing his opportunity, Jesse tucked the football tight against him, whirled, and raced for the opening.

Feinting and dodging, he avoided the first hit at the line, lowered his head, and plowed forward. With his size and strength, he was a match for most on the field, so the first solid contact slowed him but didn't take him down.

The goal line was now just a few feet away, and with a powerful surge, Jesse launched himself toward the end zone.

He was in midair when the lineman clipped his thigh.

Pain seared up his leg and into his gut as he spun around from the force of the hit.

When he landed, the impact drove the air from his lungs. Light-headed from both the lack of oxygen and the agony in his leg, he saw the lights from the stadium dance around in his vision before a shadow fell across him.

Black and white. A zebra raising its hands to signal a touchdown while more shadows came to dance in his vision. Blue and gold this time. Marauder colors.

Suddenly a voice came from directly beside him. "Jesse, man. Are you okay?"

One of his teammates in the blue and gold, only Jesse couldn't move. Couldn't think of anything but the blinding agony in his lower body.

The zebra started tweeting more loudly and waving his hands erratically. The ground beneath Jesse shook from the thundering vibrations of people racing his way.

Sucking in a breath through gritted teeth, Jesse finally focused, but when he did, the pain became overwhelming, filling his every conscious moment.

Another shadow fell across his face. Jesse turned

his head and from beyond his faceguard saw one of the trainers.

"Don't move, Jesse," the trainer said, but as he touched his hand to Jesse's thigh, pain exploded through Jesse's brain, greater than any he had ever experienced. Blinding him with its intensity until darkness overwhelmed his vision, pulling him to blessed unconsciousness.

CHAPTER 1

Jersey Shore
Two years later

Liliana Carrera stared over Carmen's shoulder at the images her friend had brought up on the monitor.

She studied the cells, smiling as she comprehended the results of the blood test. "This is good, right?"

Carmen looked up at her. "Really good. There's a noticeable reduction in the white blood cells, plus there are fewer signs of inflammation and an immuno-response."

All good, Liliana thought. It meant that the inhibitor complex they had been refining for the last several months was less toxic to Caterina's system. But less toxic wasn't necessarily enough. Liliana had to be sure the inhibitor was controlling the nonhuman genes implanted in Caterina's body by the rogue Wardwell Laboratories scientists.

"What about the gene replication? Any sign that it's slowing down?" Liliana asked.

Carmen moved away from the microscope to the end of her worktable, where assorted stacks of paper crowded the surface. "What did you notice during the physical?" Carmen questioned.

"There was some evidence of the gene expression in spots, but based on my gross examination, I would say that the patient's eye and skin tones had remained stable," Liliana replied.

Carmen tsked and shook her head. "Why, Dr. Carrera. You sound downright clinical," she chided.

She *had* sounded way too distant, Liliana realized. With a shrug, she explained. "I'm trying to keep emotion out of this, but it's hard, because I can't think of Cat as only a patient. She's my sister-in-law, and I care for her a great deal."

"And your brother loves Cat beyond words," Carmen added as she grabbed a sheath of papers and headed back to where Liliana was standing.

As Liliana waited, Carmen flipped through the reports and said, "Now you know why I like my quiet little lab. Dealing with live patients is just too damned hard."

Even though her friend lacked people skills, there was no denying Carmen was a dedicated physician. Her work in the pathology lab routinely saved others, and her assistance over the last several months in dealing with Caterina had been invaluable.

She placed her hand on Carmen's shoulder and gave an affectionate squeeze. "We wouldn't have gotten this far with Caterina if it wasn't for your help."

Carmen smiled and nodded, but her full, generous lips thinned into a tight line as she flipped to the last test analysis.

With a shake of her head, she said, "Your physical exam might not show the glowing skin caused by the genes, but we've only made a little progress in slowing down the replication."

Damn, Liliana thought, but she tried to keep positive. "Well, the good news is that our new inhibitor complex is taking less of a toll on her system—"

"And it's slowed the multiplication of the nonhuman genes somewhat," Carmen chimed in, trying to sound optimistic.

"We just have to keep on refining," Liliana said and patted her friend on the back.

"What do you want to try next?" Carmen asked, but Liliana's cell phone went off, and as Liliana checked the caller ID, she realized it was the hospital administrator.

She lifted her index finger, asking Carmen to wait for a moment, and answered.

"Dr. Carrera."

In brusque fashion, the administrator's assistant advised, "Dr. Hellman wishes to see you immediately."

"I'll be there in a few—"

"*Immediately,* Dr. Carrera. It's quite important," the assistant shot back before she abruptly ended the call.

Carmen had clearly overheard the exchange. "What bug is up his ass now?"

Liliana wished she knew. She only hoped it wasn't more blowback from her breakup with the hospital's chief of surgery. The rumors had been rampant after she ended their engagement and moved out on him, but she had kept silent about her reasons for the decision. To admit that she had been about to marry a man who liked using her as a punching bag and mentally abused her would not have instilled confidence about her ability to judge people's character.

"Don't know. I'll be back down later."

She hugged her friend and hurried through the twists and turns of the sprawling hospital grounds to the administrator's office. His assistant jerked her head of bottle blond hair in the direction of Hellman's door as soon as she saw Liliana. "Go right in. He's waiting for you."

Liliana knocked on the door and then entered at his command.

A stranger in a dark blue suit was seated before her boss, and as she walked in, he rose and faced her, hands crossed in front of him in a way that screamed cop or military. His short, neatly buzz-cut salt-and-pepper hair and tall, lean body completed the look.

Hellman stood, as well, and swept his arm in the direction of the man. "Dr. Carrera. This is—"

"Special Agent Hank Whittaker. FBI," he said, held out his hand, and smiled. It was a shark's smile, wide and toothy. No emotion showed in his flat gray eyes.

She shook his hand. A sandpaper grip was firm and dry against her palm.

Liliana wished she could say the same of her hands. Nervous sweat had erupted at the mention of his title. As she sat down, she wrung her hands, hoping he was not here about Caterina or her brother Mick. She hoped he was here about Edwards and Morales, the renegade Wardwell scientists who had kidnapped and genetically altered Caterina and were still on the loose.

"How can I help you, Special Agent?" she said while keeping a wary eye on the man.

"Four months ago your brother and Caterina Shaw were involved in an incident with Wardwell Labs."

If the murder of three people and kidnapping amounted to an "incident" in his brain, she wondered what he would consider to be a serious event.

With a hesitant nod, she confirmed his statement. "Wardwell illegally implanted a series of gene fragments in Caterina. She's currently under my care, but there's little I can say about her condition due to patient-physician confidentiality."

Her administrator coughed uneasily and said, "Dr. Carrera. Special Agent Whittaker—"

"Isn't interested in having you breach your fiduciary obligations. But the FBI *is* interested in your assistance with a similar patient."

Liliana inched up higher in her chair. "A similar patient? You've found the missing Wardwell patients?"

Whittaker shook his head. "Unfortunately not, although we believe we're close to determining where the Wardwell patients are being held captive. Luckily, another patient did manage to escape—Jesse Bradford. You may know him."

Liliana did know him, but as first impressions went, they had not been good. "I was in the ER one night. Gave him ten stitches after a local bar brawl," she said and swiped her index finger along her brow to demonstrate where she had worked on him. "A year later he came to the hospital for rehabilitation. After an injury, if I recall, but I wasn't involved with that." But she had heard the rumors about his rudeness and temper.

Whittaker inclined his head and examined her through slitted eyes. "Don't be so quick to judge, Dr. Carrera. After all, the man had just found out his multimillion-dollar career was over."

Having faced adversity more than once in her life, she was certain it was still possible to do so with class. And even if she mustered some compassion for the man, she was doubtful as to how his escape from the Wardwell scientists involved her.

"I'm a little confused, Special Agent. What does Jesse Bradford have to do with—"

"We want you to treat him and continue to work on ways to control the hybrid genes created by Wardwell. We understand you've made some progress with Ms. Shaw's condition," he stated with a confident hunch of his shoulders.

She turned her full attention to her administrator. "Is this patient presenting the same health issues as Ms. Shaw? If not, I'm not sure how I can assist."

"You and Dr. Rojas are familiar with the gene therapies and inhibitor complexes that Wardwell developed," Hellman replied, surprising her. She didn't realize he had taken such an interest in her day-to-day workload. Normally Hellman was oblivious to the routine things in the hospital.

"Plus Mr. Bradford's problem is bone-related. As an orthopedic surgery resident, that's your specialty," Hellman quickly added.

Shaking her head, Liliana faced the FBI agent. "What I can do is limited. I'm not an expert in genetic engineering or its complications."

"But you are apparently familiar with the problems created by the Wardwell gene therapies and how to control that damage," Dr. Hellman insisted.

Before she could answer, Whittaker jumped into the fray. "We need to know if Bradford's bone loss is continuing and the extent of the gene replication in his body. We may also need you to administer the inhibitor complexes and improve on them. I assume that this is similar to what you're doing with Ms. Shaw."

Liliana couldn't dispute those statements. "I do have

some familiarity with those processes, but again, it's limited. If Bradford isn't presenting the same symptoms as Ms. Shaw—"

"The FBI can help you assemble a team with more expertise in the genetic-engineering area, as well as skilled lab personnel. Since the FBI hopes to recover the other patients shortly, we'll provide the facilities and supplies, plus pay for your time and all expenses. Anything you do, however, will be need-to-know. No statements to the public or anyone other than your immediate team."

There was a tone in Whittaker's voice that had a note of finality, as if this was a done deal whether or not she agreed. Glancing at her administrator from the corner of her eye, she noted that he was nodding emphatically, as if he, too, understood there could be no argument. His next words confirmed it.

"I will make arrangements with the hospital board so that you may revise your schedule here at the hospital. Dr. Rojas, as well, if you wish for her to assist."

Heat blossomed deep in her center because she was once again being controlled by others. By men. Rising slowly from the chair, she inclined her head in Hellman's direction and then faced Special Agent Whittaker.

In measured tones, she said, "I appreciate the confidence you have in my abilities and know that this could also be a wonderful opportunity to assist Ms. Shaw."

Whittaker narrowed his eyes as he examined her. "I hear a 'but' there, Dr. Carrera."

There was definitely a big but there, and it wasn't just feeling as if she had no control over what she was expected to do. She didn't like the vibe coming from Whittaker. She suspected he was demanding and didn't tolerate differing opinions. But on top of that, she wasn't quite sure he was trustworthy. Because of her suspicions she said, "I have to think about this offer, Agent Whittaker."

Without waiting for their reply, she stormed from the office, determined to be the mistress of her own fate.

Jesse paced the short width of the cage in which he had been imprisoned for almost nine months now. It was where Edwards and Morales had taken all their former patients when they had left their facilities at Wardwell Laboratories.

They had been caged like animals, since the two scientists no longer thought of them as humans. Or maybe they never had.

More than once Jesse had tried to escape but had never made it farther than the door to the warehouse holding the cages. A combination of Taser blasts and the powerful mind-altering drugs used to control the patients had kept him a prisoner. After the third attempt and an injection that had made his brain seem like grape jelly, Jesse had stopped trying to escape, focusing instead on surviving in the hopes that someone would set them free.

And now it seemed like that moment might be at hand.

Back and forth, back and forth he paced and went slowly mad as he waited for Morales to return. He didn't much care for the little man, but the scientist was the key to his freedom and to the safety of his little sister.

So Jesse continued to pace, his anger growing with every second that passed, until his rage was so alive that it became stronger than him.

Stronger than his will.

With a blood-curdling scream, he stalked to the back of his cage, where his captors had placed a heavy body bag, and began to punch it, his big fists pummeling the inanimate bag. In his brain it was Morales he was beating to a bloody pulp.

The first few punches stung his fists, and he reminded himself of the damage such pain meant. Every little injury produced bone, even in places where bone was not meant to be. So Jesse somehow mustered control over the animal within and measured the force of his blows, relying on the quantity of them to drain him of the violence created by the genes Wardwell had implanted in his body.

A fine layer of sweat covered him by the time he finished, and deep depressions showed in the bag. Glancing down at his hands, Jesse noted they were slightly reddened but undamaged. Of course, the almost imperceptible hardening of his skin across his fists had helped protect him from further hurt. Unlike the harmful repairs on other parts of his body.

Almost absentmindedly, he ran his hand over the dense hand-sized spot on his ribs—a byproduct of Morales's little games, the assorted Taser blasts, and the wildly proliferating genes. Genes he held responsible for his anger, as well, although the little voice in his head—his father's voice—chastised him for the lie.

He had been angry before the experiments Wardwell had decided to do illegally.

Angry at losing the one thing he loved almost more than anything else—football.

Angry about his father and the way he had cut Jesse off from his family, decrying Jesse's sinful ways.

As Jesse began pacing the narrow width of the cage once again, he considered that maybe his father had been right.

It had been the sin of greed that had started him on the road to ruin. All those millions thrown at him by an upstart pro football team had made him lose sight of who he was and what he stood for.

It had been the sin of pride that made him think he could do whatever he wanted because he was the best at what he did.

Sin had been stronger than him. Stronger than the values his family had instilled over the course of his life. It was the reason his father had cut off contact, warning Jesse not to return until he had changed his ways and embraced a good Christian life once again.

The rattle and groan of the warehouse door snared his attention.

Morales and his creepy little assistant Jack entered the building. As they stepped into their makeshift laboratory, an assortment of howls, grunts, and groans rose up from the other dozen or so captive patients in the cages scattered throughout the space.

Jesse tuned out those almost inhuman noises, stopped pacing, and grabbed hold of the bars of his cage. Rattling them, he called out to Morales, "You promised to let me go."

A promise that came with a huge price tag—his little sister's life.

Morales smiled, a tight shift of his lips accompanied by a startling glitter in his eyes. If ever there was a caricature of a mad scientist, Morales fit the bill, Jesse thought. Especially when you put him together with Jack, his sniveling and kleptomaniac assistant. Jack's lab jacket pocket was filled with shiny tools and pens he had collected in their facility.

Morales strolled over, as casually as if he was taking a walk in the park, Jack trailing behind him, his hand on the precious treasures in his pocket.

"Not yet, *mi amigo*. We have to make sure everything is in place before we can let you go," he said, held out his hand, and snapped his fingers. After he did so, he peered around Jesse to the body bag at the back of his cage.

"Good. I see you've been exercising. It's important that you stay fit."

As Jesse watched, Jack wheeled another heavy bag into the large open area in the center of the warehouse. Then Jack scurried over, bringing with him the cattle prod that Morales seemed to enjoy so well.

There was only one thing the scientist enjoyed even more—the control he possessed over his captives.

"When will I be able to go?" Jesse pressed, fearful that with each day that passed, his sister's illness would advance until the damage might be irreparable.

Morales raised the cattle prod. "When all is ready."

"When is that?" Adrenaline began to pump through his system at the sight of the prod, and he felt as if his body was vibrating from within.

Morales must have registered the change in him, since he smiled and motioned for Jack to open the door. But Morales made sure to keep the cattle prod ready and to stay beyond Jesse's reach.

After so many months, Jesse knew the routine. He stepped up to the other bag and began to pummel it. With each blow, he thought about the many months of his captivity. About his family and all that he had lost, each thought increasing the strength of his punches until Jesse pounded the heavy bag with such force that a seam on the side began to split. Another strike with his rock-hard fists opened the tear even further.

Morales egged him on. "That's it, Jesse. Destroy it," the scientist urged as he stood, the cattle prod in hand, just feet away from Jesse.

Jesse remembered the sting of that device. The deadened and hard piece of what had formerly been flesh along his rib cage had repeatedly experienced the bite of the prod. He had first suffered the sting of it many months earlier, when he had been punished for interfering as another patient had murdered Morales's colleague—Dr. Rudy Wells.

Wells had seen the error of his ways, and Jesse had hoped Wells would stop the experimentation and torture being visited on him and the other patients.

Now Wells was dead and Jesse was still a captive. No one had come to save him and the others trapped alongside him in the warehouse.

At Jesse's delay, Morales picked up the prod and stepped closer. "Destroy it."

Jesse needed no further instruction. He marched up to the heavy bag, encircled it in his muscled arms, and, imagining that it was his captor, squeezed the bag in his arms like a python constricting its prey. As the seams strained, he dug his fingers into the gaps and yanked, ripping the bag open and spewing its innards along the floor of the cage much like he wanted to do with Morales.

Releasing the mangled bits of bag, Jesse staggered back, breathing heavily.

As he glanced at the scientist, Morales inched away, clearly aware of Jesse's thoughts.

"If my sister gets hurt…" Jesse began but didn't finish.

He didn't need to for the men to understand they'd better not delay much longer.

CHAPTER 2

Whittaker tracked Mick Carrera through the lens of the binoculars as Mick ran along the boardwalk in the direction of Liliana's condo. He was surprised that an ex-mercenary like Carrera had become such a creature of habit. It made him and his sister easy marks.

"Follow them. Listen in and make sure we didn't make a mistake," Whittaker said to his second-in-command.

"You think she'll say something to him?" Howard asked, tugging the black knit ski cap lower on his head and slipping on a pair of sunglasses to hide his eyes.

"Dr. Carrera is smart. I'm not sure that she's buying into this completely. If she involves her brother—"

"We've got trouble," Howard said and, with a nod, left the SUV to trail Mick.

The late fall morning was warm, the air refreshing thanks to a westerly breeze blowing in from the ocean. The scent of leaf mold mingled with that of the sea and the dying remains of a rosebush sheltered from the cold by her condo building.

Liliana waited on the corner, watching as her brother approached.

As he came up to her, he smiled and gave her a big sweaty hug. He had already been running for miles.

"Ready?" he asked as he did every morning they jogged together.

"Ready," she answered and fell into pace beside him. Or rather, it was safer to say he slowed to her pace as they crossed Ocean Avenue and jogged onto the boardwalk.

They were silent for the first few blocks as she settled into the rhythm of the run, but as they ran through the derelict remains of the Asbury Park Casino, Liliana asked, "How is Caterina today?"

"Feeling good. Your new treatment seems to be working well," Mick replied in between breaths and then glanced back over his shoulder, as if searching for something, before returning his attention to her.

"That's nice to hear." And if she accepted Whittaker's offer, Liliana might be able to improve on the inhibitor even further and possibly find a way to stop what was happening in Caterina's body due to the illegally implanted genes.

So why was she still having such doubts about the wisdom of joining up with Whittaker?

"Can we stop for a second?" Mick said and pulled up, one hand pressed against his side before he immediately bent over as if in pain.

"Are you okay?" She laid a hand on his shoulder, concern for her brother overriding all other thoughts.

He stood up and grimaced, but as he did so, he watched someone pass by them out of the corner of his eye. "Just a stitch," he replied but didn't immediately begin to jog again. Instead, he delayed for another couple of minutes, walking in a small circle as if trying to walk out a cramp.

After, he surprised her by saying, "Let's go the other way for a change."

With a nod she followed as they reversed direction, heading southward, back toward Ocean Grove and Mick's home in Bradley Beach.

"What's up?" she asked, puzzled by her brother's sudden alteration of their months' old pattern.

"Why don't you tell me?" he asked, peeking over his shoulder.

"What do you mean?" For good measure she looked toward the ruins of the casino from where they had come, but she glimpsed nothing out of the ordinary.

"We were being tailed. One man. Well built. Possibly dangerous," he advised and then motioned for them to cross onto Main Avenue and off the boardwalk.

"We're too visible here," he explained as she shot him a puzzled look.

As they jogged up the central part of town, it was relatively quiet, devoid of the crowds the summer season would bring. For good measure, Mick peered behind him once more, and as they neared the coffee shop, he pointed to it and said, "Let's sit and talk."

Given Whittaker's "need-to-know" instructions, Liliana was hesitant about what to reveal to Mick, but she didn't argue. It would only raise more concerns with her ex–Army Ranger brother, who had clearly observed that something was out of the ordinary.

They ordered coffees and then sat down, the table one row in from the window, where Mick could safely see outside but it would be harder for someone else to discern them.

"I've been asked to work on a new project, but I think it may be a big mistake to do it," Liliana said as she shifted the cup of coffee back and forth between her hands on the surface of the table.

"You have to do what feels right here and here," her brother said and tapped spots above his heart and temple with his fingers.

"It feels as if... What if I told you that it would help Caterina?"

Mick glanced away, picked up his cup, and took a long sip, obviously hesitant at her revelation. When long moments passed, she prompted him again with, "Well? What would you think?"

Mick fixed his gaze on her, his features intense. "I can't tell you what to do."

"That's a first," she teased, trying to dispel some of the gloom she sensed hanging over her older brother.

It worked. A hesitant smile came to his lips, but only briefly. "I have a vested interest, but the bottom line is— you have to do what you think is best for you."

Mick's answer was not unexpected. In his entire life, her brother had been selfless, always putting family, friends, and country ahead of himself. He had even been willing to sacrifice his life for both her and Caterina months earlier when a mercenary hired by Wardwell had tried to kill them all.

It was the realization of that selflessness that made Liliana's decision a no-brainer.

"Don't worry about me, Mick," she said. A second passed and a big black SUV cruised past on the street, its presence surprisingly menacing.

Mick nodded but reached out and laid his hand over hers. "You know you can count on me to help with anything. *Anything,* right?"

"Right," she confirmed, but she knew she wouldn't call her brother. He'd already had too much upset in recent months.

It was time for her to take care of things. And that included finding out why Whittaker was having her followed.

"This Bradford deal may be a mistake, Raymond," Morales said as he stood before Edwards in their secondary lab facility. He enjoyed the annoyance that flared to life in Edwards's gaze at his use of his first name. The superior Dr. Edwards considered himself above such familiarities, which only increased Morales's pleasure at goading him.

Edwards leaned back in his chair and ran a long, thin finger across his lips as he considered his partner's statement. "I know Bradford is one of your favorites—"

"He's unstable. The genes create rage he's barely able to control," he said.

Edwards laughed, the sound a rough cackle of disbelief. "Seriously? Seems to me he's quite capable of control, and given the incentive—"

"What if he finds out about his sister? That she's not really ill?" Morales asked, truly unhappy about losing his star patient. There was just something about Bradford's anger that he enjoyed, possibly even more than his possession of the former celebrity.

Or maybe it was just that—his possession of the jock. For too long he had suffered at the mercy of such muscle-bound idiots. Having Bradford as his plaything seemed like just compensation for all those years of misery, only his partner clearly didn't think so.

"Bradford has no contact with his family. That distance only makes it easier for us to carry out this ruse. Plus, Bradford is the most stable of all the patients. More reason he should be the sacrificial lamb," Edwards advised.

Morales wondered how much separation there could be if Bradford was willing to forfeit himself to help his sister, but as he met his partner's steely-eyed gaze, he realized his say would have no impact. The plans had already been put into motion by Edwards and the new associates he had brought into their venture.

"Whatever you say, Raymond," he replied.

"Don't screw this up, Morales," Edwards warned.

"Of course not, Raymond," he answered and hurried out, smiling as Edwards's annoyed gaze bored into his back.

Home, and yet still a prison, Jesse thought a week later.

Located on Ocean Avenue directly across from the beach, his home was an immense Wedgewood blue colonial with a large wraparound porch that opened into a gazebo on one end. Welcoming windows trimmed in white all along the front provided vistas of the beach and sea. Balconies on a second floor also allowed him to enjoy the multimillion-dollar view.

All around the home were inviting lawns and gardens, winter-dormant now, but he could picture their summer glory.

Despite the home's welcome, he was still a captive, he thought as he walked around his Spring Lake residence, familiarizing himself with the things he had left behind nearly a year ago now.

The place had been kept up in his absence. Surfaces dusted. Plants watered. Lawns mowed. Not even an old piece of mail, newspaper, or magazine in sight to testify to his absence.

Everything was in place as it should be, which saddened him.

The trappings of his life had gone on without him, as if he had been an unnecessary part of their daily existence.

The expensive furnishings; the Game Day room with an assortment of monitors, oversized and overstuffed chairs; shelves filled with his assorted trophies and awards. All just useless accessories in a life that had lost its purpose, Jesse thought, and within him came a dangerous spark of anger. Sucking in a deep breath, he willed away the desire to smash the cabinets and the worthless items within that had cost him so much.

His family.

His freedom.

His humanity, he thought, staring down at his hands and the thick, armorlike skin now covering his knuckles. Rubbing at the similar patch on his ribs, he wondered how long it would be before the rest of him became as dead and hardened.

But the pain in the center of his chest told him there was still something human left. Something that he might be able to salvage with the bargain he had struck with the scientists and Whittaker, their new partner: his cooperation in exchange for help in controlling the bone disease that was threatening his sister's life. Or at least that they *said* was hurting her, not that he trusted them. But if what they said was true, he couldn't allow his doubt to jeopardize his sister Jackie's health.

The doorbell rang, pulling him from the playroom and back out into the lavishly appointed living area.

Weird, he thought. Whittaker had at least two men positioned on the grounds to ensure Jesse followed their rules. He hadn't expected any of them to be ringing the bell if they needed to enter.

Throwing open the door, he was surprised to find a petite young woman there, looking rather prim and proper in a sedate navy suit but impossibly high heels. Fuck-me heels, he thought, thinking them out of sync with the rest of her businesslike attire.

Her irritated sigh dragged his attention back up to her face. A very attractive face, although he had to revise his estimate of her age. Maybe thirty, he guessed. Her petite stature was responsible for that initial appearance of youth.

"Jesse Bradford," she stated, nervously swinging the black bag she held in her hands. A doctor's bag. As he examined her features more carefully, he realized there was something familiar about her.

"Do we know each other?" he asked, narrowing his gaze.

She released her death grip on the bag and pointed to his left eyebrow. "Patched you up after a bar brawl while I was on call in the ER."

He rubbed at the barely noticeable scar and nodded. "Thought you looked familiar. Whittaker sent you."

She dipped her head to confirm his statement. "I'm here to do an initial exam so we can decide how to treat you."

He stepped aside to let her enter, but as he did so, he looked around outside.

Stationed at the far end of the large wraparound porch was one of Whittaker's men. He was dressed casually and sitting in a chair reading a paper, despite the chill in the air. A wire ran from one ear down to what he assumed was a radio. The man had been there all morning. Jesse had been warned that someone would be in close range at all times and that any and all communications would be monitored. Protection against his telling anyone the truth about Whittaker's operation.

Not that he would.

Without some kind of miracle from Whittaker's medical team, his sister Jackie's illness—supposedly a more severe form of his own—might not be cured. Plus, Whittaker had threatened to kill Jackie if Jesse attempted to speak to her or failed to cooperate with them.

Which made him wonder about the young doctor who had just walked into his home. How had she become a part of the illegal activities? Or maybe she didn't know the truth about the group?

He shut the door and walked to the living room where she stood, once again gripping the little black bag as she waited.

"Nice digs," she said, perusing the large open space and windows that faced the ocean. Then, "Who's he?" she asked and motioned to the man on the porch, visible through a far window.

"FBI," Jesse lied, unsure of just what she knew. "They said they would keep an eye on me 24/7 until they were able to track down Edwards and Morales."

Her full lips tightened with displeasure at the mention of the names of the fugitive scientists.

"Do you know them? The Wardwell guys?" he asked.

"My new sister-in-law was one of their patients," Liliana replied, omitting her own kidnapping by the two criminals. With what she knew of Jesse Bradford, he wouldn't much care about anything that didn't involve him, so her story would matter little.

Jesse tucked his hands into the back pockets of his jeans. It made the T-shirt he wore ride up, exposing a line of lean muscle and sandy blond hair that matched the color on his head, although those shaggy locks had sun-kissed streaks of a lighter shade. She dragged her gaze back up to his face—a very handsome one—and found him considering her with his blue-eyed gaze.

"Why don't you sit down so we can get started," she said and motioned to the sofa.

He plopped down onto the overstuffed cushions, his long legs spread-eagled before him.

She sidestepped one muscled thigh, perched on the edge of the low, espresso-colored wood coffee table, placed her bag beside her and opened it. She was removing her stethoscope and blood-pressure apparatus when he asked, "Is that how you got this gig? Your sister-in-law?"

"Gig? As in, being your physician?" She slipped the stethoscope over her neck and juggled the blood-pressure cuff in her hand as she waited for his explanation.

He shrugged shoulders so broad that it looked like he still had on his football pads. "Well, you look a little young."

"Not that I should have to explain, but I'm thirty and was currently working on my orthopedic surgery specialty."

"Was? As in, you're not now?" he pressed, mimicking her earlier statement.

"Now I'm supposed to give you priority according to Special Agent Whittaker and my hospital administrator." She grabbed hold of the large hand he had resting on his thigh and pulled his arm toward her. As she did so, she eyed the roughness along his knuckles and back of his hand.

She ran her fingers along his skin gently, but he jerked his hand away, brought it close to his chest, and rubbed it.

"Football injury?" she asked.

That intense blue-eyed gaze, the same color as the ocean outside the windows, zeroed in on her again. "What did Whittaker tell you about me?"

"Not much. Actually, nothing that I didn't already know from the news reports," she admitted.

He dragged a hand through his shaggy blond hair and looked away. "And what would that be, Dr. . . . What was your name again?"

"Carrera. Dr. Carrera."

"So, Doctor. Tell me what you know," he said, the tone of his voice growing harsh.

"Award-winning college player. Top draft pick. MVP, I think. Hell-raiser. Playboy. Degenerative bone disease that put an end to your career," Liliana recited and watched his face harden with each word she uttered.

"Seems you already know all about me, Dr. Doctor—"

"Liliana," she corrected in annoyance.

"Liliana. How about we get this over with so you can go back to your hospital and forget about me," he said and stuck out his arm.

Liliana wasted no time in getting all his vital stats and drawing the blood samples she would need for Carmen to analyze. Much like Caterina's blood, Bradford's glowed as it was exposed to the light, but the phosphorescence was duller and not as prevalent as with her sister-in-law.

After she was done, she rose, expecting him to walk her to the door, but he just sat there, muscled arms spread across the back of the sofa. An icy chill in his gaze communicated more than any words could.

"I'll be back," she said and left the house.

Jesse watched her go, relieved by her absence. He'd had enough preaching from his father about the sins of his ways. He didn't need the prim little doctor reminding him about how he had managed to screw up his life.

As he had before, the heat of rage pooled within him, only this time, he let it grow until it needed physical release.

Surging from the sofa, he stalked through his house to the gym in one of the back rooms. Throwing himself onto one of the benches, he started pressing weights. One hundred pounds. Two hundred.

It wasn't enough. He racked the pin into the bottommost notch and pressed upward, jerking the weight up and down as if it was light as a feather.

With a loud final clang, he allowed the weights to drop back onto the stack. The noise reverberated throughout the house, and a moment later, the guard from out front came running into the room.

"Jesus Christ," the guard said and whipped out a gun from behind his back.

Jesse sucked in a breath and held it. Calmed himself enough to say, "I won't hurt you, Bruno."

"You're like the fuckin' Hulk," the man said and motioned to him with the weapon.

Jesse's gaze was snared by his image in the floor-to-ceiling mirrors along one full wall of the room. His clothes were drenched in sweat from his exertions, and the muscles on his arms and chest were pumped and more pronounced from the lifting. With his six foot four inches of height and the thickness of his body, he had always been on the large side for a quarterback. His captivity and the genes Wardwell had sneaked into his body had made him even bigger. Stronger.

He understood the man's fear, but Jesse would not jeopardize helping his sister. Understanding his ability to create bone was the first step in finding a cure. He was willing to remain a guinea pig even if the uncontrolled bone production could one day take his life.

"Go away. I'm just working out," he said and faced Whittaker's goon.

Bruno scurried from the room, clearly fearful even though he had been armed.

Jesse looked down at his hands once again. Ran his fingers across the thickening, and for a moment, his rough touch became that of the doctor.

Liliana, he thought, recalling the smoothness of her skin and the gentle contact. Imagining how it might feel to have a woman touch him like that once more—with gentleness.

With caring, he thought.

It had been forever since anyone had touched him with love.

Jesse dropped to his knees and buried his head in his hands and did another thing that hadn't happened in forever.

He prayed.

CHAPTER 3

As Carmen sat at her workstation in their new lab facility, Liliana handed her the tubes with the blood samples she had taken from Bradford.

"How was he?" Carmen asked, a bit of excitement in her voice. There had been no hesitation about joining the project when Liliana had asked her. Being a fan of the Marauders team and Bradford had just made it better.

"He was...annoyed," she said, lacking the right words to describe their new patient.

"What I meant was, 'Is Jesse really hot?'" Carmen said as she took the test tubes. She frowned after a quick visual exam and then passed them under one of the lights at her workstation. A barely perceptible glow radiated from the samples.

"Weird. I wonder if they used different fluorescent proteins to track the genes," Carmen said and labeled the tubes to begin processing Bradford's blood.

"I was surprised by the lack of phosphorescence, as well," Liliana offered.

Carmen rolled her stool about a foot away from her workstation and engaged a nearby black light. She waved Bradford's blood samples beneath the bulb, and this time the glow intensified, but barely. "Interesting," she said but then quickly backtracked to their earlier conversation.

"So is he hot?"

Crossing her fingers the way two people might be joined together, Liliana said, "I thought you and Ramon—"

"We've been dating, but just because you're on a diet—"

"Doesn't mean you can't look at dessert," she finished for her friend and laughed. Shaking her head, she tried to conjure up an image of Bradford.

Large came to mind. Very, very large, with ripped muscles and amazing blue eyes. Condemning blue eyes, she thought as she recalled the way he had glared at her as she walked to the door.

"He's handsome, I guess. Big. Exceptionally big," she advised her friend and held her hands out in a guesstimate of the width of his shoulders, then lifted one hand to mark his height.

"That's because you're so tiny," Carmen teased and inclined her head in the direction of Liliana's new office space. "Messenger brought a box for you."

"I better check it out. I'll be by later to see what you've got for me." She headed to her office, just shooting a quick glance at the other scientist, who had come onto the team courtesy of the FBI financing. Dr. Gary Charles was a top genetic engineer who had lost some funding for his research project. His participation on the team would allow him to continue his research at a local university.

In addition to Dr. Charles, two other technicians had come on board to help Carmen run the various tests and procedures necessary to evaluate what was happening with Bradford.

The rather intense, slightly disturbing Mr. Bradford, she thought, hurrying into her office.

Liliana wouldn't have thought it possible, but somehow the bankers box in the middle of her desk managed to look threatening. She approached it, reminding herself that any misgivings about Whittaker could not override all the good that could happen.

They might find a way to control the genes in Caterina's body and allow her to have a normal life.

Then there were all the other patients to be helped. Whittaker thought it was just a matter of time before the FBI recovered the other Wardwell experimentation victims, and if he was right, the patients would require treatment.

It was why she had become a doctor. To help others. So why did that suddenly seem so daunting a proposition?

Maybe because of Whittaker. His highhandedness rubbed her the wrong way, as did his possible surveillance of her.

Or maybe it was because there was something unnerving about Jesse Bradford. His size, for one. His propensity for violence, the other. Possibly add to that his disregard for women, she thought, recalling his antics off the field and how he had eyed her as she stood at his door.

Based on the heat in his gaze, his thoughts had likely not been about how good a doctor she was.

Dropping her medical bag on the spare chair in her office, she grabbed scissors, sliced open the tape sealing the box, pulled off the cover, and peered within.

Bradford's medical files, and other materials marked with Wardwell's distinctive logo. She wondered how the FBI had obtained them but remembered that her own brother Mick had managed to steal similar files from the Wardwell labs. The FBI must have swooped in to grab evidence once Wardwell had been shut down due to their unlawful experiments.

Pulling the papers and folders from the box, she placed them on her desktop and sat down to read, hoping to get a better idea of what she would have to deal with, both the man and the medical.

As she flipped through the information, she was surprised to find not only Bradford's medical history, but also psychological profiles and a background check Wardwell had run prior to accepting him into their program.

She set those aside, wanting to concentrate on his medical issues. It was never good to get personally involved with a patient, although she knew some of his life story already.

A degenerative bone disease had been discovered after Bradford had been injured during a game. She remembered the hit. Recalled how he had spun around in the air like a pinwheel before landing in a heap in the end zone.

Liliana had been watching the game with her family, Ramon and Carmen. They had all been celebrating the touchdown until they realized that Bradford was not getting up. Moments later a trainer had run out, but Bradford had not left the field on his own steam. Within a few days everyone had found out that his career had come to an unexpected end.

She leaned back and considered the comments in the file about the injury to his leg and the deterioration that had been detected. Weak areas in the uninjured leg, as well as in the long bones in his body and hips.

Bradford had been lucky in that respect, she thought as

she selected one of the X-rays and held it up to the light. Had that fateful hit been higher, on one of the bones in his pelvic girdle, Bradford might have been crippled or required replacement with an artificial hip.

Not that Bradford considered himself lucky, she suspected.

Over the course of the months that followed the injury, there had been much conjecture about whether steroids had played a role. She hadn't doubted that possibility, having been personally aware of his bar brawls and aggressiveness. Such hostility could have been due to 'roid rage.

But as she read through the files, she realized that all the tests Bradford had taken ruled out steroid use. And even with the various procedures and an assortment of theories about the reason for the degeneration, his doctors had not settled on any definitive diagnosis for the bone loss.

The only thing of which the assorted physicians had been certain was that Bradford could not resume his career.

A solid reason for his anger.

Football had been his life from an early age and had been prematurely ripped away from him.

Shifting the medical file to the side, she grabbed the first volume of the various Wardwell folders, wondering how Bradford had managed to become a patient there. The FDA had fairly stringent requirements before they gave patients the right to access investigational drugs and procedures that were not yet commercially available.

Because of her terminal illness, Caterina had been able to obtain permission for such compassionate use of the experimental Wardwell gene therapies. Bradford, on the other hand, would not have qualified. His illness, while severe enough to end his career, would not have stopped him from leading a relatively normal life.

Nothing in the preliminary Wardwell notes provided any rationale for Bradford's participation in the investigational treatments.

One thing was certain, she thought as she dug through reams and reams of notations, X-rays, and test results: Wardwell had produced the response Bradford had wanted. The therapy had helped repair the weak spots in his bones, but according to the files, the implanted genes had also produced episodes of rage.

Liliana had seen similar entries before.

Caterina's file had also mentioned uncontrolled periods of anger. In Caterina's case, the notations had proven to be false and intended to frame her sister-in-law for the murder of Dr. Rudy Wells. Wells had been about to blow the whistle on the illegal activities of his two Wardwell partners—Edwards and Morales.

Despite the lies behind those entries, she had personal knowledge of another Wardwell patient with real rage issues.

Robert Santiago, a cop killer sentenced to life in prison, had been suffering from an aggressive form of diabetes, making him perfect for Wardwell's experiments. Unfortunately, the implanted genes had magnified an already violent personality.

Santiago was long buried, but Whittaker had somehow produced blood and tissue samples from the convict. Caterina had agreed to allow her samples to be used, as well.

Liliana's first order of business would be to have

Carmen and the others in the lab identify similarities, if any, among all three samples. In particular, she wanted to know if Santiago and Bradford had anything in common.

She didn't deal with violence well. Between her experience with her fiancé and being kidnapped by Wardwell, her aversion to aggression had only intensified in recent months.

Of course, having the FBI only a shout away was a relief should Bradford's violent side emerge.

Or at least she hoped having Whittaker nearby was a good thing.

With one concern alleviated, she returned to reviewing the files, determined to find out as much as she could about Bradford's illness.

Jesse stood on the second-story balcony of his home, hands braced against the white vinyl railing. A strong ocean breeze blew westward, creating waves that the local surfers would be sure to take advantage of once the sun had risen just a hair more.

Right now, the sun was only a hint of rosy pink along the horizon. The damp morning chill still lingered, yanking goose bumps to his skin as he waited for dawn on his balcony. He wore only a T-shirt and fleece sweatpants, relishing the bite of the cold air on his skin after months of being trapped indoors.

Like a dog chasing a scent, he picked up his head and deeply breathed in the ocean-kissed air and closed his eyes. The sounds around him became more alive then. The pounding of the wind-whipped surf against the shore.

The crackle and crunch of the dune grasses, and, in the distance, the blare of a train horn.

To-o-ot, toot.

He listened more carefully, and there it was again. The *toot-toot* of a train coming into a station and the clang of the warning bells at a street-level crossing.

He was surprised he could still hear it with the wind blowing in this direction, but then again, the train line bisected many of the villages along the water. As the railroad crossed through town after town it left its mark, oftentimes separating the haves from the have-nots.

Jesse knew about being from the wrong side of the tracks. He had grown up just blocks from the train. Had heard its toot and clang for most of his life. His family still lived there in the modest colonial in which he had gone from boy to man to pariah.

Feeling the sudden urge to run, he turned away and stalked through the large French doors into his bedroom. Sitting on the edge of the rumpled bed, he put on socks and sneakers, grabbed a fleece Marauders sweatshirt, and pulled it over his head.

As he did so, he experienced stiffness in his arms and winced.

He had overdone it yesterday. A dangerous thing. He ran his hands over his biceps and squeezed. Tight and hard. Rock hard, only for him that had whole new meaning.

He had to be more careful to avoid anything that would scream "injury" to his body. That would only create a flood of bone-producing genes like those that had already created the dead patch along his ribs and toughened his knuckles and the backs of his hands.

So today's run would be more like a jog. That was, if he could convince the goon watching him to come along.

He grabbed a hat and sunglasses, dashed down the stairs and into the kitchen, where Whittaker's man had already made a pot of coffee and was sitting there, reading the paper. Something that he seemed to spend a lot of time doing.

"I need to go for a jog," he said and placed his hands on his hips.

Bruno glared at him over the rim of the coffee cup. Inclining his head, he said, "There's a treadmill in the gym."

Jesse dragged a hand through his hair, pulling long strands off his face as he released a frustrated sigh. "You don't get it. I've been cooped up for too long. I need to go out."

Without waiting for the other man, he turned and took a step. The sound of metal rasping against nylon alerted him to danger.

"No, *you* don't get it, Jack," Bruno warned.

Jesse stopped dead, but the animal within him erupted at the threat.

Whirling, he surged at the man with almost inhuman speed. Before his captor could react, Jesse had grabbed his weapon and locked his arm around the other man's neck. His grip was tight as a vise, and one fast snap would end the man's life.

But he wouldn't finish the move. Too much was at stake for him to allow his personal needs to override the greater good. With a forceful shake that lifted the man, upending the chair in which he had been sitting, Jesse explained.

"For starters, the name's not Jack. Second, I could

squash you like a bug whenever I want, but I won't because of my sister."

"She's dead meat," Bruno hissed between gritted teeth, and Jesse tightened his hold.

The man flailed his hands futilely, struggling for breath.

Jesse continued. "If you so much as say her name, I'll put a world of hurt on you." Reversing his grasp, he tossed the man to the floor.

His captor kneeled there, his face nearly blue, sucking in air with long rough breaths. When the man had finally regained some semblance of control, Jesse said, "*We're* going for a jog. You've got five minutes to change. Get it?"

Bruno nodded, rose, and hurried from the kitchen.

Jesse smiled, but he knew there would be hell to pay. Whittaker wouldn't like him manhandling his team, but Jesse had to know just how far he could push the bargain he had made. It was only by determining those boundaries that he could formulate a plan, because although he wanted to help Jackie, troubled thoughts swirled in his head about his situation.

How did Whittaker know about Jackie's disease, and what if despite his sacrifice it wouldn't help his sister? Could he even trust Whittaker not to kill both of them at some point?

Pushing those doubts away, he strolled to the kitchen counter and made himself a cup of coffee. Sweet and light, the rich, nutty taste was welcome after the bitter brews they had served in captivity.

By the time he had finished the mug, Bruno had returned wearing the kind of nylon jogging suit you saw on old ladies in Atlantic City and mobsters in Little Italy. Come to think of it, he had that kind of gangster look and sound, unlike Whittaker's other team member.

Bruno had tucked his gun into a holster beneath the nylon, and the weapon created a recognizable bulge in the fabric.

Tracking Jesse's gaze, Bruno said, "No funny stuff or I'll cap your ass."

Definitely ex-mob, Jesse thought, grabbing the hat and sunglasses he had brought down and slipping them on to hide his face. Very few people knew he lived there, but there was no sense taking the risk of being discovered.

He strode through his home and outside to the winding path down to the sidewalk, all the time making sure that his mobster friend was close behind. Once on the sidewalk, he crossed the street to the boardwalk along the ocean and began jogging at a leisurely pace, uncertain of the other man's physical state, although he appeared to be in fairly good shape.

He plodded onward, keeping the pace slow. Recalling other times that he'd run along the boardwalk and streets as part of his conditioning routine. Today he just did it for the sense of freedom it gave him, but as he pressed onward, nearing Lake Como and the end of Spring Lake, something else kept him running.

Picking up his pace through Belmar, he finally crossed back and started running westward, the wind pushing at his back as if to hurry him on. From behind him erupted the rough complaint of his companion.

"Slow down, asshole."

Slow down, my ass, he thought, the memory of running these streets calling to him.

How many times had he done it? he wondered. Through elementary school, high school, and breaks home from college. In those first years before success had changed him.

How many times had he run home? he thought, ignoring the louder shouts of Whittaker's man as the familiar *toot-toot* of the horn and clang of the signal bells drew him closer.

He was almost at the tracks when a large black Suburban came barreling out of one of the side streets, nearly knocking into him as it blocked his path.

The driver's-side door flew open and Whittaker jumped out, his face an emotionless mask.

"We had a deal, Bradford."

Jesse stopped and bent, dragged in a few long slow breaths before he finally said, "Just going for a run."

Whittaker glanced over his shoulder at the tracks and the homes beyond. Slowly he faced Jesse once again.

"You make contact, your sister is dead. You breathe a word about our deal, she's dead. Piss me off again—"

"And she's dead. I get it," he said just as his running companion finally caught up and stood panting beside Jesse.

"I'm sorry, boss," Bruno said, but Whittaker only jerked his head in the direction of the Suburban.

"Get in the car."

Jesse waited for what else Whittaker would say, but suddenly Whittaker yanked something from behind his back.

A Taser.

A millisecond later, the Taser's barbs bit sharply into his side a moment before the electricity knocked him to his knees.

His body jerked as Whittaker continued administering the shocks, but Jesse was aware enough to see the other man remove something else from his jacket pocket—a syringe.

"No," Jesse said and shook his head, trying to fight off the effects of the Taser in an effort to avoid the injection.

It was a hopeless battle.

Whittaker was on him in a heartbeat, jabbing the hypodermic into Jesse's arm and slamming home the plunger.

The drugs seared fire through his nervous system, short-circuiting the few nerve endings that had somehow managed to evade the Taser's bite.

"No...stop," Jesse mumbled as dark circles swirled around in his vision and his body jerked to the tune Whittaker played with the stun gun.

Weakened, he fell to the ground, the early winter sky a crisp blue beyond his fading vision. Hard hands grabbed him and tossed him into the back of the car like last night's garbage.

So close, he thought as he finally released himself to the oblivion of the injection.

CHAPTER 4

Liliana had spent the better part of the morning at the hospital, trying to fill in the hours until her team had more information about Bradford's blood samples and the latest version of the inhibitor complex they were using to stop the gene replication in Caterina. Afterward, she headed to the laboratory Whittaker had secured for them, which was only a few miles from Bradford's Spring Lake home and near the hospital.

As she sat at her desk, she sipped the *café con leche* she had picked up at her parents' restaurant after a short lunch break and reviewed the reports that Carmen had put together. Frustration settled in.

Unlike the wild glow in Caterina's blood caused by the implanted genes, Bradford's blood was not shining as brightly, and his genes were not multiplying as quickly. In addition, while the inhibitor complex they were using to control the replication of Caterina's genes produced lots of ruptured cells and other by-products, Bradford's blood did not contain such poisons.

Discouraged, Liliana leaned back in her chair, placed her elbows on the arms, and steepled her hands in front of her as she mentally reviewed all the data her team had gathered. So little, but then again, it had been only a day since she had met Bradford up close and personal.

Up close being something her friend Carmen would surely have liked, she thought. Then her friend could have confirmed for herself whether or not Bradford was as handsome in real life as he had been on the covers of the assorted tabloids that had tracked his off-field exploits.

As for Liliana, Bradford just wasn't her type. She didn't go for those shaggy-haired, stubble-faced surfer dudes, preferring her men a little more manscaped. But despite those thoughts, the recollection of the intensity in that ocean-blue gaze sped up her heartbeat.

Okay, so maybe Bradford was attractive, but so was her ex-fiancé, and look where that had gotten her. He had been the epitome of a *GQ* cover model, but hidden beneath that smooth, elegant exterior was ugliness and brutality.

Violence being a recurring theme in her life, apparently, Liliana thought.

A knock at the door pulled her attention away from her musings.

"Come in," she called out.

Whittaker walked in and paused in front of her desk. She motioned for him to take a seat, but he remained standing.

"I'd like to know why you have someone following me, Special Agent," she said.

No surprise registered on Whittaker's face. With a shrug, he said, "I needed to make sure you weren't being tracked by anyone else—like Edwards or Morales."

She peered at him, trying to determine if he was lying, but could not. Forcing away her continuing doubts, she asked, "We've been hard at work, but I have nothing to report to you, yet."

"I'm not here for a report. I need your assistance with Bradford. We've had an incident."

She crossed her arms and stared at Whittaker. Since he continued to stand, she was forced to raise her head to meet his much greater height. She suspected his actions were intended to remind her of who was in charge in this relationship. Not that she intended to be cowed by him.

"What kind of incident?"

"Bradford attacked one of my men. We had to medicate him to regain control."

"Medicate? Did you use a sedative?" she asked, carefully watching him for any hint of lying, but there was no telltale sign that she could see as he responded.

"Traditional means don't work with Bradford. We used a formula we discovered from an earlier investigation of the Wardwell labs."

"A formula? Are you referring to Wardwell's mind-control serum? The one packed with an assortment of illegal alkaloids—"

"We used what we had to in order to protect our man," he shot back, and this time she could see a revealing tic along his jaw. He shoved his hands in his pockets and jiggled some change there, another sure gesture that he was holding back.

"That's a dangerous formula, Special Agent. And I suppose that Bradford—"

"Is barely under control. We've had to restrain him to avoid any further problems, but I'm concerned about his current physical state. I'd like for you to evaluate him. Do whatever is necessary to restore his cooperative frame of mind."

Cooperative being relative, Liliana thought, recalling her earlier encounter with Bradford.

"I'll come by the house shortly. I just need to finish up some things," she said and gestured to the papers on her desk.

"I'd prefer if you went now, Dr. Carrera," he said, not that he was truly asking for her cooperation. The command in his tone made it clear that she was to do as he asked when he asked.

She arched a brow and raised her head to a defiant degree. "Do you believe Bradford poses a danger in his current condition, either to himself or others?"

The tic came again, more pronounced than before and twice as fast, to match the increased rhythm of the rattling change. The answer, when it came, was as quick.

"Yes."

With a nod, Liliana replied, "Just let me prepare my bag."

Even though she had been to Bradford's house already, seeing it still challenged her perception of him. This was a home for a family, not for a man with Bradford's party-boy persona.

Pulling into the driveway, she parked her service-able midsized sedan before the garage doors. Whittaker stopped his large black SUV beside it a moment later.

Liliana grabbed her medical bag and slipped from her car, joining Whittaker as he waited by the bumper of his vehicle. His hands were jammed into the pockets of his black suit, and the sharp ocean breeze flapped the edges of his jacket back and forth.

The wind whipped her hair around and sneaked in beneath the collar of the lightweight parka she wore, chilling her skin.

She walked past Whittaker to the side door and yanked it open. Beyond was a large mudroom, and she hurried into the kitchen with Whittaker falling into step behind her.

The man from the porch the day before sat at the kitchen table, reading a newspaper. He jumped up as soon as they entered, a nervous look on his face. He was in shirtsleeves, providing a view of his holster and the very large gun tucked beneath his arm.

"How come you're not watching Bradford?" Whittaker asked.

"He's been quiet for about an hour. I think he fell asleep," the man answered.

Liliana hoped Bradford was asleep and not unconscious, considering that they had pumped him full of a dangerous mix of sedatives and hallucinogens.

"Where is he?" she asked.

The man jerked his head in the direction of the door leading toward the back of the home. "In the gym."

Liliana rushed through the door and down the hall, past an entrance for an oversized trophy room, and to the end of the hall, where it opened into a state-of-the-art gym. One side of the gym featured an area of free space where the floor was covered with thick mats. Bradford was lying in the middle of the mats, his legs shackled together. Another series of shackles wrapped around his hips, securing his arms to his sides.

"Is this your idea of taking care of a witness?" she asked, anger making each word escalate in volume. She was about to dash to Bradford's side when Whittaker grabbed her arm.

"He was raising such a ruckus we couldn't move him to his bedroom. He might start up again when you approach, so be careful."

He released her, and with more caution, Liliana shifted toward Bradford. As soon as her foot touched the mat, Bradford's eyes snapped open, the blue blazing brightly, almost wildly. She had seen that kind of look before—when Mick had first brought Caterina home.

She set down her medical bag, raised her hands in a sign of surrender, and calmly said, "Don't be afraid. I'm here to help you."

Despite her words, he grew even more disturbed and fought against the restraints, the muscles of his arms bulging from the force of his exertions. His wrists were already red from irritation, and if he kept on fighting the restraints, he would soon rub them raw. Considering that in his current state he was little more than an animal—thanks to the drugs Whittaker had administered—she worried he would do major damage to himself if he kept on struggling.

So she picked up her bag but continued speaking to him gently as she slowly approached.

It was a good sign that his struggles didn't increase the closer she got.

When she was about a foot away, she dropped to her knees and touched a gentle hand to the middle of his chest. "I won't hurt you."

Bradford's gaze skipped from her to Whittaker and

then back. "Needed to see them," he said, his voice husky as if he had been screaming for some time.

Maybe he had, she thought and shot a condemning look at Whittaker. Bradford wasn't a criminal, although Whittaker seemed intent on treating him like one, which made no sense to her.

"See who?" she asked as she returned her attention to Bradford and stroked her hand across his chest.

"He's not making any sense," Whittaker said from behind her and neared, causing an immediate reaction in Bradford. He started to push with his feet, driving himself a few inches away.

"Easy, Jesse," she said, using his first name to try and reestablish the rapport she had shared with him just moments before.

"Hurt me," Jesse said, digging in his heels and propelling himself farther and farther away on the mats.

Liliana looked over her shoulder at Whittaker. "It might be better if you left."

Whittaker jammed his hands on his hips, and when he did, it revealed not one but two guns tucked into holsters beneath his arms, making her wonder about the reason for the overkill.

"He's dangerous," the special agent replied as if in answer to her unspoken query.

Liliana peered back at Bradford, who had managed to move the entire distance across the mat and now sat upright, tucked into the corner of the room. His knees were drawn up protectively, his hands shackled to his hips, and the last thing he looked was dangerous.

What he looked was partly psychotic, but mostly afraid, like a child facing a too-real nightmare.

"I can handle him. Give us a little time alone," she said and patiently waited for Whittaker to leave.

The special agent glowered, but she held her ground, and with a mumbled curse, he whirled and left the room.

She moved closer to Jesse, laid a sympathetic hand on his.

"I won't hurt you, Jesse," she repeated.

Bradford knocked his head against the wall in a repetitive motion and mumbled, "Hurt me. Shot me up."

"I won't let them do that again. Where does it hurt?" she asked, still soothing her hand along his arm in a comforting gesture.

He finally stopped smashing his head and his gaze drifted downward to his left side. "Tasered me."

She wondered what he had done to prompt such action, and he immediately repeated his first words.

"Needed to see them."

"See who?" she repeated.

"My family," Bradford shot back quickly. "I just needed to see my family."

Liliana imagined that the last thing Whittaker wanted was for Bradford to have contact with anyone not in the immediate loop. But Tasering Bradford and then shooting him up with hallucinogens seemed like an extreme reaction. She was going to have to speak to Whittaker about it, but for now, her primary concern was treating her patient.

"Would you lie down for me so I can check your side?"

With a few clumsy nods, Bradford shifted from the wall and moved awkwardly to try to comply with her request.

Liliana rose and took hold of his shackled arms to help

him. Beneath her hands his body was all hard muscle, but maybe too hard, she thought. As they maneuvered together to help him lie flat, his T-shirt rode up on one side, exposing the nasty wounds and reddened area where Jesse had been electrocuted.

She mumbled a curse beneath her breath, and to her surprise, Jesse offered up a small smile and teased, "Nice mouth, doc."

Her gaze connected with his, and his intense struggle to maintain control over the drugs Whittaker had administered was visible. Placing her hand on his chest once more, she urged him on. "Focus on me, Jesse. The drugs will wear off soon," she said reassuringly, although she had no idea just how long it would take for the powerful combination of mind-altering drugs to dissipate in his system.

"Trying, Doc," he said, and beneath her hand, the tension slowly ebbed from his body.

Understanding that his reactions might be under tenuous restraint, she forewarned him about what she planned to do. "I'm going to look at your side now. Get it cleaned up. It may sting . . . a lot."

The barest hint of another smile skipped across his lips as he said, "Promise not to cry."

His humor dragged a chuckle from her. Keeping her actions nonthreatening, she removed the needed materials from her medical bag and began, her tones restful as she explained each step she took.

He jumped at the first contact of the antiseptic against the angry-looking wounds but said nothing.

Carefully she cleaned the two nasty barb marks and then slathered on an antibiotic ointment before covering the area with a large bandage. As she smoothed the tape over the area, it was hard not to notice the sculpted muscles of his abdomen or the well-defined ones in his arms.

She ripped her gaze away and sat back on her heels, wiped shaky hands along her thighs. "It may take a few days for that to feel better. I'll be back tomorrow to check on you."

"Thanks," he said and shifted his fingers slightly, as if to shake her hand.

She took his hand in hers, cradled it as she said, "We're going to make you better. I promise that."

"Will you stay?" he asked, an expectant chord coloring his words.

"Stay?"

He nodded, the action a little more coordinated than before.

"Lonely," he said and closed his eyes while continuing to hold on to her hand, the gesture so innocent it reached deep within and awakened a confusing set of emotions.

Jesse Bradford was not turning out to be quite as she expected.

A heavy tread sounded behind her, shattering the peace of the moment.

Bradford jerked awake, but at her comforting squeeze of his hand, he remained calm.

She looked over her shoulder to find Whittaker there with the other agent who had been watching Bradford. "Do you think we could move him to his bedroom?" she asked.

Whittaker inclined his head to the side as the agent whispered something to him. With a nod, as if to confirm whatever the agent had said, he replied, "Only if Bradford can get there under his own steam. I won't risk my men again."

Liliana faced Jesse and with another gentle squeeze of his hand asked, "Do you think you can stand?"

He nodded and slowly sat up, not an easy task when he couldn't use his arms, but with his impressive physical strength, he made it seem almost easy. Once he was sitting, he maneuvered to his knees but wavered a bit at that point.

Liliana quickly supported him by placing her arm around his broad shoulders. She could barely reach around him he was so massive.

He murmured his thanks and then, with a surge of power, came to his feet, Liliana at his side, continuing to steady him.

Jesse fought a wave of dizziness, and the suddenly wild colors swirling around in his vision. It had been a long time since Wardwell had used the mind-control drugs on him, mainly because he had stopped fighting Morales in the hopes of finding a way to escape. Now the drugs wreaked havoc on his mind once again. He lost his balance but suddenly encountered Liliana's sympathetic weight at his side.

As he glanced down at her from nearly a foot more in height, she looked like a fierce angel with her dark hair and her eyes blazing with emotion. "I'm okay," he said and took a wobbly step toward the door, where Whittaker and his goon awaited them.

Even with the psychedelic vision from the hallucinogens, he detected the way both men reached for their weapons. Would they shoot? he wondered, although if they did, all their plans would go awry.

But so would his, he forced himself to remember as the animal instinct to escape rose up sharply. He tamped down that desire. He had to stay to help his sister. Whittaker and this odd little doctor were the key to that.

He took another unsteady step, and Liliana was immediately there, balancing him as he leaned on her. Together they took one step and then another until they were safely past Whittaker and on their way up to his bedroom.

The bed would be a welcome change from the hard mats in the gym.

In his bedroom, they shuffled over to the large king-sized bed, hips bumping as they moved.

Her hips were soft and wide. He could imagine holding them in his hands, curving them around to cup her deliciously formed ass as he drove into her.

"Fuck," he muttered beneath his breath as his erection roared to life with his uncontrolled imaginings.

She pulled away from him then and he plopped onto the bed, shaking his head to drive away the visions.

"Are you okay?" she asked with concern, and he reared away as she reached for him.

"Okay," he said, his eyes closed to avoid any further temptation from her proximity.

A second later, hard hands were pulling him up into the center of the bed. Whittaker and Bruno, he realized as he peered through half-closed eyes.

"Can you undo the shackles so I can tend to those abrasions?" she asked, but he immediately shouted, "No," at the same time as his captors.

"Not safe," he added and gazed at her, pleading for her to understand.

Maybe she did, because she didn't press further. Instead

she said, "I need to take some more blood samples. I'll only be a second."

With efficient movements she prepared a syringe and removed several vials of blood while sitting on the edge of the bed. After, she grabbed a tube of antibiotic ointment and, with her index finger, gently applied the salve all over the abraded spots on his ankles and wrists.

"That should help a little," she said and rose from the bed.

She hesitated, and her gaze was clouded with confusion, but with a nod of her head, almost as if she was answering some unspoken question, she said, "I'll be back tomorrow to see how you're doing."

She turned and walked to where Whittaker was standing by the door.

"If you want me to continue to help you, you won't treat him like an animal. And you won't use those mind-control drugs again. He's not a criminal."

Whittaker narrowed his eyes as he considered her, but he seemed to understand she was serious in her demand. With a curt bop of his head, he said, "We'll do our best, Dr. Carrera."

Carrera, Jesse thought. Like the race car, but the only sleek thing about the doctor had been the thick masses of her shoulder-length hair. The rest of her was more like a race track—all dangerous curves.

Not even the mind-controlling drugs could make him forget that, he thought with a smile as he relaxed his tenuous hold on reality and slipped away to more pleasant imaginings.

Liliana's gentle touch, growing bolder as it skimmed along his muscles. The deep cocoa of her eyes darkening with desire, and that soft husky voice saying his name with need.

His mind retrieved the feel of her rounded, womanly hips, and he pictured placing his hands on them. Urging her closer. Wrapping up that petite but curvy body in his embrace.

Jesse groaned with need as his body responded. He snapped open his eyes and glanced around, hoping that no one was observing.

The room was blessedly empty.

With a smile of relief, Jesse allowed his mind to wander back to thoughts of Liliana.

Gentle, caring, rebellious Liliana.

He had never met a woman quite like her. Maybe that was the reason she haunted his mind as he lay there. As his body refused to let go of thoughts of her close to him. Beneath him as all those womanly curves accepted his hardness. Welcomed the union of his body with hers.

He groaned again, the sound loud in the emptiness of his room.

An emptiness that had been a part of his life for far too long, he acknowledged, although...

With Liliana beside him, that bleakness had lessened a bit. Surprising, considering she was a virtual stranger.

For now.

As Jesse awkwardly rolled over onto his stomach, willing away his unwanted erection, he was certain of one thing.

He didn't want Liliana to stay a stranger.

CHAPTER 5

So how's this new gig going?" Ramon asked as he captured one of the tacos on the plate Liliana's mother had brought to the table just minutes earlier.

"Not much is happening yet," Liliana replied. Although she had provided her family some initial information, she could not reveal any more to her cousin because of Whittaker's "need-to-know" directive.

When Ramon glanced at Carmen, as if expecting her to provide a different answer, Carmen only echoed Liliana's earlier statement, which clearly displeased Ramon.

"I get that you can't talk about it. Just remember that if you need anything, I'm always here," he said as he finally brought the taco to his mouth and took a big bite.

Liliana nodded, feeling slightly guilty about keeping anything from him. Ramon had spent so much time in her house while they were growing up that he was like a brother. She had no doubt she could count on him. With his being the police chief in one of the nearby towns, that support could come in handy.

When he zeroed in on a second taco, she slapped his hand playfully. "Wait your turn, *primo*."

He smiled and waved at the plate. "After you, ladies,

but make it quick. I have to be back at the stationhouse in about forty minutes."

Liliana's mother returned to the table, this time with an assortment of drinks for them. "Can I get you anything else?" she asked.

Liliana glanced around the restaurant. It was late in the afternoon. Too late for lunch and too early for dinner, which meant there was only a couple in the far corner. "Why don't you join us, *mami?*"

Her mother smiled and shook her head. "I'd love to, *mi'ja*, but I've got to make sure your father finishes making the tortillas for tonight's dinner rush."

Dropping a kiss on Liliana's cheek, her mother waddled away, painfully favoring one leg. For over a year Liliana had been trying to convince her to go for a knee replacement, but her mother insisted that money was too scarce for the operation.

Having to move out of the condo with her fiancé and into a new place had unfortunately eaten up some of the money Liliana had been setting aside to help pay for the procedure.

Ramon must have noticed the focus of her attention, since he smothered her hand with his comforting touch. In low tones he said, "Don't worry, *chica*. She's going to be fine."

"Seriously, Lil. Your *mami* will agree to have the operation eventually. Don't let it wear you down," Carmen added, because her friend understood, maybe better than most, just how much Liliana hated to see anyone in pain.

Which brought back memories of Jesse Bradford.

He had been seriously hurting earlier that day thanks to Whittaker and his men. She couldn't understand how anyone would treat a witness like that—as if he was a prisoner. Which made her wonder what kinds of rules they had about handling detainees.

"Have you ever Tasered someone?" she asked her cousin.

He paused with a taco halfway to his mouth and then put it back down. With a shrug, he said, "On occasion. If I've got someone who's an emotionally disturbed person and I can't control them..."

"You stun-gun them—"

"Rather than shoot them or have one of my men injured. Yes. I know it sounds harsh, but it beats the alternatives," Ramon finished for her.

His explanation wasn't far from Whittaker's, and yet... There was something about what Jesse had said. That all he had wanted to do was see his family. She wondered how it had gone from that to requiring the use of a Taser.

"Something wrong, Lil?" Carmen prompted, picking up on her distress.

Unfortunately, her earlier negative vibes about Whittaker were only growing.

She shook her head and reached for one of the tacos before Ramon finished devouring them. As she brought it to her mouth, her gaze connected with her cousin's and she knew that he, too, had sensed her concern.

"If you need me for anything, you know you can count on me," he reiterated.

Liliana had no doubt about that. And because Mick and Caterina already had too much upset in their lives, Ramon would be her go-to-guy with any concerns. Like the ones she was having right now.

"Could you find out if anyone reported anything

unusual? Like someone being abducted in the area?" she asked. Beside her, Carmen sat up straighter, clearly surprised, although she remained silent.

Ramon's dark gaze settled on her face, inquisitive, but he seemed to understand there was a limit to how much she could tell him. So instead he said, "Any particular area?"

Liliana thought of Jesse's words about wanting to see his family. She wondered just how close he had gotten to them. "Lake Como. Belmar. That area."

"Will do," Ramon confirmed, and because all of them comprehended that further discussion was out of the question, they turned their attention to the meal Liliana's mother and father had made for them.

Carmen had prepped the blood from the day before for a more detailed analysis. As with the earlier samples, there was a decided difference in the rate of replication in the gene fragments that had been introduced into Bradford from those in Caterina's system.

Liliana sat beside Carmen at her workstation, reviewing what little they knew so far. *Little* being the operative word. They still had yet to discover an explanation for what the x-rays and her gross examination of Bradford's body had shown.

"So you say his body was hard, as in—"

"Rigid. Like nothing I've felt before. Granted, his muscles were more developed than most I've encountered—"

"Hence the expression 'rock hard,' " Carmen reminded.

Liliana thought back to the roughness on the tops of Bradford's hands and the dense feel of his arms beneath her palms. Was her imagination running away from her? Was it possible the patches on his hands were nothing other than the calluses of someone who used their hands often? And that those ripped muscles were just more defined than any she had ever felt before?

Unlikely, given that she regularly examined athletes in her line of work. And how would someone get calluses on the *back* of his hands?

"If I get a skin sample later, would you have time to analyze it?"

Carmen nodded. "Sure. In the meantime, I'll keep on working on the blood samples you've brought. There's something funky about them, but I can't put my finger on it yet."

Liliana shot a glance at her watch. Barely nine in the morning. She had planned on returning to Bradford's home to see how he had passed the night, but first she wanted to speak to his family to develop a medical history that might assist with their investigations.

"I have some running around to do but may be back in time for lunch. Do you want to grab a bite together?"

A light flush of pink blossomed across Carmen's cheeks. "Actually, I have a date to go eat lunch with Ramon."

Based on the blush, Liliana suspected there was more going on than just lunch but was glad for her friend, as well as for her cousin. They would be good together.

"Then maybe I'll see you later," she said and headed to her office.

At her desk, she logged on to the hospital network to review Bradford's earlier hospital files to get more information, since the Wardwell files had lacked certain details. As was standard procedure, the hospital records for Jesse's earlier visit had all of Bradford's personal information, including whom to contact in the event of an emergency.

His family lived nearby, just a few miles away on the other side of the tracks, which would make it easy for her to pay a visit. The one problem with that was Whittaker's instruction that all information about this project be confidential and that Jesse's recovery be kept secret.

It would make it harder to speak with his family, but she had to do it if they were going to figure out what might be causing Jesse's bone problems and how to deal with whatever Wardwell had done to him.

She picked up the phone and dialed the number, and a woman answered.

"Mrs. Bradford?" she asked, and the woman confirmed it, a dull, almost tired cadence to her voice.

"I'm calling about your son."

"You've found Jesse. Sweet Lord, you've found Jesse," she said excitedly and with such hope that it almost hurt Liliana to dash that expectation.

"I'm sorry, but that's not why I'm calling," she said, wishing she could tell his mother the truth.

The earlier excitement fled, replaced by disappointment. "Oh, I'm sorry. It's just that...I keep on praying Jesse will come home."

He almost did, she thought, recalling the punishment he had received because of his desire to see his family. Trying to comfort the other woman, she said, "I'm sure Jesse would if he could. When he's found..."

Liliana stopped and sucked in a deep breath, hating

the lies she was spewing, even if they were necessary. When she had regained control, she continued. "I'm with a team dealing with another of the Wardwell patients—Caterina Shaw. We're gathering medical histories of all the patients participating in the experiments so that we'll be ready to treat them when they're found. I was hoping you could spare some time to meet with me about Jesse's condition."

"Anything I can do to help, I will. When would you like to chat?"

It would take her only about fifteen minutes to get to the Bradford family home. It wasn't far from the lab or from Jesse's home in Spring Lake, making her wonder if that's why he had bought the large colonial along the oceanfront. If that home had been intended not just for him, but for the family he seemed to care so much about—something else she hadn't expected from what she knew of him from the tabloids.

"Will ten be too soon?" she asked.

"No, not at all," the woman replied and rattled off her address. The same one in the hospital file.

"See you then," Liliana confirmed and hung up.

She turned her attention back to the remaining Wardwell papers on Jesse and continued adding notes to those she had previously gotten from the other volumes. Nothing in them, however, gave her a clue as to how Jesse had gotten in their program or whether Edwards or Morales had discovered the reason for Jesse's unexplained bone loss.

Odd, but then again, Morales and Edwards, the ones responsible for the illegal experimentation, had clearly not been interested in helping their patients.

At least, not at the end.

But Liliana was committed to helping Caterina and Jesse or any of the other patients that the FBI might soon find.

Tucking her spiral-bound journal into her purse, she grabbed her keys and left the office for her meeting with the Bradfords.

The Bradford family home was a small ranch house on a postage-stamp-sized yard west of the railroad tracks. It looked like it had been recently renovated and landscaped, as did many of the nearby homes on the narrow street. Many of the houses and cars along the road boasted Mauraders flags and emblems. A tribute to their hometown hero, Liliana guessed.

Overall, the working-class homes on the block were in much better condition than those on the surrounding streets.

She parked her car in front of the home and walked up the curving cement walkway. She gave the doorbell a quick push and heard it resonate within. Barely a few seconds passed before the door opened.

A tall, lean woman stood there, her sandy blond hair streaked with white. Her cornflower blue eyes—eyes so much like Jesse's—intently traveled over Liliana's face as the woman waited behind the protection of a storm door.

"Mrs. Bradford?" she asked and, at the woman's nod, identified herself. "I'm Dr. Carrera. I spoke with you earlier."

"Mary Bradford. Please come in." She opened the door and held out her hand to invite Liliana in. As Liliana entered, she noticed the careful arrangement of photos along the top of an old upright piano. There wasn't a single picture of Jesse, although the young woman in the photos bore a strong resemblance to him.

A cough alerted her to the presence of someone else in the room.

A man sat on the sofa in the space. He rose and gave a polite dip of his head as he said, "My wife tells me you want to talk about Jesse."

She held out her hand and said, "I assume you're Jesse's dad. I'm Dr. Carrera. Liliana, if you'd prefer."

The man didn't shake her hand. Instead he motioned her to a nearby chair and sat back down as his wife joined them. She hovered nearby, nervously wringing her hands until her husband said, "Mary, please sit down."

The "please" in the sentence did nothing to eliminate the command in the words, making Liliana wonder about Jesse's father.

He sat across from her, body militarily straight. The strong line of his jaw and nose much like Jesse's, although Jesse seemed to favor his mother more.

Jesse's father had on worn, but clean and precisely pressed, dark slacks with a starched white shirt that was open at the neck. The pants were shiny from the iron, and the tip of one collar was slightly threadbare.

His hands rested on his knees. Large hands bearing the nicks and scars of a man who used them to earn a living. What, then, was he doing at home during the day?

"I'm sorry to take you away from work—"

"I'm retired now. Spend my days puttering around the house," he said and gripped his knees with his hands as if uncomfortable with that statement. Maybe because he seemed too young to be retired. Late fifties at best, Liliana thought and began the discussion once more.

"As I mentioned to Mary, I'm dealing with another Wardwell patient and would like to talk to you about Jesse's medical condition."

"No condition, Dr. Carrera. It was God's punishment for my son's sinful ways."

"Sinful ways?" she asked, curious about what he meant.

"Drinking. Whoring. Forgetting the values we instilled in him at home," Mr. Bradford replied sharply and drummed the fingers of one hand against his knee.

His wife reached out and stopped the angry motion, her touch gentling. "Jesse's not a bad boy, John. He just lost his way."

Liliana recalled the brawls, different daily girlfriends, and assorted gossip about Jesse in the supermarket magazines. As she glanced back at his parents, she noted the ornate crucifix on a far wall of the room beside a needle-pointed Lord's Prayer with an Irish flag stitched beneath. If they were as zealous as they seemed, she could understand their reluctance to condone Jesse's actions.

"I'm not here to judge Jesse—"

"God has already judged my son," his father intoned, his voice rising as if he was getting ready to launch into a sermon.

Liliana fought back unexpected emotions as a mix of pity and anger awoke within her. Mustering patience, a trait she possessed in very short supply, she said, "Did anyone in your family ever have any signs of a bone- or joint-related disease? Arthritis? Osteoporosis? Anything like that?"

"Nothing. It's why Jesse's disease was so odd," Mary quickly replied.

As John drew in a long breath, apparently prepping for a tirade once again, Mary patted his hand and said, "Why don't you go out back, John. Liliana and I don't want to waste your time."

With a grunt and a resigned sigh, Jesse's dad popped up off the sofa and stalked out of the room.

After he was gone, Mary twined her fingers together and said, "No one in the family has any history of problems. The Bradfords are sturdy stock. So is my family."

"What about Jesse's sister?" Liliana asked, pulling her journal from her purse to jot down some notes.

"Jackie is healthy as an ox. Athletic like her brother." Mary rose from the sofa, walked over to the upright, and grabbed a frame from its surface. She returned and handed it to Liliana.

"She's going to school thanks to Jesse. He's paid for it, and he set up a scholarship there so others could go to college…" Her voice trailed off for a moment and then she gestured to the photo and said, "That's Jackie playing soccer."

Jesse's sister radiated strength and health in the action shot of her kicking a ball, but then again, Jesse had exhibited no symptoms until many years after graduating college.

Liliana handed the photo back to Mary and resumed her questioning. "Has Jackie had any tests to confirm whether she's suffering any kind of bone loss? Did either she or Jesse have any unusual illnesses?"

"No tests other than routine physicals. And both my children were quite healthy, although I had a couple of miscarriages between them. I was blessed to be able to carry Jackie to term, the doctors said." Mary stroked her hand lovingly across the surface of the photo, almost as if it was her daughter standing before her.

Making a note of that in her journal, Liliana asked, "Any reasons for the miscarriages?"

"It was just God's way. But it wasn't easy for me or for Jesse. Especially with the baby before Jackie. I had to lay up in bed for nearly two months, and I still lost the baby," Mary said, and her hands fidgeted against the edge of the frame.

Liliana hated to see her discomfiture, so she rose and sat on the edge of the coffee table in front of the sofa. Placed a consoling hand on the other woman's to quiet the anxious motion. "Why was it so hard for Jesse?"

Mary hunched her shoulders and looked away, but her eyes were wet with tears. "Jesse was six and an active boy. But he seemed to sense there was something wrong from the very beginning. He became more withdrawn as soon as he found out I was pregnant. From the moment I had to take bed rest, he was at my side, keeping me company."

She patted Mary's hand. "He was a good boy for you, then."

"Always," his mother replied with vehemence and met Liliana's gaze. "He never gave us any trouble until..."

Until he started playing pro ball and everything changed, Liliana thought. Sin had been stronger than the values with which he had been raised.

Liliana didn't want to stir up any more painful memories. Rising from the coffee table, she said, "If you can think of anything else—anything—please call me." She took a card from a pocket in her journal and handed it to her.

"I will, only ... Do you think you could do me a favor?" Mary asked, her voice suddenly soft and timid in contrast to her earlier outburst.

"Sure," Liliana said.

With a nod, she left the room and then came back holding a large black garbage bag that clanked loudly as she carried it along.

"When you find Jesse, could you make sure he gets this?" She handed it to Liliana.

It was heavier than Liliana had thought and filled with hard, oddly shaped objects. As she opened the top to peer within, she realized it was packed with trophies and awards.

Jesse's accomplishments being tossed out like yesterday's rubbish.

"I'll make sure your son gets his things if we find him," she said, her voice tight with the emotions she suppressed. She carefully carried the bag, not wanting to damage the contents.

Anger rose up as she left the Bradford home. While there was a lot about Jesse's past of which she did not approve, nothing she knew about Jesse so far warranted the kind of harsh judgment his father dispensed. If anything, there was more to Jesse than she had expected, but still so much she did not know about him.

Her one hope for later was that she would be able to deal with the consequences of presenting Jesse with his mother's package.

CHAPTER 6

The overload of sensations buffeting Jesse's mind had gradually subsided through the course of the night and morning. A long night where he had battled back the rage building at his center, stronger now because of the effects of the drugs. In the year of his captivity, he had discovered that finding something on which to focus helped contain that emotion. Whether it was physical exertion like his workouts or a person, place, or thing, concentrating on it restored balance.

Liliana had been the object of his attention through the night and morning. Her gentle touch against his body and the soothing tones of her voice. The feel of her against him, so feminine and enticing. He replayed scenes of her in his mind, over and over, using them to hold back the overwhelming sensations created by the drugs.

Desire. Sadness. Hope. Need, since the petite doctor seemed to have made an indelible impression on his psyche.

Jesse heard Liliana's voice again, stronger this time. Not in his brain, he realized.

She had returned, and within him came a surge of excitement.

He half opened his eyes and waited for her, listening to the lilt of her voice and noticing for the first time a slight singsong quality that came from another language. With her looks and name, he guessed she was either Latina or Italian.

The sound of her voice became stronger, more forceful as she came up the stairs. The clink and clank of something metallic seemed to keep pace with her steps. Then he heard Whittaker's voice, just as powerful and raised in outrage.

Jesse forced away the remaining cobwebs in his brain and finally eased his eyes open. As he turned toward the door, he experienced a twinge of pain. Stiffness had set into his muscles from the lack of mobility created by his restraints.

Liliana hurried in, carrying an oversized trash bag. The odd metallic noises on the stairs had come from something inside that bag.

Whittaker was hot on her heels, his body visibly vibrating with rage.

"What don't you get about 'need-to-know'?" he shouted at her and scraped a hand across his salt-and-pepper buzz cut.

Liliana dropped the bag on the ground with a noisy clatter and whirled to face Whittaker.

"What you don't get is that I need to find out what's going on with Jesse."

Jesse smiled at the sound of his name on her lips. So much nicer spilling from the real Liliana rather than his dream woman.

"You disobeyed my orders, Dr. Carrera. No one is supposed to know—"

"No one *does* know. I did not tell Jesse's family that he's been found."

His family. She had seen his family, he thought and tried to sit up, but couldn't with the ache in his muscles, the awkward way his hands were still bound to his hips and the manner in which the bed gave beneath him. He groaned at the distress in his body and squeezed his eyes shut against the pain.

A second later, her calming touch came against his chest, but it was immediately followed by Whittaker's curt, "When I give an order—"

"I am not your slave, Special Agent Whittaker. You hired me to find out what's going on with Jesse. To do so, I needed a more detailed medical history."

Spunk. She had spunk, and that brought a smile to his face.

"Are you awake, Jesse?" she asked, apparently noticing that grin.

"Yeah, I'm awake," he said, his voice rusty from the night of disuse.

"Please open your eyes for me."

He did, and a moment later, she was leaning over him, her gaze connecting with his. Inquisitive and intelligent, she straight away moved back and said, "Your little cocktail seems to have worn off, Special Agent. Could you please release him?"

Whittaker strode up to her and snagged her arm, yanking her around to face him. "Are you crazy? Release him?"

With cold fury glittering in her amazing brown eyes and her body trembling, Liliana glanced down at Whittaker's hand on her arm. "Release *me*, Special Agent. I'm not your prisoner. Come to think of it, neither is Jesse."

Whittaker hesitated a moment but then did as she asked while also questioning her. "Meaning?"

"He shouldn't be treated worse than a criminal," she shot back.

Score one for the doc, Jesse thought but wondered at her reaction to the agent's manhandling. Almost an overreaction.

"Please unchain Jesse so I can treat those abrasions and get the samples I need to continue our research."

With a frustrated sigh and a false smile on his face, Whittaker asked, "Is that a 'pretty please'?"

Liliana grasped her hands in front of her and shot him a patently bogus grin. "Pretty please."

Whittaker nodded. "I'll send Bruno up to undo the shackles, but he'll stand guard at the door in case you need him. Understand this: You disobey my orders again and this whole project gets scrapped."

Jesse bit back his reaction, but fear dug its ugly claws into his gut at the threat. He had committed to this farce because of his sister and his desire to find a cure for the disease that Whittaker had said would decimate her body.

He couldn't let the project be scrapped.

"I'll be good," he said and hated the almost childlike way it came across.

"I know you will, Jesse," Liliana replied. She sounded as if she was speaking to someone who was mentally challenged.

Though her tone ignited a small spark of irritation inside him, he strangled it by focusing on her face. An expressive face filled with a mix of emotions, although he didn't know her well enough to discern all of them. The one he could decipher was pity, and that was the last thing he wanted from the pretty doctor.

Bruno came into the room, swinging a ring of keys that jangled in time with his gait. He approached Jesse and searched for the key to the shackles. When he unlocked them, he said, "Next time it's a bullet, Bradford."

"Special Agent," Liliana complained, only Jesse was quick to intercede.

"Ignore him, Doc. He must be an Eagles fan."

The comment dragged a surprised chuckle from Liliana and even Bruno. "Lost a bundle on that last playoff game thanks to you," Bruno said and quickly undid the rest of the restraints.

Bruno left them and took up a spot right outside the door.

Jesse gingerly sat up, his bones and muscles protesting the movement. When he got vertical, the room started to spin wildly. He pressed fists to his head and leaned his elbows on his thighs to try and regain balance.

Liliana was immediately before him. "Take a slow breath and hold it."

He did as she instructed and then repeated the process until the room stabilized. Then he straightened and glanced at her, meeting her concerned gaze.

"Thanks."

"Do you think you can walk around?" Her eyes narrowed as she considered him, clearly doubtful.

"I think I can," he said, and with great care, and one hand on the mattress to steady himself, he slowly stood. As soon as he was on his feet, she slipped beneath his one arm, offering support as he took his first hesitant step and then a second.

Hips bumping yet again, reminding him of her assistance the other day and his dreams of the night before. Bringing that same unwanted reaction to her nearness, only today it was even worse. He was more aware of the feminine feel of her and her scent, alluring beneath the vanilla-almond smells of hand wash.

He breathed in that scent deeply, hungry for it after so much time alone.

"Are you okay?" she asked as she noted his exaggerated inhalations.

"Fine. I think I can do this by myself now." He shifted away from her. From her natural perfume and the enticement of her body.

With any other woman all he would have to do was flash an inviting smile and they'd be in bed, but he suspected Liliana wasn't like the other women he'd had in his life.

He faced her and raised his arms over his head, twined his fingers together, and pressed upward, attempting to alleviate the stiffness in his muscles and joints. Part of it was due to his inactivity, but he suspected a larger part of it was a by-product of the Wardwell genes in his body.

"You're looking better," she said as she returned to the bed and opened her medical bag.

"Feeling better," he confirmed and walked to her side, where he waited for her instruction.

"Would you mind sitting down again so I can tend to those abrasions, get some more blood and skin samples?"

He eased back down onto the edge of the bed and held out his arm. "You wouldn't be a vampire, would you? Because you sure seem to need a lot of blood."

An inviting flush erupted across her cheeks, and her

hand trembled against his skin while she wrapped the rubber hose around his bicep. "I'm sorry, Jesse. We're seeing a big difference between your blood and Caterina's. We need to figure out why."

"Caterina?" He tried to recall the other patients who had been with him. A face popped into memory. Beautiful and haunted.

"I remember her. She escaped the night Dr. Wells was killed."

Liliana paused with the needle right on his skin. "How do you know that?"

"I was fighting with another patient. A big hulking guy—"

"Rob Santiago. The police think he killed Dr. Wells," she said and finally pricked his skin to draw the blood.

Jesse nodded, remembering the immense man prone to incredible, nearly uncontrollable bouts of rage. The one difference between their fits of anger—Santiago seemed to get off on the violence.

"Wells came in when Morales had us fighting. Morales liked to do that—pit us against each other as if we were junkyard dogs," he said, recalling the little scientist's vicious fun.

Liliana finished drawing the blood, slipped an alcohol-soaked cotton ball on the wound, and urged his arm upward to apply pressure. Then she began tending to the abrasions on his ankles and wrists. "So you were fighting with Santiago?"

"At first the sparring was just to satisfy Morales. But when Wells came in that night, I knew something was up. Wells wanted to blow the whistle on the illegal project."

Liliana finished bandaging his ankles and sat down

beside him once again, her gaze trained on his face, obviously eager to hear more. "What happened then?"

Jesse shrugged and dropped his arm. The small pinprick was already healed over, another by-product of the Wardwell genes.

"I guess I shouldn't have worried about your scrapes," she said as she noticed and urged him to continue with a delicate flick of her hand.

"Morales commanded Santiago to kill Wells. I jumped in, trying to stop him. I figured if I could overpower Santiago and Wells got away..."

Only Wells hadn't escaped, but Caterina had, he thought.

"I'm sorry that it took so long for you to be free," she said and once again laid a hand on his arm. She was definitely the touchy-feely type, but he shrugged off the contact, unable to deal with the needs it roused.

"I got away. Maybe in time we'll find the others," he replied, repeating the lie as Whittaker had instructed. Although he had his doubts about the other man, for now he had to play by Whittaker's rules to safeguard his sister's life.

Liliana tucked the blood sample into her bag and removed another test tube and scalpel.

"What's that for?"

"A skin sample. I thought I noticed some hard patches on your hands."

He placed his hands before him and spread out his fingers, displaying an assortment of scars from playing football, as well as the denser, deadened flesh along his knuckles. "It's from the body bag," he explained.

"The body bag?"

With another nonchalant shrug, he met her gaze. "Ever since they stuck these genes in me, I get angry and need to vent. I punch the body bag, but..." He ran his fingers along the back of his other hand, the sensation deadened thanks to the thicker skin.

"May I?" she asked and, at his nod, grasped his big hand in hers. She ran the pads of her fingers along the same spots he had just seconds before.

Only this time he experienced her touch like a jolt of electricity and yanked his hand away.

"I'm sorry, I didn't mean to hurt you," she said, but as their gazes connected she realized the reason behind his skittishness. That becoming blush erupted along her high cheekbones again and she stammered, "I'm sorry. I didn't—"

"Hard not to resist the first woman in a long time, Doc."

Her gaze narrowed, and she tightened her lips into a thin line. "I'm not a woman. I'm your physician."

He laughed at her annoyance. "Sorry, Doc, but you are definitely all woman."

She sputtered in indignation but quickly recovered. "Your hand, please, Mr. Bradford. I promise it won't hurt."

He offered her his hand, and she carefully scraped off samples of skin from each of his knuckles into the test tube. Then she sealed it up and placed everything back in her bag.

Back stiff, she rose from the bed and said, "I'll be by later to see how you're doing."

He rose, as well, although the gentlemanly gesture cost him as his body protested the movement. He grimaced and looked away from her, caught sight of the bag she had been dragging around earlier.

"What's that?" he asked and walked toward it, his long strides eating up ground as Liliana followed him, but she placed her index finger on her lips to signal him to be discreet, since Bruno was within hearing distance just outside the room.

Jesse bent and opened the top of the bag. Realized what it contained. Reaching in, he retrieved one of the trophies and read the engraving.

New Jersey All-State Champions 2000.

"Where did you get this?" he whispered, gently placing the trophy on the floor and then pulling another from the bag.

"Your mother asked that I give them to you. I told her we hadn't found you yet, but I suspect she knows there's more to the story I provided."

He nodded, battling back the emotions roiling in him. The dangerous soul-deep hurt, and worse, self-pity. Dragging in a deep breath through the tight constriction in his throat, he continued removing all the items until the floor around him was littered with the debris of his past.

She stood beside him quietly the entire time until he finally looked up at her.

This time there was no denying what he saw.

"I don't need a pity party," he said, rising to his feet, his hands clenched at his sides as he battled his own emotions.

"No, you don't," she said, surprising him. Pointing to the awards and trophies lying along the floor she said, "You should be proud of all you accomplished, only it's time to leave the past behind."

"Is that what you think I do? Live in the past?" he nearly shouted and took a step toward her.

She flinched, almost as if he had hit her, and stepped back. Coupled with her earlier reaction to Whittaker, he wondered what had happened to her. An abusive relationship, maybe, he thought and because of that, he tempered his actions.

"What's in *your* past, Doc? Why are you afraid of me?"

She lowered her gaze and shook her head, sending the shoulder-length strands of her hair into motion. Thick, silky locks that hid her face from him.

When he moved toward her again, he did so cautiously and she didn't move away. Raising his hand, he cupped her chin and gently urged her face upward.

She was beautiful, he thought. Strong, as well, but he could see that she had suffered. Her eyes spoke volumes. The urge rose up in him to protect her, although he suspected she wouldn't like that, either.

"I won't hurt you, Liliana" he said, repeating his earlier vow. Savoring the way her name tasted on his lips.

"I'm going to try and believe that, Jesse. But there's something else I need to know."

Beneath his fingers, he sensed the tension in her. Knew that despite her words, she feared his response to the question. Because of that, he dropped his hand and took a step back. Opening his arms wide, he invited her query.

"Ask away, Doc."

She nodded and clasped her hands before her. Peering upward to meet his gaze, she said, "All the other patients in the Wardwell program were beyond help. It's why they qualified for the experiments. But you ... How did you get into the tests?"

Jesse jammed his hands on his hips and considered lying. Not that it would help, since in time, she was bound to find out. So he admitted to his shame. To the sin of pride that had whittled away his common sense and brought more pain and loss than he had ever thought possible.

"I bribed my way into the program."

CHAPTER 7

Liliana heard his words and yet had to repeat them to be sure. "You bribed your way into experimental tests."

He leaned toward her, and he was so large it would have been scary except for the pleading look in his gaze. "Try to understand."

"Understand? You could have lived a normal life—"

"I've done normal, Liliana," he said and blew out an exasperated sigh before dragging a hand through his hair and continuing. "I grew up on the wrong side of town. I watched my mother and father struggle every day to provide for us. I wanted better. For me. For them. For others."

Liliana thought back to the home she had visited just hours before. Clean and newly renovated. Surrounded by homes in a similar state in an area that otherwise was a little dated. The Mauraders flags and decals everywhere. She knew then what he had done and why they boasted his colors. It matched the generosity he had shown with the scholarships he had created.

"You fixed up your parents' home. Your neighbors' homes."

He shrugged casually, as if it had been nothing. "They were always good to me. It was the least I could do."

She imagined the punishment his body took out on the ball field. The pain and effort he had endured for that "least" he had provided for his family and friends. For the students at his old alma mater. He had allowed himself to become a guinea pig, only...

"Do you think they would have wanted you to make this kind of sacrifice for them?"

With a sad tilt of his head, he half turned and pointed to the detritus of his life sitting on the floor of his bedroom. "What do you think?"

Liliana couldn't deny what was staring her in the face or the disgust his father had exhibited that morning. But his mother had seemed to feel differently. Maybe his sister also.

"I think you can't judge everyone by what your dad thinks."

"Or what you think. Admit it, Doc. You know the real me, don't you? The brawler, party animal, and playboy," he challenged, stalking away from her and back to the trophies and awards littering the floor.

She had thought she knew the real Jesse Bradford. Now she wasn't so certain that she did. But she couldn't let herself get personally involved any further. She already was getting to know more than was maybe good. He was her patient, and he was prone to violence.

She had to remain objective.

"I've got to go, Jesse. There's a lot to do," she said as he bent and started putting the trophies back into the bag.

"You do that, Doc. It's important. For the other patients."

She wanted to tell him that it was important for him, as well, but couldn't give him false hope. She had been battling the genes replicating in Caterina's body for months now, and it was a difficult struggle. One that she hoped she could win, but there were no guarantees.

"I'll be back," she said, although she wasn't sure he heard her. He seemed engrossed in his task, pausing to examine each of his prizes as he placed them back in the bag.

As he hopefully let go of the past.

Carmen had prepped the skin samples, and the specimens provided a clear picture of what was going on along Jesse's knuckles. It wasn't good, Liliana thought as she examined the slides.

The cells from his skin were packed with far more genetic material than was typical. Plus, there was an abnormal amount of the various cells necessary for producing compact bone in the human body, but not in skin, Liliana thought.

Bone was her specialty, and yet she had never witnessed anything close to what she just had on the slide.

"What's up, Doc?" Carmen teased as she walked out of the clean room where the geneticist was still hard at work on the various blood samples Liliana had brought them.

"Don't call me 'Doc,'" she snapped. It reminded her too much of Jesse.

"That good, huh?" Carmen asked and came right up to her, shot her a gentle hip check to get her to move away from the microscope.

"Whoa. Amazing bone formation," her friend said, then straightened, a puzzled look on her face. "Wait, this was his skin sample, right?"

Liliana nodded. "Right. He says this started after Wardwell implanted the genes."

Carmen plopped down onto a lab stool beside Liliana. She held a number of papers in her hand that she tapped against her leg repeatedly while she considered what Liliana had just said and then inched over to take another peek into the microscope. "If this is happening all over his body—"

"Not all over. At least, not that I can tell from what I've seen," Liliana explained.

Carmen fought back a grin. "So you've seen a good amount of his body?"

Liliana shook her head in exasperation. "No, Carmen. I haven't, but I guess it makes sense to do a full physical exam."

"Definitely, but if you don't want to, I'd be happy to volunteer," Carmen teased.

Liliana bit back a rebuke about staying professional, as well as an unexpected pang of jealousy. Hiding that emotion, she teased, "I may have to mention to Ramon that you have this recurring desire to see Jesse Bradford naked."

Carmen laughed and nudged Liliana with her knee. "You do that and I'll never forgive you, *amiga*. And I won't let you see these," she said and brandished the papers she had in her hand.

Liliana snagged them midwave and then laid them out beside the microscope along the surface of Carmen's workstation. She organized them into piles. DNA tests. Blood tests.

As with Caterina, the DNA analysis pointed to the presence of nonhuman genes in Jesse's body.

Liliana motioned to the results on the various exams. "Do we have any idea what kinds of genes produced this?"

"Not yet. We're not getting the kind of replication that we had with Caterina, so we're dealing with a limited amount of DNA to analyze."

Liliana rounded up the tests and asked, "Why do you think that is?"

Carmen shrugged. "Maybe the samples are bad? They sure aren't glowing in the same way as Caterina's blood specimens."

"Or maybe they used different fluorescent proteins to track the genes?" Liliana suggested.

"Possibly. Or maybe we need a different sample," Carmen said and reached for the DNA tests. She flipped through them, so rapidly that Liliana wondered what she could possibly see, but then Carmen said, "Bone marrow."

Bone marrow was responsible for the production of the cells that eventually led to bone formation. "Taking a bone marrow specimen is painful. Maybe even risky, since we don't know what's really happening in his body."

Carmen raised her hands as if in surrender. "Just putting it out there, Lil."

"Noted," Liliana said and then reviewed the blood tests. As Carmen had observed, there was a decided lack of fluorescent proteins. Admittedly Caterina's disease—brain cancer—and the genes to regenerate what the cancer had destroyed had been different. But there was one similarity with Jesse: his white blood cells were reacting to the foreign genes and causing cell destruction. In time Jesse might need an injection of the inhibitor complex to slow down the gene replication, as well as a plasmapheresis treatment to remove the poisons that could threaten his health.

The tests had also shown elevated protein levels. "Can we tell what kinds of proteins these are?"

Carmen nodded. "Already working on it. My guess based on everything I've seen so far is that they're—"

"Bone morphogenetic proteins," she said, thinking the same thing. Given the unusual bone on Jesse's knuckles, elevated proteins might explain that bizarre behavior.

Jesse's words replayed in her head. "Bradford says that the hardness on his knuckles started happening when he punched the body bag. Inflammation occurs at the site of injury, and that leads to bone formation."

"So any injury—"

Let's hope that it's not any *injury,* Liliana thought. That would mean that little by little, more and more of Jesse's body might become ossified until . . .

"Please do the analysis. I'm going to go back and see about doing a full physical exam. And talk to Jesse about getting a bone marrow specimen."

Carmen nodded and rounded up the last of the papers. After she did so, she said with a smile, "Do you want to hear the latest about the inhibitor complex?"

CHAPTER 8

Jesse stood on the balcony, staring outward at the dark ocean. It was calm today, with barely a ripple disrupting its moon-silvered surface. Unusual for this time of year, when late fall winds often whipped up waves and sent them crashing against the shoreline.

The ocean's peacefulness helped tame the conflict within his soul roused by Liliana and her visit earlier that day.

She had seen his family. Talked to them. Or at least to his mother and father.

He wondered how they were. If his sister was okay. Whether his father had lessened his intractable stance against him. And his mother...Did she still kowtow to his father's every whim?

Funny in a way. As much as he despised his father's control over his mother, he had behaved no better in his relationships with women. They had been things to be used, to serve his needs and then be discarded.

He suspected the intriguing doctor would not tolerate that kind of treatment, based on her behavior this morning.

A car came down Ocean Avenue and pulled into the

driveway. A boring, nondescript sedan driven by none other than the woman who had ensnared his thoughts for the better part of the day.

The car screamed dependable, making him ponder if it matched Liliana's personality. Possibly accurate from what he knew of her so far.

Except for that exciting streak of spunk she exhibited around Whittaker.

She exited the car and glanced upward. He tried not to hope that she was looking for him, but as she saw him standing on the balcony, a smile came to her lips. She waved hesitantly before walking up the steps to the wraparound porch and front door.

He didn't wait for the doorbell. Bruno had been in the gazebo at the far end of the space, reading his paper again. Or at least he guessed that's what he was doing, since all he could see were Bruno's feet from his position up on the balcony. Whittaker's man had risen as the car had arrived, presumably headed toward the front door, ever vigilant.

That vigilance was part of the reason Jesse hadn't tried to escape. How far could he get without them noticing? Without them taking action against his sister or family? Against Liliana and her people, now that they were involved?

Not far, he thought as he hurried down the stairs and got to the front door just as she was coming in with Bruno, her medical bag in hand.

He stopped at the entry to the foyer. "Need some more blood, Doc?"

A slight grimace crossed her face, and he knew then it would be something far worse than a blood or skin sample.

"Mind if we get a bite first? Maybe even go for a walk?" Jesse asked.

Bruno immediately shook his head. "No walk until we eat. I'm starving."

Liliana's stomach grumbled as well, and she quickly covered it with her hand and offered an apology. "I've been on the run all day. I haven't had a chance to eat."

"I can make something," Jesse said and motioned toward the kitchen.

"This I've got to see," Bruno said and walked to the kitchen ahead of them.

Jesse sauntered up to Liliana, placed his hand at the small of her back, but paused. "Is that okay with you? We've been eating mostly takeout, and I'm a little tired of it."

"I'll help if you want," she replied.

"Deal." He applied gentle pressure to urge her forward, and they entered the kitchen, where she placed her bag on a far counter and removed her suit jacket.

A dangerous move, he thought, glancing at her full figure from the corner of his eye. Noticing the way Bruno also appreciated the sight. "Put your eyes back in your head," he warned the other man.

Bruno chuckled. "That's rich coming from you, Bradford."

Liliana snared an apron from a hook by one wall. "Gentlemen—and I use that term loosely—I don't appreciate your ogling."

"Sorry," they both said in unison, although the apologies were clearly insincere.

Jesse opted to get past the moment by motioning to the fridge. "I think there's some chicken in there."

Liliana opened the refrigerator. Inside were prepackaged chicken cutlets, half-and-half, and a big chunk of Parmesan cheese.

"How about some chicken Alfredo?"

Jesse walked up to her and peered over her shoulder. "We've got all the makings. I'll grill while you make the sauce?"

Liliana looked up at him. He was too close. She felt surrounded by all his blatant masculinity, and it was unsettling. Slipping beneath his arm to get away from him, she said, "Since you offered to cook, I'll grill and you make the sauce."

She expected an argument but got none. Instead, Jesse grabbed all the ingredients from the fridge and headed to the counter, where he laid them out. Efficiently he set about readying pots and pans to boil the pasta and make the Alfredo sauce.

He was clearly comfortable around a kitchen, she thought as she reached over, grabbed the cutlets, and worked on her part of the bargain. While Jesse labored at the stove, she fired up the indoor grill and the fan overhead. Prepped the cutlets and got them cooking.

"How domestic," Bruno said, and she glanced over her shoulder at him. He lounged at the table, killing time until someone waited on him.

"How about you move your ass and get the table ready," she called out to him.

The man chuckled again and then mumbled, "Nothing worse than a demanding woman."

Despite his complaint, he did as she asked and set the table. Even went into another room and came back with a bottle of wine.

Beside her, Jesse was comfortably working on the sauce.

"You do this a lot?" she asked, arching a brow.

As he stirred the butter and added some flour, he nodded but then hesitated. "If you think this is part of a whole seduction routine—"

"I do."

"Then you'd be wrong," he said while adding some half-and-half that he had warmed in the microwave to the roux. Shooting her a glance out of the corner of his eye, he said, "My mom and dad worked hard during the day. My mom would come home dead tired. I learned to cook to help her out."

"Totally understand. I helped my parents in their restaurant kitchen all the time."

"You worked there?" he questioned as he moved from the sauce to add pasta to the boiling water.

"We all worked there, even as children. We'd go to school and come home to the restaurant. After we finished our homework, we'd help out in any way we could. Preparing the cutlery and napkins. Making tortillas or shredding the chicken or beef for the dishes."

He heard what she wasn't saying with her words—that it had been hard at times. He understood. "My dad worked at a mill shop when I was a kid. The owner used to pay me to sweep up the sawdust and round up all the scrap pieces of wood. I was eight, maybe nine."

"So we have something in common."

"Maybe more than you think," he said with a grin before continuing. "I used to work at a restaurant also—Vic's."

"You were a waiter?"

"I started as a dishwasher, then became a busboy, and

eventually worked my way to waiter," he replied and pulled the sauce off the stove to wait for the pasta.

"I bet you were popular with the female customers," she teased and he actually felt a flush of heat spread across his face.

"I was a good waiter," he said in defense and offered her a sampling of the sauce from the stirring spoon.

She took a taste, but their gazes met and he could see the devilment in her eyes. "Seriously, I never dropped a dish on anyone," he replied.

"But did anyone ever complain about a wrong order?" she kidded.

"That's like the pot calling the kettle black. I'm sure none of your male customers ever complained to you."

The sparkle in her eyes faded and her smile tightened. He understood without her saying a word. She'd probably had more than one customer who had treated her like a foreigner who didn't comprehend the insults they were tossing at her.

"People are stupid," he said and passed the back of his hand across her cheek.

The action surprised her, caring as it was. She hadn't expected such understanding and tenderness in him.

Needing physical space, she moved away to check the cutlets on the grill but found herself wanting to know more about him.

"What about your sister? Did she help? She's a lot younger than you."

He shrugged while stirring the pasta, utterly masculine while at the decidedly domestic task. "A lot younger, but I found ways for her to help so she didn't feel left out. You didn't meet Jackie, did you?"

"Easy, Bradford," Bruno jumped in, reminding her that they weren't alone. She had been getting so comfortable with Jesse that she had forgotten about the presence of the bodyguard. But she also wondered about the warning vibe in the man's voice.

"Done already, Bruno?" she asked and turned, but the man had finished the table. The uncorked bottle of wine and glasses completed his contribution to the meal.

"Don't get too comfy, Doc. This is only a temporary arrangement," Bruno said again, some of his earlier friendliness gone.

"Temporary because Bruno and his FBI pals should find the other patients soon," Jesse explained, although an underlying tone hinted at something more ominous.

She wanted to press, but a cautioning glance from Jesse urged her not to do so.

At least not yet.

She flipped the cutlets, which were close to done. The hiss of the stove warned that the linguini would soon be ready as the water boiled over. Jesse quickly whipped off the cover to quell the roiling water.

"Almost done there?" he asked, returning the sauce to the stove and expertly flipping it around in the low sauté pan.

"Almost," she said, and a few minutes later, she was pulling the cutlets off the grill and slicing them. Jesse had prepared three plates with linguine drenched with his creamy sauce.

She brought over the cutting board with the grilled chicken slices and arranged them over the pasta. "Voilà," she said with a flourish of her hand.

"Looks good," he replied and grabbed two of the

plates, arranged them on one arm, then snagged the third, displaying the skills he had learned as a waiter.

She followed him to the table, and he gallantly placed the first plate in front of her, then Bruno, and finally himself before sitting down at the table.

Hunger ruled, making for silence as they ate first. After the edge was off, however, she had to compliment him. "This is really good. Thanks."

"My sister thanks you, since it's her recipe," Jesse said.

Bruno twitched beside him, and his fork stilled halfway to his mouth, but when Jesse said nothing else, Bruno continued eating.

Liliana decided this was one case where discretion was warranted. Besides, once she took Jesse upstairs for her examination, she'd be alone with him and would be better able to get a sense of what was causing the strange undercurrents she was feeling.

When they had finished eating, Jesse leaned back from the table and rubbed his flat midsection. "Nothing like a home-cooked meal."

Unexpected again, she thought, imagining that a man of his means and fame regularly spent a great deal of time eating out.

"Very tasty. Maybe I can make you some Mexican food next time," she offered.

"So you're Mexican? You looked like a *paesan* to me," Bruno said, wiping some sauce off his lips with a napkin.

"Were you born there?" Jesse asked, shifting back toward the table and leaning his elbows on its surface.

Liliana nodded. "I was born in Mérida, a beautiful little city on the Yucatán peninsula. My parents got a visa to move to the States when I was five."

"So you're not a wetback," Bruno interjected crudely.

"Stuff it, Bruno," Jesse said.

She bit back her own response, used to Bruno's kind of ignorance. Funny given that his Italian ancestors had probably come over only a generation before hers.

"You know what the rule was in my house, Bruno. Whoever cooks, the other person cleans, so I guess that means you're 'it,' " Liliana said.

She didn't wait for his answer. She tossed her napkin on the table, rose, and grabbed her bag from the counter on her way out the door.

From behind her she heard Jesse's amused chuckle, followed by, "I cooked, too."

She grinned and strode down the hall toward the gym. The massage table there would make a good place for her to examine Jesse and discuss the bone marrow sample with him.

He was immediately behind her, following close. Teasing her with, "You've got brass, Doc."

She hadn't had it in the past, she thought, recalling how she had allowed her ex to abuse her. But she had rediscovered the Liliana she had lost for a little while.

"Just standing up for myself."

"I like that in a woman."

She stopped short, and he had to grab her to keep from bowling her over. The contact brought instant electricity, and as she looked up at him, she realized it was mutual. And because it was wrong on so many levels, she brought her hands to his and extricated herself physically. Then she created needed mental distance.

"Really? I thought you liked a different kind of woman. Blond, beautiful, and brainless."

A sad smile slipped to his lips. "Maybe in the past, but who says an old dog can't learn new tricks?"

"You're younger than I am," she said, whirled on one foot, and took the last few steps to the gym.

"I could be your boy toy," he said, but there was no doubting the teasing tones in his voice, and she was hard-pressed to battle the smile it yanked to her face.

"For now, you can be my anatomy model," she said and slapped the leather surface of the massage table.

"Excuse me?" he said and rested his butt on the edge of the table.

"I need to do a physical exam. Strip off your T-shirt and sweats and jump up here for me." She slapped the surface of the table again, but instead Jesse moved away from her. He stood a few feet away, arms across his chest in a defensive stance, clearly upset by the request.

"Jesse?" she questioned, wanting to understand.

Jesse planted one hand on his hip and, in a gesture that was becoming familiar, dragged back the longish strands of his blond hair with the other.

"I don't think so, Doc," he said when he finally answered.

"Why not?" she blurted out.

With a shrug of his massive shoulders, he said, "You must know what's happening, otherwise why would you ask?"

"To confirm what you think I know. To understand just how bad it is—"

"It's not that bad," he immediately countered.

"Why don't you let me be the judge of that, Jesse? I can't treat you or anyone else if I don't know what's actually happening."

It was the "anyone else" that breached Jesse's reticence to have her examine him. If having Liliana see the damage to his body would help her find a way to help others, like his sister, he could endure the exam and her touch.

First the pants, he thought, stalking to the massage table. He peeled off the sweats and tossed them aside. Then he pulled off his T-shirt, revealing the worst of the damage to his body, and lay down on the table.

Sucking in a breath through gritted teeth, he said, "Do your worst, Doc."

CHAPTER 9

Somehow she managed to control the various elements of shock running rampant through her mind.

First there was the sheer perfection of his body. Long, beautifully muscled legs. Narrow hips and a flat, sculpted midsection. A broad, well-defined chest that flared into even broader shoulders. Ripped muscles in his arms completed the package.

Well, almost completed the package, since she refused to dwell too much on the very obvious length of him beneath the bikini briefs he wore.

But marring all that masculine perfection were the signs of both past and present injuries. A thin white scar along his right thigh gave testament to the fracture that had ended his football career. If memory served her right, they'd had to insert several pins into his femur to join the pieces together.

Farther up, along his left side, were the Taser marks she had treated. The wounds inflicted by the barbs were sealed up, but with skin that looked way too white.

Maybe because it wasn't skin, but developing bone, she thought. Just to confirm, she ran a finger along the paler skin. Encountered the denser surface that she had first noticed on his knuckles.

But the worst of the injuries to his body appeared to be on the other side, and she stepped around the massage table to better examine the area.

This time she could not control a shocked gasp from escaping.

He finally glanced at her, his face set in hard lines, almost as hard as the bone that appeared to have developed along a larger-than-hand-sized section of his right rib cage.

"May I?" she asked even as she was touching that smooth surface. Feeling the almost slick, rigid shell beneath her fingers.

"What happened here?" she asked, still exploring the area with her fingers.

He snagged her hand to stop her.

"Morales used a cattle prod to get me to fight Santiago. After the first blast, my side was red and inflamed. By the next day, it was numb. Then Morales shocked me again a few days later. It got worse. It took a few more prods before I realized what was happening."

"But you couldn't stop it," she said, twining her fingers with his rather than releasing his hand.

"I couldn't stop it, but I could try to let him hit me in the same spot. After a while, the effects of the cattle prod lessened, probably because my ribs had gotten so hard. It's bone, isn't it?" he asked and reached over, ran his free hand across the area.

"Yes. Some kind of compact bone. Your body seems to be producing it in response to certain kinds of inflammation or injury."

Jesse nodded and looked back up at the ceiling, avoiding her gaze. "So I guess that's it. Don't get hurt and I don't get any bone, right?"

"Possibly. Except that your body is making too many bone-producing proteins. If we can't get that under control—"

"But if you could, it would help someone with the problem I had—fragile bones."

She didn't miss the hopefulness in his voice, but she couldn't give him false expectations. "There are so many diseases that eat away bone. We don't know what caused your bone loss—"

"But you know I'm building bone. Just look at me," he said, pulling his hand out of hers and sitting up.

She did look at him. At the dichotomy of his male beauty and the ugliness of the damage.

Somewhere within him lay the key to both his curse and a possible cure. The problem would be finding out which before the mechanisms in his body got totally out of control and turned him into cold, hard bone.

Inside, her stomach twisted at the thought of that. At the possibility that if she and her team couldn't find out what was going on, he might die.

She felt compelled to touch him again, as if her touch could somehow soothe the hurt and damage he had suffered. And so she cupped his jaw. Strong and straight and masculinely perfect.

With him sitting on the table, their faces were closer to level, providing her an amazing view of the blue of his eyes, like the ocean he craved outside his window. And like the ocean when a storm came, his gaze grew a dark gray as it met hers and he mimicked her action, cradling her cheek with his large hand.

"I know you can help me, Liliana," he said and traced the line of her cheekbone with his thumb.

"I will try, Jesse, only—"

He silenced her by moving his thumb down across her lips. Her heartbeat kicked up a notch as he ran his finger along the edges of her lips, a prelude to a kiss. When he slowly bent toward her, she skipped back and away from his touch, sure of only one thing.

She was attracted to him.

What right-minded woman wouldn't be, she thought, reconsidering her whole "not into the surfer dude" thing.

But he was her patient, and he was capable of violence. Extreme violence. He had confessed as much himself when he had explained about his need to vent his anger on the body bag. And to him, she was probably just another conquest.

All of those factors outweighed any kind of physical attraction from which she was suffering.

"I need to run another test," she said to put things back on track.

Jesse smiled, both amused and saddened by her reaction to him. She found him desirable, but then again, he was used to that reaction from women. After a while it got stale without anything more behind it. He had found that out the hard way after a parade of unsatisfying relationships.

And she was also still wary of him. Not that he blamed her. She was aware of his capacity for violence and unaware of the secrets he was keeping. Plus there was his past. He had done little to reassure her that he was a changed man from the one with whom she was familiar: the Jesse Bradford of the tabloids, with his brawling and womanizing ways.

"What kind of test, Doc?" he asked, acknowledging

that she was back to hiding behind professionalism. He preferred Liliana the woman but would settle for Liliana the doctor for now.

"Just like that, Jesse? What kind of test?" she asked, narrowing her deep brown gaze to consider him.

"What choice do I have, Doc? Let you use me for a pincushion or turn to bone?" he said, mindful also of the bargain with Whittaker that he had to keep. One that he knew the beautiful doctor would not like. At that thought, guilt set in that he was deceiving her by allowing her to believe that Whittaker and his friends were actually good guys, when all they wanted was a way to improve the humans they planned to sell as weapons.

She must have sensed his guilt, since her expression remained thoughtful, as if she didn't quite believe he could be that cooperative. But he had little choice. If he didn't help Whittaker, his sister would pay the price. So he pressed Liliana again, "What kind of test?"

"The blood we drew from you isn't exhibiting the same behavior as the other samples we have."

"The other samples being from Caterina Shaw?"

Liliana nodded. "Wardwell was a leader in creating fluorescent proteins for tracking genes. They used them in the genes transplanted into Caterina and Santiago, producing fairly obvious ways to see the gene expression."

"Translation, please, for us non-science types," he teased, although he found her kind of sexy in scientist mode. Brains and beauty were a potent mix.

"Caterina's blood glows. The glow was starting to become visible on her skin and in her eyes because of how the genes were multiplying."

"And you're not seeing that in my blood?" he said and

rested his forearms on his thighs as he sat on the edge of the massage table, swinging his legs back and forth.

Liliana moved away from him to root in her medical bag. She withdrew a test tube with some clear liquid, a long, thick needle, and a syringe. She faced him once again and said, "There is some glow in your blood, but not what we expected to see."

He gestured to the needle. "I suppose you think that might help?"

She nodded. "There are bone-producing proteins in your marrow. We think the genes that are expressing—"

"As in glowing?" he interjected and leaned back on his elbows.

Her gaze flitted across his body for a moment, bringing a flush of pink to her olive skin and a stammer when she spoke. "The test . . . a bone marrow procedure, will help us get a sample to see if that's where Wardwell's genes are working."

He sat up and held his hands out wide in a gesture of surrender. "What do you need me to do?"

Liliana considered him. So damn handsome. Too damn agreeable, but then again, his life depended on his helping her. Maybe whatever vibes she was picking up about his willingness to be poked and prodded were wrong.

"Lie down on your stomach. I'm going to make a little incision below the small of your back near your ilium. It's the best place to get a sample," she explained.

"Will it hurt?" he asked as he turned onto his stomach and brought all of his body to rest on the table.

Finally some hesitation on his part. *Good,* she thought as she went on with the explanation. "The cut will be minor and the needle shouldn't hurt all that much. You may have some pain when I connect the syringe and extract the marrow."

"You may want to get Bruno in here, then," he said, resting his face on its side so he could see her.

"Why?" she asked as she plucked a scalpel from her medical kit along with some alcohol pads, butterfly bandages and gauze.

"Pain brings anger. The greater the pain, the worse the reaction, so just in case..."

She recalled the notations in the Wardwell file and his words about fighting Santiago. She had personal experience with that psycho and his rage. If Jesse could fight someone that powerful...

Fear settled in her gut.

She took him up on his suggestion, walking back to the kitchen to get Bruno and have him escort her to the gym.

Jesse was still lying there, facing her as she approached the massage table. She grabbed the scalpel she had left by his side, raised it, and said, "Are you ready?"

A footfall came behind her, and Jesse's gaze shifted to Bruno as he entered. "Don't be afraid to use that cap gun if you need to," Jesse said.

Bruno laid his hand on his gun, but his next words diminished the menace in that gesture. "And kill Whittaker's golden goose? No way."

Whittaker's golden goose? Liliana thought, the words distracting her until Jesse urged her on.

"I'm ready for you, Doc."

CHAPTER 10

Morales, Edwards, and Whittaker stared at the patient's body as it rested on the stainless steel table in their laboratory warehouse. A "Y" incision marred the patient's colorful skin and was pulled back to reveal the tangle of organs beneath the vibrant flesh.

"You're sure about what's happening?" Whittaker questioned, jangling the change in his pocket as he glanced at Morales in his blood-stained white lab coat.

"Massive organ failure. Genes were replicating too quickly and the plasmapheresis couldn't clean the blood."

Edwards tsked and leaned toward the body. Peered within. "How many others are exhibiting these symptoms?"

Morales walked to a worktable a short distance away and snared a clipboard from its surface. He flipped through the papers on it, then peered at his partners. "One other patient is close to organ failure. Then there are another four with similar problems. We may lose the one, but it will likely take at least another week or so before the others become critical," he said.

Whittaker stalked away to the cages holding the assorted patients, who began to whimper, whine, or scream depending on their physical and mental conditions. He paused before one cage where a man lay quietly on a narrow cot. He reached in through the bars and nudged the patient with his foot.

The patient didn't respond.

He hurried back toward his partners, hands jammed into his pockets. The change silent as he held himself still against the frustration building in his body. "We can't afford to lose any more of them. It'll make the buyers antsy if they think they're too fragile."

"We need a different inhibitor complex. One that controls the replication with fewer side effects," Edwards advised.

"Now, why didn't I think of that? Oh, wait, I did," Morales chimed in snidely, looking upward and tapping his lips for effect.

"The complex that Carrera has developed—"

"Has to be better than the crap we have. Just look at Shaw. She's not on a slab yet," Morales said and jerked his hand in the direction of their dead patient.

"Not yet," Edwards replied and rubbed his lip with his finger before facing Whittaker. "Can you get us a sample of Carrera's inhibitor complex?"

Whittaker shrugged. "Carrera hasn't needed to use it on Bradford yet. Why is that?"

Edwards shook his head and considered all that he knew about Bradford's case. The genes implanted would be replicating, likely as fast as with the others, only ...

"The replication isn't going to be as visible as with the other patients. Because of that, it may take Carrera a little time to figure out what's happening."

Morales immediately added his assessment. "But she

will have to do something to keep Bradford's bones from becoming too dense—"

"And having other parts of him turn to bone," Whittaker said, recalling what he had seen of Bradford's body.

Morales smiled in seeming pleasure at the mention of the unusual bone forming on Bradford. "Beautiful, isn't it?"

Whittaker glared at Morales. "You're a sick bastard, aren't you?"

His condemnation earned an amused chuckle from the other man, who replied, "And I suppose you consider yourself a Boy Scout?"

Whittaker jangled the change in his pockets and said, "I'll get you the inhibitor."

Edwards elegantly crossed his arms over his chest, rumpling the expensive wool of his suit. He turned and faced the cages with the patients.

"If it takes too long, we may need more test subjects," he said.

Whittaker shrugged off that request. "There are plenty more where they came from," he said, thinking of how easy it was just to snag a few more homeless from the streets of nearby Camden or Philadelphia.

Edwards tapped his lip with his finger and finally said, "Then consider this a request to get us a few more."

Jesse sucked in a breath at the chill as Liliana sprayed a topical anesthetic along his back.

"You'll experience pressure from the scalpel." She sprayed the area again and he jumped slightly but then settled down.

"I'm going to cut now," she said, leaned over him, and carefully made the incision near the dimple beside the small of his back.

"So far, so good, Doc," Jesse replied.

Liliana exchanged the scalpel for the long needle needed to pierce through his bone and extract the sample. She also placed the test tube for Jesse's bone marrow sample nearby.

As she had done before, she warned Jesse about the next step in the process. "I'm going to insert the bone probe now. You may feel some pressure again, possibly some pain when I remove the sample."

"Thanks for letting me know," he said and dropped his hands close to the legs of the massage table. Loosely wrapped them around the legs.

Liliana inhaled deeply and inserted the probe into the incision she had made. Jesse shifted a bit, and his hands grasped the legs of the table a little more tightly. She pressed the needle through the small distance to his hip bone and, when it hit something hard, increased the force of her invasion to pierce the bone. A little bit more pressure than was normally necessary, since she still felt the resistance of dense, hard bone rather than marrow.

Jesse was now gripping the legs tightly, and his breathing had grown choppy.

"Almost done," she said, sympathizing with the pain he might be experiencing from the procedure. With a gentle final push, the needle slipped into the marrow and she quickly attached the syringe to remove the sample.

Jesse groaned. His body was visibly trembling from the strain, and a thin line of blood trickled down the side of his hip from the incision she had made. A second later, however, she watched as the bleeding stopped and the wound seemed to be closing up.

Another moan erupted from Jesse, and his hands on the legs of the table were a bloodless white from the pressure he was exerting.

"Jesse?" she questioned, unsure of what was happening, since the worst of the procedure was already over.

"Hurts, Doc," he replied, his breathing rough. His body shaking.

Liliana made a quick visual observation of the bone marrow sample she had taken, noting the bright phosphorescent glow before transferring the sample to the test tube. She quickly placed the sample in her bag and turned her attention to dealing with Jesse.

"Where is the pain, Jesse?"

"Hip. Back. Head," he said, groaned, and began to bang his head against the padded top of the table.

Liliana examined the site of the incision. A pale white line was starting to form along the cut, and as she palpated the area around the incision, she could feel a slight hardness that said additional bone was forming beneath. Probably all along the path of the probe and at his hip.

He moaned again and warned, "Move her back, Bruno."

Jesse staggered to his feet, holding his head with his hands and looking almost wild-eyed.

"Jesse?" she said, but Bruno was yanking her away and to a far side of the room.

"It's the pain. It makes him lose control."

Jesse lurched forward toward the gym equipment and grabbed hold of the handle for the bench press to steady himself. A few feet away was a body bag suspended from a chain in the ceiling. Jesse attacked it, brutally punching the bag.

Liliana flinched at the sound and the force of his blows, imagining the destruction he could wreak on a human body. Despite that, she realized that if there was one thing that Jesse had it was control, contrary to Bruno's statement. Despite his very obvious pain, he had managed to turn the response away from her and Bruno and to the inanimate body bag.

The muscles in his body trembled and rippled as he struck at it, and fear took hold in Liliana, but a different kind of fear than she had expected.

It wasn't the violence making her worry. It was the reality that the test she had done and the beating Jesse was administering were going to create inflammation and injury. And if she was right about her earlier assessment, that was going to create even more destruction in Jesse's body. Unless they could control the bone formation.

It suddenly occurred to her just what they had to do.

She jerked away from Bruno and to the massage table. Grabbed her cell phone from her medical bag and dialed Carmen. Her friend answered almost instantly.

"How'd it go, *amiga?*" Carmen asked.

"Not good," Liliana admitted. "Can you create a filter for those bone proteins we detected in Jesse? Enough to get the plasmapheresis setup working?"

"I think I can," Carmen replied.

"I need that done ASAP, and clear the lab. Just you, me—"

"And our special patient?" Carmen piped in, which meant someone was in the lab that hadn't been cleared to know about Jesse.

"Yes. How long will it take?"

"An hour or two."

Jesse was still pounding the bag, although not as force-fully. Sweat dripped from his body, and he was near the edge of physical exhaustion, probably the only thing that worked to control the anger and the pain.

"Make it happen. We'll see you soon," Liliana said.

"I don't know if that's possible," Bruno advised and approached her.

She shot a glance at Jesse as he dropped to his knees, hugging the bottom of the bag for support. She jabbed her finger at Bruno and said, "You want to lose the golden goose?"

Bruno paled beneath his olive-colored skin. "That can't happen. Doc. Whittaker—"

"Will demote your ass if it does. Which means I have to get Jesse to the lab." She crossed her arms and raised her chin to get her point across. And for good measure, she said, "And don't call me 'Doc.'"

Bruno glanced at Jesse as he kneeled before the bag, sweat dripping from his body. His breathing rough from his exertions.

"Fuck it. I'll be waiting in the garage for you. Make sure he covers up his face," Bruno said.

She walked over to the massage table and grabbed the sweats Jesse had been wearing earlier. She also snagged a few towels from a storage unit next to a water cooler. Gin-gerly she approached Jesse, unsure of how he would react.

"Did you hear the plan, Jesse?" She stopped about a foot away from him.

He glanced up at her, a dead look in his crystal blue eyes. "Not sure I can move."

At least he seemed aware and in control. She took a step closer, dropped his sweats by his body, and knelt beside him. She handed him a towel, which he grasped in one unsteady hand. She kept another and tenderly ran it down his arm.

"There's no rush, Jesse. When you feel strong enough," she said and continued her ministrations, drying his body little by little.

Her touch was torture, Jesse thought. Each slight pass of the towel roused emotions more painful than the physical exertions that had taxed his body. It had been too long since someone had cared for him like this. Since someone had worried about him.

He dried his face and then somehow mustered the strength to reach up and swipe the towel along the back of his neck. His muscles were stiffening. He worried that he had overdone it, only the pain of the procedure had been so great that if he hadn't tired himself, the rage might have overpowered him.

That he had acted selflessly didn't make the ache any less painful, he thought as he reached up and attempted to work out the kinks by rubbing his arm.

He groaned at the discomfort, and a second later, she brushed away his hand and commenced a gentler massage. As their gazes connected, she asked, "Can you tolerate any NSAIDS?"

Morales had occasionally given him painkillers, so he nodded. She was suddenly in action, returning to her medical bag, grabbing a bottle, and then pouring a glass of water from the cooler. She returned and gave him the medication, then resumed the massage, extending it to other parts of his body as she dried him.

Whether it was the medication or her touch, in a few short minutes he was better and stronger. She must have sensed it, since she paused and handed him his sweats.

"I'll help you get dressed."

She assisted him, although he would have preferred her help in undressing much, much more, he thought.

Luckily she missed the wayward turn of his attention and eased beneath his arm without hesitation to help him up onto his feet. He wavered for a moment, physically depleted, but her presence steadied him.

Together they did the short walk to the garage, where Bruno waited in a large Suburban with windows tinted so black, only his silhouette was visible behind the wheel. By the door, Jesse paused at a hanging organizer where assorted keys dangled along with a pair of Oakley sunglasses and a Mauraders hat.

He slipped on the hat and glasses.

No one would know who he was, she thought. The glasses hid his eyes and wrapped around to hide a goodly portion of his face. The hat and shaggy hair added to the disguise, leaving few recognizable features. Just the small cleft in his chin and his firm masculine lips.

Beautiful lips, she thought, and a second later a dimple erupted beside that luscious mouth, as if Jesse had guessed at the nature of her thoughts and approved.

"In your dreams," she goaded.

"It would be a shame to limit it just to dreams," he immediately retorted.

She jerked her finger in the direction of the car. "Get in the back. I'll ride shotgun with our friend Bruno."

Jesse opened the door and she discovered another of Whittaker's goons—Howard—was in the back seat. The heavy tinted glass had hidden his presence. Jesse slipped into the back seat, and she climbed into the SUV for the short ride to the lab.

Bruno locked the doors with a loud *kathunk* and peered into the rearview mirror. "No funny business, Bradford."

Jesse tossed his hands up into the air. "Does it look like I can do much of anything?"

Neither Bruno nor his partner said anything else as Bruno pulled out of the garage, shut it with a remote, and then eased onto Ocean Avenue before heading westward toward the FBI laboratory and the hospital. The proximity to the hospital brought her some relief. If anything went wrong with any of the medications she gave Jesse, or the plasmapheresis, being nearby was good in case of an emergency.

She only hoped that wouldn't be necessary and glanced at her watch. It had taken them more than half an hour to cool down and dry Jesse. He seemed more relaxed, less uncomfortable than he had earlier, she thought as she peered over her shoulder at him. His head was resting against the back of the seat, and his long legs were stretched out as far as possible. His hands were propped on his thighs, but loosely and absent any signs of pain.

Blessfully peaceful, she thought, recalling the earlier violence he had directed against the body bag.

Violence to be feared, she reminded herself, driving away the empathy she was feeling for him. One of her teachers in medical school had warned her that she sometimes got too emotionally involved with her patients. She was on the brink of it this time and forced herself to recall the risks involved with Jesse.

His violent strength.

The possibility that he might die if they couldn't stop the bone production.

His immense size, daunting for anyone, but in particular for her, since he topped her by at least a foot.

His physical presence nearly overwhelmed her when she was beside him, and yet there was something about that difference that also pulled at her. She could imagine the peace of being surrounded in those strong arms, or the way he might lift her as if she weighed nearly nothing.

Not that she did, she thought, shooting a glance down at her ample curves before driving such thoughts from her mind.

Jesse Bradford might be attractive, but his many faults and issues outweighed that masculine beauty.

The car stopped. She had been so lost in her contemplation that she hadn't realized they had reached the facility. Withdrawing a key card from her purse, she walked to the door, Jesse following behind her. He was flanked on either side by Whittaker's men.

She swiped the card and they entered the laboratory.

Carmen was at her workstation, bent over the microscope. She rose and faced them as they entered. A smile erupted on her friend's face as she glanced beyond Liliana to Jesse.

"Is the treatment ready?" Liliana walked up to Carmen and gently nudged her to get her attention.

Carmen motioned to the treatment room. "Almost. You can get set up in there. I shouldn't be much longer."

Liliana turned, but Jesse and his two guards were already in motion. Liliana joined them, but between the equipment in the room and all the bodies, it was a tight fit.

"Could the two of you wait outside?" she said to Bruno and Howard.

They shared an uneasy glance, obviously hesitant until Liliana said, "He can't go anywhere. You can wait by the door."

Reluctantly they took up spots on either side of the entrance, earning another dimpled smile from Jesse. "Doc, you sure know how to get your way."

Too bad she didn't know how to get her way with him.

She pointed to the borrowed hospital bed, and Jesse eased onto the edge of it while peeling off the sunglasses and hat. His bright blue gaze glittered intensely as his smile widened and he patted the bed beside him in invitation.

This was the Jesse the media loved, she realized. The one with a string of female conquests that meant nothing. Another negative to add to her list.

"Not on a bet, Jesse." She walked over and asserted gentle pressure on his shoulder to get him to lie down.

All business, she wheeled over a table with a pulse oximeter to track his pulse and oxygen levels as she said, "You may want to take off your sneakers and get comfortable. This could take a couple of hours."

"A couple of hours with you sounds like heaven, Doc," he replied with a wink but did as she asked.

Liliana shifted the plasmapheresis machine to reach all the wires and tubes she would need to connect to Jesse. With them in hand, she sat on the edge of the bed and he sighed dramatically.

"Finally got you where I want you," he teased and his smile broadened.

There was something about his humor that was hard to resist, even though it was sexist and disrespectful. Maybe it was that she sensed he was doing it just to push her buttons. So she decided to push back.

"So why don't you do something about it? Like take your shirt off for me?" She pitched the tones of her voice low, hoping for sexy.

He chuckled, aware of her ploy, but played along. Humming a tune suitable for a striptease, he pulled one arm out of his sweatshirt and then another, leaving the shirt over his body until with a triumphant, "Ta-da," he ripped it off.

"*Dios mio.*"

Carmen froze in the doorway, eyes wide at the sight of Jesse's body.

Jesse glared at her, arching an eyebrow, and Carmen immediately snapped out of her daze. She approached the bed and grabbed some of the wires from Liliana.

"Let me help get you the anticoagulant and IV drip ready," Carmen said.

"What are they for?" Jesse asked as Liliana wrapped a rubber hose around his bicep and tapped his arm to expose a vein.

"We need to keep your blood from clotting as it flows through the machine. The IV drip will stabilize any drop in blood volume and pressure," she said, all traces of the earlier playfulness gone.

Jesse quietly watched as the two women efficiently got him hooked up to the plasmapheresis unit, inserting needles as well as the IV drip into his two arms. Liliana clipped the pulse oximeter on his index finger and then kicked on the unit.

He was fine for a few minutes, but soon light-headedness set in. Liliana seemed to notice his discomfort and covered his hand with hers.

"It'll pass in a bit. Close your eyes and try to rest, since this will take some time."

He did as she said, but the whirling sensation continued, reminding him of the beginning stages of the mind control drugs Whittaker had used on him. Hating that sensation, he opened his eyes and realized the two women had left the room.

From his position in the bed, he could observe them at a workstation, examining something with a microscope.

His marrow sample? he wondered. A moment later, Liliana's colleague waved a blue light over something and a slight yellow-green became visible near the bottom of the microscope. As she passed it over a nearby test tube, the color became a bright phosphorescent neon green.

Liliana patted her friend on the back. They discussed something, but it was impossible for him to hear what it was.

The light-headedness intensified, creating a disturbing whirl that had him wanting to vomit. Taking a deep breath, he closed his eyes and tried to combat the nausea.

Whittaker listened to the message Bruno had left him.

Fate was working in his favor for a change.

If Carrera had taken Bradford to the lab, it was possible she was administering the inhibitor, and none too soon. He might be able to save at least a few of the subjects they had so diligently engineered for sale if he could get his hands on her inhibitor.

He parked his Suburban in front of the building, walked to the secured door, and swiped his key to enter.

Inside, Bruno and Howard were at a far door, guarding what looked to be a sleeping Bradford. He paused briefly for their report, but they advised that nothing unusual had happened.

Whittaker continued into the lab. Carrera and her colleague Dr. Rojas were examining a vial of something that was glowing brightly under a black light.

"Is that Bradford's blood?" he asked, pointing to the test tube.

"A bone marrow sample. That seems to be the place where the Wardwell genes have been incorporated," Dr. Rojas advised.

"And where they're producing the proteins that are creating the ossification in Jesse's body," Liliana tacked on.

"What about the glow in the blood?" he questioned, recalling the bits of light in the earlier samples Carrera had drawn.

"Free-floating marrow and osteoblasts. Both were likely produced by the hybrid genes in Jesse's system," Liliana answered and motioned to the door to the treatment room. "We're filtering his blood to attempt to cut down on the number of bone-producing proteins. That should help control the damage to his body."

Whittaker nodded and glanced toward the door. Bradford had not moved since he had entered a few minutes earlier. *Playing possum?* he thought but then returned his attention to the physicians.

"You'll also be using the inhibitor to control the genes?" And when they did, he would snag a sample somehow.

"Not yet." Liliana held up a test tube with glittering bits

floating in it. "We don't know if the inhibitor will contain the replication in his marrow because of the difference with what's happening with Caterina."

"Different? How?" he asked and jammed his hands in his pockets, playing with his change as he waited for an answer.

"With Caterina we needed to control the replication of the hybrid genes, but the cells being produced were not essential for life-sustaining functions," Dr. Rojas began.

"In Jesse's case, we can't inhibit bone marrow formation. The marrow produces too many necessary cells. So for now, no inhibitor. We'll just eliminate the excess proteins from his blood," Liliana finished.

Fuck, Whittaker thought and rubbed his hand across his buzz cut. "When will you know?"

"When we've done enough testing," Liliana advised in the tone he recognized as her don't-mess-with-me stand. Grudgingly he admired her tenacity, but he had to find a way to get the inhibitor.

"Since Bradford's down for the count, I'm going to grab a dinner break. Howard, come with me so you can take over for Bruno later."

Liliana stood silent until the two men had left. Then she faced her friend and the tube that she held. "Can you set up some kind of test of what the inhibitor will do to the marrow?"

Carmen brought Jesse's marrow sample up to the room light. Even without the black light, the glow was bright. "I can clone it. Analyze how it reacts."

She hated sounding like Whittaker, but she had to know. "How long will that take?"

Carmen shrugged. "Can't say. In the meantime, maybe

you should assess just where these genes are at work besides the marrow. Give us an idea how serious his condition is."

She thought of her visual exam and the bony parts it had revealed. Wondered how she would expand on that assessment when Carmen handed her a handheld black light.

"Run it over his body. Whatever glows—"

"We'll know where something is up."

With a nod, Liliana grabbed the portable unit and headed into the treatment room to examine Jesse.

CHAPTER 11

Jesse's eyes were shut tight, and his breathing had the slow, measured cadence of sleep.

The clink of glass and metal, Carmen stirring something probably, filtered into the room. Liliana shut the door to block out any sound.

Jesse was lying on top of the covers, his upper body exposed and connected to the cell separator by the tubes carrying his blood into the machine. Within the unit were a series of filters specifically chosen to remove the dangerous proteins from Jesse's blood. Liliana hoped that would contain the bone formation.

She approached cautiously, anxious about disturbing his rest. At his side, she flipped on the black light, and immediately parts of his body began to gleam with a paler, less dense version of the yellow-green of his marrow.

The hardened knuckles and back of his hand.

The injury along his left side where he had been recently Tasered, now nearly healed with a coating of something other than skin.

She walked to his other side, and the larger batch along his ribs phosphoresced. More pronounced and shining brightly beneath the black light.

As she moved, the light played across the IV tubes and bits of yellow-green shone back in his blood.

So much contamination, she thought, and when she turned back, the black light skimmed along his skin and her breath whistled out in surprise. She leaned close to his arm and focused the beam on his bicep.

Was she imagining the glow lying just beneath the surface of his skin?

She snapped off the light and laid her hand on his arm, gently palpated the muscle beneath. Harder than just muscle. Rock hard, but with Jesse that expression had an entirely new meaning.

He was turning to bone, and she had little idea on how to stop it. And if she didn't...

She looked up at his face—that movie star face. Tears welled up in her eyes as she imagined that visage hard and still in a death mask of bone. Imagined that playful dimple gone forever.

She laid her hand on the strong line of his jaw, traced the spot where that dimple would come out and play.

Jesse opened his eyes slowly, but as he saw who it was, he fixed his gaze on her face and smiled until he realized she was crying.

He awkwardly took hold of her hand but grimaced, probably as the needles in his arm pinched with the motion.

"You're not crying for me, are you, Liliana?"

She liked the sound of her name on his lips. The way his eyes had darkened to the gray of storm clouds as he noted her upset.

"What if I was?" she said defensively, although it seemed to be a losing battle to guard her heart.

He smiled again and shifted his hand to bring hers to

his lips. A whisper of a kiss across her knuckles created a flutter in her midsection as he said, "You have the hands of a healer."

When he opened her hand and dropped another kiss in the center of her palm, her stomach did a somersault that kick-started a more dangerous response farther down.

"Don't care about me," he whispered against her palm.

"Why not?" She sat on the edge of the bed, leaning toward him.

The smile on his lips faded, and he released her hand as he said, "Because I'm not worth the pain I'll bring into your life."

It was crazy. *Madly and certifiably crazy,* she thought only a second before she said, "Why don't you let me be the judge of that."

And then she was closing the distance between them until her lips hovered close to his and their gazes locked.

Inquisitive.

Determined.

Alive with doubt about that next step.

Jesse slipped his hand to the back of her head, cradled it in his hand, his fingers tunneling into the thick, silky strands of her hair. Urging her closer until his lips played on hers.

So smooth, he thought, rubbing his mouth along her lips.

So sweet as he allowed himself a taste.

Shock filled her warm brown gaze before her eyelids fluttered closed and she released herself entirely to the kiss. Her mouth moving along his, exploring it. Opening, the wetness of her tongue passing over the edges of his mouth, dragging a groan from him as his body responded.

From somewhere, a persistent beeping penetrated his brain and was followed by the jangle of the doorknob.

They broke apart, breathing heavily, but seemingly in control as Carmen entered the room.

"I heard the warning signal from the pulse oximeter," Carmen said, glancing at where their hands were still joined. Where Jesse's hand was now minus the finger sensor for the monitoring device.

Liliana fumbled with the sensor. "I was just checking it out," she lied, earning a knowing smile from her friend.

"*Sí,* I can tell you were just checking things out," Carmen replied, choking back a chuckle.

Liliana glanced at her watch. The plasmapheresis had already been running for nearly an hour. Just another hour to go. "Let me just double-check Jesse's vitals, and then you and I can go over what you've got."

"You're the boss," Carmen said, but before she could leave the room, Whittaker returned with the other agent, who positioned himself by the door inside the room with them.

"Actually, *I'm* the boss," Whittaker clarified, earning a glare from Carmen as she exited, brushing past the blond-haired hulk at the door.

"Then maybe you can do something important, like ask Bruno to pick us up some dinner. Jesse will be hungry by the time this therapy is done," Liliana said, clearly also displeased with Whittaker's high-handedness.

A dull rose color spread up from the collar of Whittaker's starched white shirt. "Just give Bruno your order on your way out, Dr. Carrera."

"Thank you, Special Agent. Is there anything else you need tonight?" she asked, pointedly arching a brow.

"I need to speak with Mr. Bradford. Privately, if you don't mind."

Liliana took a glimpse at Jesse, a slight furrow marring her brow. "Are you feeling up to it?"

He peered past her to Whittaker, noting the chill in the man's gray gaze and the tight set of his jaw. Whether or not he was feeling up to it, Jesse would endure whatever was necessary to keep Whittaker's fallout from landing on Liliana.

"I'm fine. Just a little light-headed."

Preferably from her kisses and not the treatment.

With a sharp bop of her head, she rose from the bed and departed, closing the door behind her.

Whittaker crossed the room, hands jammed into his pockets and jingling the change in a habit that Jesse was finding to be increasingly annoying.

"What do you want?" Jesse asked.

"You seem to be getting quite friendly with Dr. Carrera," the black-ops leader said.

Carelessly, Jesse swiped at his mouth and looked for any sign of lipstick, not realizing the import of what he had done until a sly grin came to Whittaker's face.

"Very friendly, I gather," the other man said.

"Nothing's happened," Jesse lied, grasping his hands together to keep away from any other incriminating actions.

"Actually, it's very good that she's getting to like you. Maybe even trusting you."

Jesse wasn't keen on where Whittaker was going. "What do you want?"

"The two doctors have an inhibitor complex they've been using on Caterina Shaw, apparently with some success," Whittaker advised and approached the IV lines running into Jesse's arm.

"That's good, right?" Jesse asked and flinched as Whittaker negligently flicked his finger against one of the lines, causing the needle in his arm to pinch painfully.

"They don't plan on using it on you. At least not yet, so—"

"We wait. I'm not feeling all that bad," Jesse advised, but Whittaker got in his face.

"*We* can't wait. I need that complex for the patients back at the lab. Your sister will need that complex eventually, so you're going to get it for me."

"How can I do that?" Jesse asked, unprepared for Whittaker's response.

CHAPTER 12

Whittaker jabbed his index finger into Jesse's chest, the tip of it painfully sharp. "Figure it out. The vials are on the lab table."

"You expect me to just snatch them?" Jesse asked, narrowing his eyes as he judged the other man's intent.

Whittaker cocked his head to the side. "I thought the sportscasters said you had the best hands in the NFL. Put them to use on something besides Dr. Carrera."

Without waiting for a response, Whittaker hurried from the room, leaving Jesse to watch his retreating back and endure the smirk of the goon still standing by the door.

From his spot in bed, Jesse was able to observe Liliana and her friend as they moved back and forth between the microscope and two racks of test tubes a few feet away. He wondered if one of the racks contained the medication that Whittaker wanted him to grab.

The two women repeatedly huddled over the equipment, until after a few minutes, Liliana raised her face and shot a glance in his direction.

As she noted his attention, she smiled, but it was a tired smile and didn't quite reach up into her eyes.

Carmen must have realized she no longer had Liliana's

attention. Once she tracked her friend's gaze and confirmed what had caught her friend's eye, she nudged Liliana playfully, urging her in the direction of the treatment room.

Liliana rolled her eyes, handed Carmen the file in her hand, and walked toward Jesse.

Was he imagining the sexy sway in her hips? Before he could decide, Whittaker's instructions came rushing back.

Grab the vials. Steal them from Liliana.

Rob Liliana of the inviting walk and eyes as warm as freshly baked chocolate brownies. Those full lips, ends turned up in a smile, which had felt so wonderful beneath his.

Her touch. Tender. Caring.

Whittaker wanted him to steal from her. To lie to her. Again.

A sick feeling gelled in his gut, and Liliana was quick to move to his side. Uninhibited as she placed her hand over his, she took a spot on the edge of the bed and asked, "Are you okay?"

No, he wasn't.

He might have been a womanizer and occasional drunk. He might have let fame get to his head and become a jerk, but . . .

He had never been a thief. Not even as a poor kid.

But if he didn't get the inhibitor . . .

"Jesse?" she pressed again and gently squeezed his hand, her touch reassuring and kind.

It only increased the tension within him. If he didn't get the drug, other patients might die. His sister might not get it when she needed it.

"Just feeling a little woozy still," he fibbed, imagining that he might be able to use a bit of weakness quite effectively during his subterfuge.

She patted his hand and hurried around to where the pulse oximeter registered his vitals. Examining them, she shook her head. "Oxygen saturation and pulse seem normal."

Snagging a stethoscope hanging from the cart, as well as a manual blood pressure device, she eased the cuff around his arm and measured his blood pressure.

"Also normal."

He shrugged. "Maybe I'm just weak from hunger," he teased, trying to keep things lighthearted to avoid any suspicions on her part.

She dropped her hands into her lap, still holding the stethoscope and blood pressure device, and peered at him intently. It was the kind of look a mother might shoot an ailing child on a school day. A school day with an upcoming test, he thought, afraid she was not quite buying his act. But then she nodded and said, "We ordered some food from my parents' restaurant. We'll pick it up on the way home."

Home, he thought, liking the way she said it. Allowing himself to imagine for the briefest of moments what it might be like to have a home with a woman like Liliana.

"Sounds good." He relaxed back against the pillows and closed his eyes, unable to keep his gaze on her for fear that she would see through his deceit.

The caring pass of her hand along his face awoke need and guilt. Made him realize how long it had been since someone had shown any kind of real emotion toward him. Made him acknowledge that this was just another relationship he was going to fuck up.

He kept his eyes closed as he mentally counted down the minutes and listened to the sounds of activity outside the room. The soft murmur of the voices of the two women and the clink and clatter of the equipment as they worked.

He heard a softly muttered, "It's time," and wondered if they were talking about him.

He half opened his eyes. Liliana was approaching, the stethoscope draped around her neck. The ends dangled close to her breasts, and he dragged his gaze from them and up to her face.

She was staring at him. Her expression concerned, intense.

"Hey, Doc." He shot her a smile.

She sat on the bed and grinned, but as he had noted before, it didn't quite reach up into her eyes. He could understand why.

"It's been a rough day for you," he said and cupped the side of her face in his hand.

"Not as hard as for you."

He shot a half glance at the connections running in and out of his body and shrugged. "I'll take this over being sacked by the defensive line any day."

Her smile brightened with that, awakening glittering bits of gold in her otherwise dark brown eyes. "My brother Tony probably would agree with you. He was a quarterback in high school."

Her affection for her brother was obvious. Jesse wanted to hear more. "Does he still play?"

Liliana shook her head. "He's concentrating on school now. And working at the restaurant. It's the only way to make ends meet."

"I understand," he said, and he did. He had lived that kind of life early on, always struggling to keep ahead. The battle to just survive had been a major driving force in his desire to be the best so he could change things for his family.

"I know you do," she replied and touched a sympathetic hand to his. Her hand was so small and delicate. So trusting, which only made his gut tighten with disgust at what he would have to do.

Her eyes narrowed for a moment. She was too keen an observer and had likely noticed the tension in him, so he brushed it off by saying, "Just thinking about my sis. I miss her."

Liliana bought his explanation and relaxed. Slipped her hand into his, urging it from her face and down to rest in her lap as she sat beside him.

"I'm sure your sister thinks about you. Worries how you are. Maybe when this is all over—"

"I'll call her," he said, hoping that he would still be alive when this was all over.

"I'm going to disconnect you from the machines and take another blood sample while I'm doing it. Then we'll get you patched up, pick up dinner, and get you home."

"You're the boss," he said and smiled, dragging a reluctant grin to her lips.

"Don't let Whittaker hear you say that."

"Fuck Whittaker," he groused, wishing he actually could tell the black-ops leader to take a flying leap.

"Stuff it, Bradford," Whittaker's guard said from his spot at the door.

Liliana rolled her eyes and said, "Let's get going." In her no-nonsense way, she made short work of getting him disconnected, taking the blood sample, and helping him dress so they could leave.

As he let his legs slide over the edge of the bed, he didn't have to feign a sudden bout of dizziness. The room spun for a few seconds. She rushed to his side, providing her shoulder so he could steady himself.

"It may be a few days while your body readjusts to the change in blood volume. No exercise or intense activity. You've also got to watch for bruising of any kind, because we gave you an anticoagulant."

"Got you, Doc," he said and gingerly stood, relying on her assistance for balance.

When he stabilized, he cautiously trudged out to the lab. Bruno and Howard immediately fell in step behind him. As he neared the worktable in the middle of the lab, he spotted the two racks of test tubes. One set glowed with neon color, while the tubes in the other rack contained a clear liquid.

The inhibitor complex.

Beside him, Liliana took a step toward those racks, the test tubes with the blood samples she had taken in her hand. As she laid the tubes on the counter, he made his move, faking a stumble. His one hand skidded across the surface of the worktable and upended the racks with all the samples, sending test tubes skittering across the surface of the table and onto the floor of the lab.

Liliana was instantly at his side, steadying him. Her obvious concern was for him and not the materials he had sent flying.

"Are you okay?" she said, allowing her gaze to travel over his face while her hands grasped his sides.

His hand was only an inch from one of the test tubes Whittaker wanted. Just an inch away, only . . .

He couldn't do it.

He couldn't betray her trust, fragile as it was.

Suddenly firm hands were on him, grabbing his shoulders and hauling him upright. Yanking him away from the samples he was supposed to steal.

"I've got him," Bruno said and jerked his head in Howard's direction. "Help the docs clean up while I get Bradford to the car."

A pained look crossed Jesse's face, forcing Liliana to admonish Bruno. "Take it easy. Jesse's still weak from the plasmapheresis."

"Yeah, right," Bruno said and dragged Jesse away.

Liliana turned to help Carmen clean the mess, but Howard was immediately there and snapped up his hand. "Careful. There's broken glass all over. I'll take care of this."

Howard then carefully collected the scattered tubes that were salvageable and placed them back in the racks.

Carmen advised Liliana, "I can see that you're worried. Why don't you go see what's up with Jesse while we finish up in here."

Liliana didn't hesitate. She grabbed her purse and medical bag and hurried outside to where the big black Suburban was parked in front of the lab building. With the dark-tinted windows, she couldn't see what was happening, so she walked to the driver's-side door and rapped on the glass with her knuckles.

The glass inched down guardedly, and at her questioning stare, Bruno said, "He's in the back passenger seat."

Liliana popped open the door behind Bruno and sat next to Jesse. His eyes were closed and his hand rested on the seat, palm up. She eased her hand into his. A chill lingered on his skin, probably from a combination of the cold in the treatment room and a possible drop in blood pressure.

"How are you feeling?"

Like a royal shit, Jesse wanted to say as he faced her. He had almost betrayed her, but in not doing so, he had possibly harmed the other patients and his sister.

"I'm okay."

Her eyes narrowed as she observed him, obviously concerned, intensifying his guilt. With a quick dip of her head that sent the silky locks of her hair waving with the action, she said, "Maybe you'll feel better after you've had a chance to eat."

Howard pulled open the front passenger door and jumped up into the seat. "We're set to go," he said and tapped the dash several times in a signal to his partner to get a move on.

Bruno whipped onto the roadway. Early evening had little traffic volume, and in no time they had made it to Liliana's parents' restaurant.

El Mirador was on the main drag in Bradley Beach, and there wasn't an empty spot anywhere nearby. Bruno pulled up into the alley behind the restaurant.

"I'll be back in a second," she said, exited the car, and entered through the service entrance straight into the kitchen.

Her mother was prepping a plate but smiled as she noticed Liliana. *"Mi'ja,"* she said and wrapped her arms around her daughter.

Liliana hugged her back hard and, after they separated, pointed to a bag on a nearby table. "I'm assuming that's for me."

Her mother pressed the paper bag into her hands. "I made some of my special *sopa de pollo* for your friend. To help him feel better."

She grinned and shook her head. Her *mami* always thought food could cure most anything. "I know he'll love it," she replied and hugged her mother good-bye.

"I'll be by tomorrow," she tossed out as she paused to hug her father and then exited.

The Suburban waited in the lot, intimidating in the growing dark of the night.

She jumped back into the passenger seat, and the aromas of dinner quickly escaped the container, seasoning the air with the enticing scents from the food her parents had prepared.

"It smells wonderful," Jesse said and rubbed his flat midsection as if in anticipation of the meal.

She grinned back. "It is, and *Mami* even made some soup just for you."

His brows knitted together. "Just for me? Why?"

"It's super special. Sure to cure the common cold and an assortment of ailments."

Jesse's grin widened, bringing alive the engaging dimple to the side of his enticing lips. "I could use something like that right now."

She eased her hand back into his and squeezed gently. "You'll feel better in no time."

Jesse twined his fingers with hers, enjoying the repartee, with his guilt somewhat diminished. He hadn't stolen the inhibitor, which would displease Whittaker. But he hadn't betrayed her trust.

At least not tonight.

They traveled in silent camaraderie for the remaining

few minutes to his home. Howard and Bruno were quick to urge them from the vehicle, with Bruno providing minimal assistance to Jesse.

Jesse plopped into a chair by the kitchen table while Bruno, once again displaying his domestic abilities, laid out the placemats, dishes, and cutlery. Howard assumed a place just beyond the table, hands held before him in that stereotypical cop pose.

She brought the plastic takeout trays to the table and uncovered them, releasing even more of the aromatic fragrances from the dishes.

Enchiladas. Chicken in a rich mole sauce garnished with toasted pumpkin seeds. Neatly wrapped flautas topped with some *queso fresco*. Not to mention the chicken soup and a trio of side dishes. Refried beans, yellow rice, and ripe plantains drizzled with sour cream and more *queso fresco*.

"That looks and smells great," Jesse replied as she grabbed a ladle Bruno had provided and spooned soup into his bowl.

"She and dad are great cooks. It's made the restaurant a big success, only..."

Bruno sat beside Jesse and said, "Only what?"

"They had a fire some years back. Nearly put them out of business."

"Sorry to hear that," Bruno said, and a muffled cough erupted from Howard.

Bruno looked over at him. "Not joining us?"

"Ate already. You should watch what you eat," Howard cautioned.

Bruno, who Liliana was beginning to suspect was not the brightest bulb, looked down at the slight bulge in his midsection and then glared at Howard. "I'm not fat, man."

Howard said nothing else, just remained in the pose, staring straight ahead as if the three of them were not sitting only a few feet away. Unnerving, and in the back of her brain, it occurred to her that Howard's earlier warning had to do with more than the food.

Was he worried Bruno was getting too friendly with them? And what if he was? They weren't criminals.

"Soup's delicious," Jesse said as he brought another spoonful up to his mouth.

"I'll let *Mami* know."

Jesse savored the richness of the dish and wondered if it was possible that the love it had been prepared with somehow made it tastier. He hoped that one day he would be able to thank Liliana's mother himself for the meal.

Probably unlikely, but then again, he had to have something to look forward to besides helping his sister. The latter still seemed like a long shot, given everything happening with his body and the people with whom he was dealing. Although he had agreed to assist Whittaker, he didn't really trust he would keep his word. For that matter, he still wasn't sure that he could rely on Whittaker's assertion that his sister was sick. But he would not let his doubts possibly endanger Jackie.

Spooning up more of the soup, he considered whether Liliana was a woman of her word, and the answer was immediate.

Yes.

Which made him consider whether telling Liliana the truth would help in any way. Whether it would abate his guilt about deceiving her.

But as she sat beside him, quietly eating, he realized that if he told her the truth now and she wouldn't play along with him, he would be risking his sister's well-being and possibly even Liliana's life.

So instead, he finished off the bowl of soup and afterward felt amazingly recharged. "This *is* a cure," he said, rubbing his hand across his stomach.

"There's more," she said and would have risen to remove the soup bowls, but Jesse stood instead.

"Let me." He quickly cleared off the three bowls, and by the time he returned to the table, Liliana had served each of them an assortment of the dishes.

As he watched Liliana, Jesse thought about how different she was from the women in his past. Women who had warmed his bed—but not his heart, he reluctantly acknowledged—and who had all been alike. The same false smiles and equally plastic parts.

Unlike Liliana, he thought, shooting a glance out of the corner of his eye at her generous curves. Provided by nature, of that he had no doubt. The comely doctor would likely not approve of enhancing herself physically, since she prized other, more important traits.

Intelligence. Dedication. Honor.

In the short time they had spent together, he knew more about her than the many women who had passed through his life.

She faced him, her fork halfway to her mouth, and paused. A furrow developed in the middle of her forehead as she considered him. "Is everything okay?"

He wanted to say that it wasn't. That he had so much to tell her. That he needed to kiss her again and find satisfaction with her like none he had experienced.

But the words failed him.

"Everything is fine. The food is...amazing. I've never had anything like it."

"Me neither," Bruno advised and pushed away from the table. He rose and gestured to Howard, who had remained silently passive throughout their entire meal.

"You sure you don't want some of this?" Bruno asked the other guard.

The distant rumble of the garage door opening snared Howard's attention. "Whittaker's here."

Beside her, Liliana sensed the immediate tension that entered Jesse's body, but before she could say anything, Howard barked out an order.

"Bruno. Get Bradford settled upstairs. He probably needs some rest."

Jesse pushed off abruptly from the table. "I think I can find the way to my own bedroom."

He held out his hand to her.

She glanced at the three men, wondering at the hostility she sensed among them. Footsteps sounded in the hall, approaching briskly, and a moment later, Whittaker appeared at the far door to the kitchen.

He jammed his hands on his hips, which pulled back his suit jacket, revealing the double holster beneath with the menacing grips of his gun.

He arched a brow and asked, "Something wrong?"

CHAPTER 13

Tired. I'm going upstairs to rest," Jesse replied, and before Whittaker could protest that statement, Jesse was in motion, leaving the room—and her—behind.

Whittaker glared at her. "How did the treatment go?"

"It drained him physically, but I'm hopeful that the samples we took after the therapy will show a reduction in the bone-morphogenic proteins in his blood."

"What about his marrow? When will you test the inhibitor?" Whittaker snapped.

Liliana rose from the table, intending to follow Jesse as soon as she could finish with the FBI agent's questioning. "Dr. Rojas should still be at the lab, cloning the marrow specimens so that we have enough material—"

"And when will that be?" Whittaker barked.

Anger ground through her at his attitude. She wasn't one of his men he could order around or a criminal he was trying to intimidate. Which made her wonder yet again why it was that Jesse was being treated like a prisoner.

"Special Agent Whittaker. I assure you that we are working as quickly as possible and in accordance with accepted protocols."

He didn't miss the chill rebuke in her tone. With an

exasperated sigh, he ran his fingers over his buzz cut and shook his head. "I understand."

Liliana supposed that was about as close to an apology as she would ever get from the taciturn agent.

"If you'll excuse me, I'm going to check on Jesse one last time before heading home."

She left Whittaker staring at his two men. He waited until he could hear her footsteps on the stairs and then questioned them.

"Did Bradford get the inhibitor?"

A puzzled look came to Bruno's face, but Howard quickly answered, "He went for it but then chickened out."

"Damn," Whittaker cursed.

"Not to worry, boss," Howard replied, reached into his suit jacket pocket, and pulled out two test tubes.

"The inhibitor?" Whittaker questioned and waggled his fingers for the tubes.

"Yes, sir. When Bradford failed to fulfill his mission, I stepped in," Howard said as he placed them in his boss's hand.

Whittaker held the test tubes up to the light. They were filled with clear liquid. Hopefully enough for Morales and Edwards to not only use on the patients, but to analyze and synthesize more.

"Did they see you take them?" he asked as he pocketed the medication.

Howard shook his head. "No, and I don't think they'll notice that they're gone. Bradford knocked over the racks and quite a few of the tubes broke."

"There was glass all over the place," Bruno jumped in, but Howard shot him a dirty look.

"No thanks to you. I think we have a problem with Bruno. He's getting a little too friendly with Bradford and the doctors," Howard warned.

Whittaker glared at his other man, who squirmed beneath his observation.

"I know what I have to do, boss. Just say the word and they're all history," Bruno replied, a whiny tone weeding through his words.

"For now, keep things normal. Even let Bradford out and about, as long as you keep an eye on him. Dr. Carrera is already uneasy, and we must not let her think there's anything unusual going on."

Whittaker raised his hand, crooked his forefinger at Howard. "Come with me. I may need assistance at our other location."

Whittaker shot a withering glare at Bruno. "Make sure Bradford is tucked in for the night and that Dr. Carrera is satisfied that all is in order."

"Yes, sir," Bruno replied, mimicking Howard's earlier tone. Not that it would help, Whittaker thought. Bruno came from the streets and lacked the spit and polish Howard had acquired from his many years of serving beside him in the military. Whittaker would trust Howard with his life, and as for Bruno...

He was as expendable as the people he was guarding.

"We'll check back later," Whittaker said and exited with Howard.

Bruno watched them go, an unsettling feeling in his gut. He didn't much like the way either of the two men treated him, as if he was inferior. And despite his assertion that he'd kill either Bradford or the doc without hesitation, well...

He wasn't quite sure it would be all that easy to do, not that he hadn't disposed of his share of miscreants in the past when it was necessary. But the doctor and Bradford were different.

Different, but still dead meat as far as Whittaker was concerned.

With that in mind, he hurried upstairs to make sure all was in order as Whittaker had instructed.

Liliana listened to the beat of Jesse's pulse and glanced at the pressure gauge. Perfectly normal, which brought a smile to her face.

"Everything is fine," she said, completing the exam.

"And *I* feel fine," he said, trying to relieve her of any concerns after the little spell he had faked back at the lab.

"Glad to hear that." She was just putting away the blood-pressure device when Bruno appeared in the doorway, a stern and yet almost comical look on his face.

"Something wrong?" she asked.

"Just wanted to make sure everything was okay up here," Bruno replied and glanced between the two of them.

"Everything's okay, thanks. I won't be much longer," she answered. Although she was done with her assessment, she wasn't quite ready to leave Jesse for the night.

Bruno turned his attention to Jesse, who said, "Could you please see the doctor to her car after she's done?"

"Sure thing, Jesse. I'll give you two a little time alone," he said and, with a conspiratorial wink, closed the door behind him.

"He's not your typical FBI agent, is he?" Liliana asked, both amused and puzzled by Bruno's behavior.

"Maybe he got pistol-whipped once too often," Jesse teased, leaning back into the pillows, although his gaze never wavered from her face.

His too-earnest attention was a little disconcerting, and she averted her gaze as she put everything back into her medical bag. She zipped it shut and was about to rise when Jesse lovingly placed his hand on her arm.

She followed the long, strong line of his arm up to his face, which had grown serious.

"About the kiss, Doc..."

She waved him off. "No need to apologize."

He chuckled, and a hint of mischief glittered in his gaze. "Not apologizing, Liliana."

She shouldn't like the way her name sounded on his lips. He was her patient and therefore off-limits. He was unpredictable, with violence just a hair's breadth away at any moment. And he might be dying. Dying unless...

"I need to keep a level head. Maintain order and balance," she cautioned, maybe more for her own welfare than his.

The glitter intensified in his gaze, and the dimple winked at her as his smile emerged. "Do I upset that order and balance?"

He cupped her cheek and ran his finger along an ever-intensifying flush. The heat of it warmed her skin, especially when he dipped his thumb down to trace the edge of her lips.

She needed distance.

Immediately.

There was just one way to get it.

"I can't trust you, Jesse. Your anger and your past. The future you may not have if I can't—"

"Maintain order and balance," he said, all of his earlier playfulness receding.

His gaze was colder now, an icy blue that froze her out. A hard, granite-like set to his features.

"I'm sorry, Jesse."

"No need to apologize, Doc. I guess I'll see you some-time tomorrow," Jesse replied, hands fisted at his sides to keep from reaching out for her again. He wanted to shake her until she admitted her feelings, but then again, she expected that kind of behavior from him. Uncontrolled. Even violent, as she had seen earlier in the day.

It took all of his willpower to curb the twined serpents of anger and need roiling in his gut. But he did. Because he wanted to prove something to her. Because he needed to prove it to himself.

He could be better than he had been before.

She made him want to be a better man.

She seemed to understand he was at the edge, since she gave a curt jerk of her head and her short strides carried her from his bedroom.

Liliana's soft footfalls came on the stairs, followed by a muffled conversation with Bruno, the distant rumble of the garage door opening, and a car starting.

She was on her way home.

Somehow with her gone, his house felt even less like a home. Maybe because in the short time she had spent with him, something had changed.

Something he wasn't sure he could live without again.

He closed his eyes, imagining how different his life could be if he had someone who cared for him. Maybe even someone who could love him. Envisioning that one day he might be the kind of man worthy of such affection.

But no matter what he imagined, Liliana was always in the picture. Always by his side, providing love.

An impossible future, Jesse thought, running his hand over the patch of bone on his side. Trailing it upward to rest directly above his heart as he imagined it hardening, as well.

Love was not meant for him. Especially with a woman like Liliana, he thought, but somehow she came to him in his dreams once again.

And as he had before, Jesse welcomed her embrace.

CHAPTER 14

Liliana phoned the lab just to make sure Carmen would soon be on her way home. Her friend was notorious for getting so involved in a project that she lost all sense of time. More than once Carmen had worked through the night on an analysis or had forgotten to get something to eat.

Carmen answered on the first ring, and Liliana admonished her to call it a night.

"Don't worry. Ramon is coming by to get me when he gets off duty. We're going to grab a bite before heading home," Carmen replied.

"Heading home? As in your home, or his?" she kidded while wondering if her cousin and Carmen had gotten to the spending-the-night-together phase. If so, she wondered why she hadn't noticed it before.

"That's TMI for now, Liliana. I'll see you in the morning," Carmen confirmed and hung up.

Too much information, huh? Carmen had never been one to keep any kind of info from her before, but then again, in all the time they had known each other, Carmen had not been seriously dating anyone.

And if she had to pick someone for her best friend, she couldn't think of anyone better than her cousin Ramon.

Liliana strolled to her bedroom and changed into comfortable flannel pajamas. Even with their heavier weight there was a nip in the air, so she grabbed a robe and slipped it on.

Although she'd had a long and demanding day, she was too wired to sleep. In the living room, she snapped on the ten-o'clock news, but as she sat there, only half listening, her mind busy processing the overload of the day's events, she stared out the window.

Must be a full moon, she thought, noticing the glint of silver on the waves and the brightness of the occasional wind-blown whitecaps.

A full moon might explain her earlier lunacy, she surmised and headed out to the small balcony off the living room. Her condo was located on the side of the building, just one unit away from those that faced the ocean. Luckily that was forward enough to still give her a view of the water.

Out on the balcony, a strong wind blew off the ocean, crisp and bringing the first warning that winter would soon arrive. Out beyond the boardwalk, the dune grasses danced wildly in the wind while the pennants strung between a strip of stores and the casino in Asbury Park fluttered and snapped.

A lone pedestrian, head tucked down into a heavy jacket, braved the boardwalk, his steps brisk as he hurried from Asbury Park and deeper into the heart of Ocean Grove.

In the dim illumination from the streetlights, Liliana could make out the shape of the cross on the beach before her. It was just one of several along the beach, a testament to God's Little Square Mile on the Shore, as the town was proud to say.

She reached up and took hold of the gold crucifix she had worn all her life. It was cold beneath her hand, the surface smooth from wear and prayer.

She needed prayer tonight. For guidance on what to do in her confusion about Jesse.

Her heart told her to trust, but her heart had been wrong before. She had loved and trusted her ex-fiancé, and he had both mentally and physically abused her. If not for her brother Mick and for Caterina, it might have taken her longer to find the strength to put an end to that relationship.

But she had found the strength.

And she hoped that she had become a better judge of a man's character, but if she had, why did she find herself attracted to Jesse?

An even stronger gust of wind whipped down the street, lifting the hem of her robe and snaking beneath to chill her to the bone.

Time to go in, but as she settled down on her sofa, ready to let the monotones of the nightly news lull her to sleep, her troubled mind continued to race.

She grabbed her laptop from the coffee table and powered it up. As it finished booting, a tiny prompt flared to life in the corner, indicating that her sister Bobbie was online.

She launched Skype and called her, and soon Bobbie's voice came across the computer speakers.

"*Hola, hermanita,*" Bobbie said, the tone of her voice morning bright, but then again, it was well into the day in Iraq, where her sister was serving another tour.

Hopefully her last tour before coming home for college.

A second later, the video clicked to life, too, and there

Bobbie was, dressed in camo. Behind her sister, other female soldiers milled about and the framework of bunks and neatly made beds were visible.

"*Hola,* Bobbie. How's my lil' sis?"

"Better than you, I think. You look tired, Lil," Bobbie replied, leaning toward the web camera as if by doing so she might get a better look.

"It was a long day. How are things there?" she asked, worry creeping in as it always did when she thought about the way her sister risked her life.

"Things are okay. I can't really say much, Lil," Bobbie replied, and Liliana understood.

"I know," she said with an intense sigh that her computer faithfully picked up and transmitted to her sister.

"But things aren't okay with you, I can tell. What's up? Troubles at work?" she asked, and a moment later, a burst of laughter erupted behind Bobbie. Her sister turned, checked it out, and then returned her attention to her computer.

"So, is it work?" Bobbie prompted again.

With a shrug, Liliana replied, "You might say that. He's a patient."

Bobbie grimaced. "Tough one. Hippocratic oath and all that."

All that. Jesse was definitely all that, but also so much more that confused her. "He's very handsome," she told Bobbie and quickly added, "And younger."

"Legal, I hope," Bobbie kidded, dragging a laugh from her sister.

"Definitely legal, *hermanita.*"

Bobbie's brows knitted together. "Will he be your patient for long? Can you wait it out?"

Images of Jesse's body with its patches of bone and

the wildly glowing plug of bone marrow flashed into her brain. She didn't know how to control that. At least not yet, but even if she did...

"Hell, no, Lil. Don't tell me he's dying," Bobbie shot out, concern coloring her tones despite her harsh words.

No, Jesse wasn't dying on her watch. But she also didn't know how long it would be before he stopped being her patient.

"It's complicated," she said, totally uncertain.

Bobbie's brows became even deeper furrows. "Complicated? Tell me the first word that pops into your brain when you think of him."

Shock and awe, Bobbie's stock in trade.

"Sexy," she shot back, grinning devilishly at the stunned look on her baby sister's face.

Bobbie shook her head and then chuckled. "Got me. So what's the second thing you think?"

Liliana shifted her gaze away from the webcam as she pondered it. Word after word popped into her brain before they all coalesced into one apropos description.

"Unpredictable."

Hooting and clapping her hands in amusement, Bobbie replied, "Unpredictable. To a woman who thrives on being practical—"

"Not necessarily," she said, but Bobbie quickly countered with, "You own a ten-year-old sedan that no one under sixty would be caught dead driving."

"It's reliable." A predictable and boring response from a predictable and boring woman. Liliana only hoped that the webcam couldn't pick up the blush of embarrassment on her cheeks.

A loud sound came across the connection and Bobbie

turned to look over her shoulder. Bodies rushed back and forth in the background and Bobbie leaned closer to the camera.

"Gotta roll, *hermanita*. Be careful with Mr. Unpredictable."

"Stay safe." A moment later she was staring at a blank screen where her sister's beautiful face had once been.

Worry for her sister's well-being piled onto all her other concerns. Grabbing her cross, she murmured a quick prayer for her sister and then turned her attention to the television screen. She flipped through channels until she found one where a narrator was providing excruciating and monotonous detail about some nearly extinct furry creature living in some little-known forest. Leaning back against the arm of the sofa, she pulled the blanket up to her chin and closed her eyes.

Half listening to the *blah-blah-blah* of the speaker, she allowed her mind to wander.

Predictably it roamed to thoughts of Jesse, but she didn't battle them. Maybe dealing with him in her dreams would help her handle him in real life.

Carmen was just locking up the lab when Ramon pulled his police cruiser into the parking lot.

Even in the dark she could see his perfectly white teeth in a broad smile. As she hurried to the driver's side of the car, he opened his window and leaned out slightly. From inside the car came the aroma of something spicy.

She inhaled deeply. "Hmm. That smells good."

"I had Tia Mariel make up a sampler from their daily specials. Do you want to go to my place or yours?"

Her place was positively spartan, with few amenities for comfort, possibly because up until Ramon, she had spent most of her time either in the hospital or helping out with some cancer research at a local university laboratory.

"Your place," she replied without hesitation.

Ramon laughed and wagged his head. "One of these days we're going to go shopping and get you some toys."

"Why? You've got enough of them for both of us. Besides, I like spending time with you at your place."

Ramon shot a look at the bulging knapsack she was carrying and pointed to it. "Does that mean you've got a change of clothes in there 'cause you plan to spend the night?"

"It does," she answered without guile. Man-woman things, like patient-doctor things, were out of her arena. She preferred directness in her life, including her relationship with him.

She liked that he was just as direct.

"Good. My house—and my bed—are way closer than yours."

She walked around to the passenger-side door and opened it. Sitting on the seat were a dozen red roses.

"For me?" she asked as she tossed her knapsack onto the floor of the car.

"Didn't want you to think it was all about the sex. I like you. A lot," he said, grabbed hold of the roses, and urged her to take them.

The last time she had gotten flowers was from her father at her med school graduation. Tears stung her eyes as she slipped onto the seat, took hold of the flowers, and pressed them to her chest.

"*Gracias,*" she said, her voice husky with emotion.

Ramon leaned over, grabbed her seat belt, and snapped it shut. After, he brushed his lips against hers and whispered, "Have to take care of my girl."

The feminist in her wanted to rear up, demand that he acknowledge she was a woman and quite capable of taking care of herself. Hell, she'd been doing so for quite some time.

But as her gaze met his, all she could see was caring and not a desire for subjugation. Cradling the straight line of his jaw, she leaned forward and kissed him, leaving no doubt in his mind about what was in her heart. About what she wanted.

When they broke apart, they were both breathing heavily and Ramon shot a half glance at the bag with the take-out food in the backseat.

"Do you think that'll keep in the oven?"

Carmen smiled, reached down, and covered the very obvious proof of his need beneath the khaki of his police uniform. "I think it can wait."

Ramon's eyelids fluttered as she caressed him until desire dragged them close and a rough groan escaped his lips. "*Dios,* you'll get us arrested if you keep this up."

With a final stroke, she primly sat back into her seat. "I've heard handcuffs are quite popular—"

He silenced her by gently placing his finger on her lips. "Don't go there—otherwise I don't think we'll ever make it to my place."

She kissed the tip of his finger and said, "Then please hurry home. I'm hungry."

"Me, too," Ramon replied, but from the wicked grin on his face, she knew it wasn't about the food. It was about

her, something new and decidedly different in her life—
being the center of someone's attention.

She kind of liked it.

Liked him and let her brain wander to whether he
might let her try the handcuffs later that night.

CHAPTER 15

Jesse had been dreaming of her when he fell asleep. Fantasizing about her in the middle of the night when his desire had become so strong, it had woken him. He hadn't been able to go back to sleep since. Every time he closed his eyes, she was there waiting for him. Arms opened wide to hold him close to her silky-smooth skin. Her ample breasts crushed to his chest as he encircled her with his arms and brought her body flush to his.

He gulped in a breath and opened his eyes, painfully erect once again. Or maybe his erection had never ebbed during the course of the long night. It made him wonder if he should do as all those annoying commercials instructed and call a doctor, since it had to have been hours that he was aroused.

Problem was there was only one doctor who could take care of this particular problem.

Rising, he noted out his window that the bright colors of the dawn were pushing away the night sky. In no time at all, the sun would be full, and so he decided it was time to get up anyway. Maybe a nice warm shower would help him get rid of his little problem.

Well, not so little, he thought pridefully.

Shoving aside the sheets, he ambled to the shower, pulling his hair off his face. Scrubbed his morning beard, which rasped loudly in the quiet of the morning.

In the bathroom he stared into the mirror. Considered how he might appear to her. With his shaggy hair and stubble, he was likely not her type. She probably was used to those carefully manicured types in expensive designer suits.

He brushed his teeth, and as he was scrounging around for his deodorant, he noticed the scissors in the drawer. He reached for them almost before he knew what he was doing.

Grabbing his hair in bunches, he snipped and measured. Trimmed a few inches here and there, shaped it as best as he could until it seemed a trifle neater. Then he shaved, scraping off the stubble to reveal the clear skin beneath.

Passing a hand across his face, he nodded in approval and headed for the shower.

With the water as hot as he could stand it, he let the liquid cascade down his shoulders and across his midsection from the jets along the sides of the stall. Soaping up, he ran his hands across his body, flinching as he encountered the large patch on his right side and the smaller but just as troubling spot on his left.

Those physical reminders of his damaged state worked more effectively than any cold shower.

Damaged goods wouldn't appeal to any woman.

Rinsing off quickly, he stepped out of the shower, toweled down with brisk strokes, and returned to his bedroom to dress.

Whittaker was there, Bruno and Howard beside him.

In his hand Whittaker held a small kraft envelope. Howard grasped a black rod that looked way too much like the cattle prod Morales employed in his twisted games. But then Howard whipped his arm and the rod extended to about two feet in length.

Two feet of hard, threatening metal.

"Something wrong?" he asked, striding right up to the trio. If there was one thing he'd learned over his many years of competition, it was to never show your fear.

Whittaker got straight to the point. "I gave you a mission yesterday."

"I tried—"

Howard snapped the steel rod across his left side, just below the bony patch. The blow pounded into his ribs, bringing punishing pain.

The force of the strike was enough to drop him to his knees. Nausea came on strongly, making him dry heave before the embers of anger flared to life.

He was on his knees, struggling for control, when Whittaker opened the kraft envelope and removed something from within.

Photos, he realized, and then the embers the beating had stoked smoldered more powerfully as Whittaker flashed the images of his younger sister before his eyes.

"She's looking good. Howard snapped these last night," Whittaker said and tossed them to the floor before Jesse.

Howard whipped him again, this time across his back.

Jesse went down on all fours from the wallop, his head hanging down, facing the photos of his sister.

Whittaker leaned close and whispered in his ear, "Next time you fail, she's toast."

The rage he had been trying to bank erupted like a backdraft denied air for too long.

He lunged forward, tackling Whittaker to the ground with a thud that shook the floor.

Howard was quickly on Jesse, striking at him with the steel rod, but Jesse blocked the blow and, with a swipe of his leg, took down Howard, as well.

He jumped to his feet, met Bruno's stunned gaze. Before Bruno could reach for his gun, Jesse knocked him out cold with one punch.

Bruno's body had barely hit the ground when Whittaker and Howard were both on him, pummeling him with their fists and landing another powerful swipe that brought him to the ground.

They then began to kick at him, raining blow after blow until Jesse managed to grab Whittaker's leg and force him down once again. He landed a jab that stunned the other man and thought all he had to do was get past Howard and—

Howard hit him hard, across the side of the head.

The crack of the steel rod sent him staggering backward as the warmth of blood trailed down the side of his face.

His knees hit the bed and he crumpled to the ground. Black circles danced before his eyes, and he was having trouble breathing. Each inhalation brought excruciating pain in his side.

He was going to die.

And he was going to have failed his sister, he thought as darkness threatened to overtake him. He sucked air through his nose, trying to lessen the pain, and pushed back at unconsciousness.

With blurry eyes he saw Howard approaching, his nose bloody. A purpling bruise was already forming on the side of his face and he held the long, lethal rod in his hand.

He raised it, and Jesse prepared for the blow, but suddenly Liliana called out, "What the hell is going on?"

CHAPTER 16

*L*iliana.

A moment later she was at his side, her hand at his neck, feeling for his pulse.

Liliana, he thought again.

"I'm here, Jesse," she said, and he realized then that he had said her name.

He dragged in a breath, groaning as his ribs protested the movement, slight as it was.

"Try not to breathe so deeply. You may have a broken rib or two," Liliana warned as she ran her hand across his side, where a deep purple bruise had already formed.

Fear gripped her hard as she noted all the other contusions on his body.

Glaring up at Howard, who still stood by threateningly, a dangerous-looking rod in his hand, she commanded, "Back off."

Howard held his ground while Whittaker scrambled to his feet. The FBI agent approached, looking not much better than Howard. An angry scrape stretched across one cheekbone. One eye sported a shiner, and blood dripped from the side of his mouth.

"I need to get Jesse to a hospital," she said, worried

about his assorted injuries and how his body would react
to the damage. Her one hope was that the plasmapheresis treatment they had run the night before had filtered
out enough of the bone-producing proteins to prevent the
formation of any bone at the various points of damage.

"No. He's a risk to others and to this assignment."

"He may die—"

"But many more may die if this mission is compromised," Whittaker countered.

"He's right," Jesse said, the words weak and choppy.

She stared at Jesse. Like Whittaker, he had an assortment of bruises on his face and a gash on the side of his
head, which was bleeding profusely.

She grabbed a piece of gauze from her medical bag
and placed it over the gash. Applied gentle pressure and
Jesse flinched.

"If we don't get you to a hospital—"

"It's okay. I'll be okay," he replied and moaned from
the pain of speaking.

Liliana rose from where she had been kneeling by Jesse's side.

"Help me get him into bed. Gently. If his ribs are broken, they could puncture a lung."

"Serve the bastard right," Howard muttered beneath his
breath, but a second later, he and Bruno—who had finally
gotten to his feet—were slowly lifting Jesse onto the bed.

Behind them, Whittaker hastily plucked some papers
from the floor and stuffed them into his jacket pocket.

Liliana left Jesse's side and stalked right up to Whittaker. She was so close her nose nearly bumped the bottom of his chin. "What happened here?" she asked.

"Bradford just went crazy," Whittaker said, but he

looked down and to the left, and a little tic played at the corner of his mouth. Sure signs that he was lying.

"What if I can't treat his injuries here?"

"I won't authorize a trip to the hospital," Whittaker reiterated, glancing over her head to where his two men were placing Jesse on the bed.

With a lean forefinger, Whittaker pointed to them. "Time for you to get to work. Maybe call Dr. Rojas for some of that inhibitor."

An uneasy feeling crept into her gut. Not only had he lied to her about the reason for the beating, this was the second time in as many days that he had brought up the medication that she and Carmen had been refining.

As his probing gaze met hers, she worried that he sensed her disquiet and so she quickly looked away, but not before dangling the carrot before him.

"It may be necessary to stop the gene replication in his body with the inhibitor complex. Hopefully our overnight tests with his bone marrow will confirm that it's safe to use on Jesse."

From the corner of her eye, she detected the sly smile before he controlled it. Apprehension settled in more deeply as she returned to Jesse's side. Whittaker wanted the complex enough to beat Jesse even while knowing that such a beating might kill him.

Why would he want the inhibitor? For other patients? But if they had found the other gene therapy patients, why wasn't he telling her so that she could help them?

Maybe because the FBI agent had something to hide.

She sat on the edge of Jesse's bed, but before she started working on Jesse she said, "I suggest the three of you get cleaned up. I'll let you know if I need your help."

Whittaker jerked his head toward the door. "Bruno, stand guard. Howard, you're with me."

Both men snapped to do his bidding, but once they had left, Liliana walked to the door and shut it.

Hurrying back to Jesse, she worked on the gash on his head, which was still bleeding more than she liked. She cleaned the cut with some antiseptic pads from her bag and then closed the wound with butterfly bandages. Blood leaked from the sealed edges for just a moment but then stopped, relieving some of her concern that they had filtered needed clotting elements from Jesse's blood along with the bone proteins.

"Don't worry," Jesse said and patted her thigh before resting his hand there.

The weight of it was comforting, until she noticed the raw abrasions on his knuckles from punching the other men.

"Did you go crazy, Jesse? Because you don't seem very crazy to me right now."

"Doesn't matter," he replied and grimaced as he tried to draw a deeper breath.

It did matter to her. If one of them was lying, she wanted to know who and why.

And she hoped it wasn't Jesse lying, although she sensed she wouldn't get the complete story from either him or Whittaker.

Leaning over Jesse, she placed her hand along the bony patch on his right side.

Jesse reacted immediately, grabbing hold of her hand.

She glanced at him, and his discomfort was clear. He didn't want her to feel that part of him. That inhuman part of him.

"I need to examine you."

Jesse shifted her hand downward, to a narrow line of deep purple bruising beneath the damaged area. Carefully Liliana ran her hand across the rib beneath. The bone appeared to be in one piece.

"It's not broken," she confirmed.

"Hurts like a bitch," he said and covered her hand with his as it rested against his side.

"Tell me what happened, Jesse," she pressed again, pulling her hand away to examine the various other injuries on his body. Worrying that at each site he would soon be developing bone like that on both sides of his ribs and hands.

"Got angry. Went after Whittaker."

This time she didn't doubt him. Nothing about his demeanor suggested he was lying, but despite that, she still knew he was holding back.

That bothered her. A lot. More than it should, maybe because she had wanted more from him.

Jesse could see the disappointment on her face. The emotion replaced her earlier concern over him and her anger with Whittaker.

She was saddened by his actions, and he could understand why.

She didn't like violence. That much had become evident to him over their many meetings.

"It won't happen again, Liliana," he promised, laying his hand over hers once more as it rested on her thigh.

She murmured her acceptance of his statement, then began tending to the abrasions on his hands by carefully smearing antiseptic cream along his knuckles.

He closed his eyes as she cared for him, relishing that gentle touch. Wishing for more of it.

"Jesse," she said.

He popped open his eyes and tracked the line of her sight, aware of what she was eyeing even before his gaze landed on his very obvious erection.

"I'm sorry, but you're a beautiful woman, and sometimes I can't control what I'm feeling." As in most of the time when she touched him or he thought of her, he couldn't control himself.

She shook her head, and the glint of tears there caught his attention.

He cupped her jaw, applied gentle pressure so that she was facing him. "Why the tears, Liliana?"

She tossed her hands up, then laid them on her thighs, where she rubbed her legs nervously. "What you feel... What *I* feel isn't going to ever lead anywhere for us, Jesse."

Score one, he thought. She did have some feelings for him. Woman kinds of feelings.

"I know I'm your patient—"

"It's not that, Jesse. And it's not what's happening to your body or the violence," she said, her voice husky with suppressed emotion.

"Then what is it?" he replied and traced his thumb along her cheek to swipe away the tear that had finally escaped from her eye.

"I don't trust you. And without trust..."

Without trust there was nothing, he knew, and he fisted his hands at his side as he said, "I guess you should finish up then and go home, Doc."

CHAPTER 17

Liliana completed her assessment of Jesse, her initial worries receding as it became apparent his bruises were remaining normal. Ugly as they were, and as troubling as they were, there was no immediate sign of the injuries turning to bone.

The plasmapheresis had made a difference.

A sample would confirm it, but she was hesitant to do anything else to hurt him.

Jesse faced her, wondering why she had stopped, but then again, she had finished checking him out. Doctor-wise, that was. After that initial flare of female interest, every glance and touch had been clinical.

"Something wrong, Doc?" He arched a brow for emphasis. Regretted it as the butterfly bandages close to his temple pulled and pain radiated from the spot of the blow.

"That may be tender for a while," Liliana said and motioned to it.

"And that's a good thing, right?"

She shrugged, expressing her uncertainty about his condition with that simple gesture.

He covered both her hands with his one large one. "What do you need to confirm what's happening?"

"Some samples."

Samples. Giving more blood. Another cut or slice of his body. More damage, but what did it matter? He was damaged goods any way you looked at it.

He held his hands open wide in a go-for-it gesture. "I'm yours."

Liliana drew in a shaky breath. She'd never had a man tell her that. Her ex-fiancé had turned out to be a man who cared only about himself and dominating her. He would never have relinquished control as Jesse had.

"Liliana?" he asked at her prolonged delay.

She wagged her head in chastisement. "Just thinking about where to take the skin sample."

Jesse chuckled, tucked his thumb under her chin, and applied light pressure to raise her gaze to his. "You're not a good liar."

"Neither are you. I don't doubt you went after Whittaker—"

"I did and I'm sorry for it."

She scrutinized his face carefully and let out a rough chuckle. "You're not sorry, Jesse. I suspect you'd do it again, which makes me wonder what he did to piss you off."

This time Jesse was the one who broke eye contact. "Take your pound of flesh, Doc. I'd like to take a nap."

"A sample from your hand will do. And as for a nap, that's a big no with that head injury."

"Will you keep me company?" he asked, faking a little-boy-lost look even as he held out his right hand for her to take her specimen for testing.

"I've got to get to the lab, but I'll be back later."

She efficiently took a small piece of abraded skin from

his knuckle and dropped it into a test tube. Then she drew another vial of blood from him. As she was tucking everything into her medical bag, she dropped one of the tubes. Bending, she reached down for it, and something caught her eye beneath the bed.

She pulled it out and realized it was a photo of a young woman—Jesse's sister. It looked like the kind of photo a private detective would take. The back of the photo was blurry, and the photographer had caught his sister talking to another young girl in front of a brick building. Jackie had a knapsack slung over one shoulder. Judging from the books in the arms of the two girls, the shot had been taken at her college.

A date stamp on the photograph indicated that the photo had been snapped the day before.

"This is your sister, right?" she asked and handed Jesse the photo.

The color slid from his face along with all the earlier good humor that he had mustered despite his injuries. A hard slash replaced his smile as he accepted the photo. Tenderly he ran his fingers along the surface.

"It's Jackie. Whittaker wanted to show me how she was doing."

A dead tone rang in his voice. One that chilled her to the bone and sent warning vibes throughout her body. She suspected Whittaker had had other reasons for the photos and suddenly suspected what had set Jesse off earlier: a threat to his sister.

"That was nice of him," she replied, forced neutrality in her voice.

She knew, Jesse thought, half glancing at her while he stared at the photo of Jackie. The photos had gone flying when he had pounced on Whittaker. In the aftermath of Liliana's arrival, he had seen the other man scrambling to pick them up, but he must have missed this one.

"Very nice," he lied and remembered her words about trust. Or the lack thereof. It would take just a few words from him. Just a few to let her know what was really going on, only...

A few words would risk not only his sister's life, but Liliana's. Instead he said, "I guess you should get going. Maybe ask Bruno to keep me company."

She swung her medical bag back and forth in that nervous gesture that was becoming endearingly familiar. Pursing her lips, she considered him again, suddenly reminding him of his sixth-grade teacher.

Not a good memory. He had to drag up that image next time his wanderings were leading to dangerous thoughts of Liliana.

"See you later," she said, and with a quick dip of her head, she left him with the photo of Jackie.

His little sister looked good. Looked happy.

If she was sick, as Whittaker had said, it was hard to tell that from the photo.

Of course, he hadn't known he was sick, either. Not until the hit that had changed his life.

From outside his door came Bruno's heavy tread up the stairs. He allowed himself one last glimpse of the photo before tucking it into the nightstand drawer for safekeeping.

Bruno stopped at the door to the room, a murderous glare in his eyes. Eyes already showing hints of purple beside a nose nearly twice its normal size.

"Sorry, dude. I couldn't handle three-to-one."

Bruno only grunted and walked over, stood by the bed silently while he eyeballed Jesse's body.

"Must hurt like a bitch."

Jesse tried to sit up, but pain erupted down his one side along with dizziness. Falling back onto the pillows, he said, "Definitely hurts like a bitch."

"Good," Bruno said, pulled up a chair, and plopped down beside the bed.

Jesse screwed his eyes shut to battle the way the room was spinning. "Tell me a story, Bruno."

"There once was a jock and a doc . . ."

CHAPTER 18

Liliana drummed her fingers against the steering wheel, contemplating Whittaker, Jesse, and the fight that had ensued as she drove to the lab.

The only thing that rang true with her was Jesse's assertion that he had gone crazy and attacked Whittaker. But she'd be lying to herself if she said the violence didn't bother her.

It did.

Jesse did.

Maybe because she sensed he'd had a very good reason for losing his cool—his sister.

Jesse had attempted to spin it. Okay, maybe *spin* was a euphemism for what he had really done.

He'd lied.

Another thing Liliana was none too happy about.

The light turned red and Liliana slowed to a halt. She had been so distracted she hadn't realized she was blocks away from both her parents' restaurant and Ramon's station house. And as eager as she was to take Jesse's skin and blood samples to Carmen for examination, something else called to her more.

When the light went green, she executed a couple of

turns, and within a few minutes she was sitting in the parking lot of the police station.

She hesitated, debating what she was about to do. If her concerns about Whittaker and Jesse revealed problems, she needed someone who could deal with those issues. Normally she would have relied on her older brother, Mick. But she had already almost lost him months earlier, and she didn't want to interfere with all the good things going on in his life. Especially when she knew Ramon was capable of handling what she wanted.

Confident that the specimens from Jesse would keep in the chill of the car, she locked it up and walked the short distance to the front door. As she entered, the officer manning the front desk inched her head up and smiled.

"Dr. Carrera. How are you today?"

She leaned on the counter and her gaze skipped around the officers in the station. "Fine, Sylvia. I was wondering if the chief was around?"

Sylvia nodded, inclined her head in the direction of the back of the office, and picked up the end of the counter to allow her to enter the bullpen.

Liliana greeted the various officers at their desks on her way to Ramon's office at the far end of the room. She paused at his door, since he was on the phone and jotting down notes.

"Got it, Mayor. I'll make sure the barricades are in place for the antiques fair on Sunday."

Typical for the shore, she thought. Festivals and fairs, boardwalks and beachgoers to protect. Not to mention policing the various shore homes that sometimes sat vacant over the winter months.

Ramon noticed her standing at his door and grinned,

dipped his head in greeting. "Yes, Mayor. We've got the situation under control."

With that he hung up and hurried to the door, where he wrapped her up in a big bear hug. Built much like her brother Mick, Ramon was tall and muscularly lean, a holdover of his time in the military.

"What can I do for you, *prima?*"

He returned to his chair and offered her a seat.

Liliana entered but closed the door as she did, drawing raised eyebrows from Ramon.

"Something serious?"

"I need your help, only..." She drew in a long breath, and her hands plucked at the air as if she could find the words there.

Ramon folded his hands on the surface of his desk and leaned forward. "Anything you tell me is between the two of us, if that's what's worrying you."

She breathed a sigh of relief. "It is. I'm not even sure I should involve you."

Reclining back in his chair, Ramon leaned his elbow on the arm of his chair and scrubbed one big hand across his face as he considered her. Then he popped back up and said, "I know you, Lil. I trust your gut. If it's saying something is wrong..."

She wished she could trust herself as much as her cousin did. Ever since her debacle with her ex-fiancé, she had doubted her instincts. Even now, with the confused feelings she was experiencing about Jesse, she had her misgivings.

But there was one thing of which she was certain: something was wrong about Whittaker.

"I need you to find out more about someone. An FBI agent."

Tilting his head, Ramon set aside the notes on his desk and grabbed his notepad. "Got a name for me?"

"Hank Whittaker. I assume 'Hank' is short for Henry," she advised.

Ramon wrote down the name. "Do you know what office he's in? Newark? Philadelphia? New York?"

She shook her head. "No."

"Age and general description?"

"Fifties. Salt-and-pepper buzz cut. Definitely ex-military," she said, and Ramon arched a brow at that.

"How can you tell?"

Liliana smiled and pointed at him. "The stance. Attitude. He just smells of military, no offense intended."

"No offense taken. Anything else you can give me?"

"Whittaker has two other agents with him. Howard and Bruno. No last names. Howard is like Whittaker. Bruno is straight out of a wise guy movie."

Ramon finished his note taking and faced her full-on. "Are you okay? Are these guys the only things troubling you?"

Liliana twined her fingers together to restrain her nervousness. She wished it would be as easy to twist together her tongue and lips, because she wanted to spill her guts to Ramon. For all of her life he had been there, more like a brother than a cousin. And much like a brother, she knew her confidences would stay with him. Knew he would protect her against harm, but…

This danger involved her heart. Because of that, she kept it secret.

"I'm okay. But as soon as you find out anything—"

"I'll let you know."

*   *   *

One bright moment in an otherwise troubling day, Liliana thought as she glanced at the slides Carmen had prepared from Jesse's blood and skin.

"No bone formation in the skin. Drastically reduced levels of bone proteins and free-floating marrow in the blood."

"On the money. The plasmapheresis made a huge difference," Carmen advised, hovering nearby as Liliana slipped the slides into the microscope and cautiously reviewed them once more.

"I have to wonder how long these effects will last," Liliana said before pushing away from the microscope and swiveling the stool to face Carmen.

"How did Jesse's bone marrow respond to the inhibitor?"

Carmen shrugged, but Liliana behind that simple action, knew there was serious concern.

"Carmen? What's up?"

Her friend avoided her gaze, forcing Liliana to bend and insinuate herself into Carmen's line of sight.

"The inhibitor stopped replication. All replication, not just the bone-forming cells," Carmen advised.

Liliana sat up, gripped her thighs, and stroked her hands back and forth as she considered the report. If the inhibitor blocked *all* cell growth in Jesse's marrow, it also affected red and white blood cells, platelets, and a number of other processes regulated within his bones. Fat and mineral storage, detox, and blood pH balance could all be affected.

Lethally affected.

"So we won't be able to use this version of the inhibitor on Jesse?" Liliana offered, and Carmen confirmed it.

"No, we won't. We'll have to find a different way to stop production of only the mesenchymal stem cells in the marrow," Carmen replied.

That prospect reduced Liliana's concern, but not by much. Monkeying with those cells could still have detrimental effects on Jesse's muscles and cartilage.

"Do you have enough specimens to continue testing?" Liliana asked, worried about taking another bone marrow sample.

"I kept some of Jesse's cells. Plus, I can order some artificial bone marrow that we can use for preliminary testing."

"What about identifying the nature of the genes that have been mixed with Jesse's?" Liliana questioned.

Carmen raised her forefinger and smiled. "Score one for us. Based on the DNA tests, we were able to confirm that one of the nonhuman gene strands implanted in Jesse is the same one in Caterina. The amphibian genes—"

"Used to regenerate tissues in a way that's identical to the original tissue," Liliana finished for her.

Carmen placed the results of the DNA tests on the workstation table and motioned to the spikes created by the amphibian genes. "If they're using that gene to produce the stem cells, we may be able to target that specific gene and slow the process."

"Get on it. In the meantime, I'm going to check in on Jesse. See how his injuries are doing," Liliana advised.

"They beat him up pretty bad?" Carmen asked, a crease forming in her forehead with worry.

"Bruises. Nasty gash on his head and possibly a mild

concussion." She picked up her journal with the notes she had taken and was about to walk away when Carmen stopped her by shooting up her hand like a schoolgirl in class.

"You're holding out on me. Something is going on," Carmen said.

Even if Liliana had tried, she wouldn't have been able to fool her friend. "I'm worried about Whittaker and his men. He's rubbed me the wrong way from the beginning, and now he's got me totally worried."

"Thank God," Carmen said with a relieved sigh. "I know I'm not the best at reading people. I thought it was just me."

"It's not just you. I asked Ramon to check out Whittaker."

Carmen nodded, and some of the tension in her body fled. "Thanks for keeping me in the loop about Ramon, but there's still more, isn't there? Something you're not saying?"

Liliana stared hard at her friend. Her best friend.

Carmen had helped her out during her problem with her ex-fiancé. Had offered support during a difficult time. Because of that, she sat back down on the stool and placed her journal on the workbench.

Lacing her fingers together, she plopped her hands in her lap, glanced up at her friend, and said, "I think I've lost my objectivity about Jesse."

"Do tell," Carmen said, eyes wide with surprise.

After expelling a long, hesitant sigh, Liliana did just that.

CHAPTER 19

Jesse wasn't in his bed when Liliana walked into the room.

Closing the door and locking it behind her, she glanced around the large suite and noticed that he was out on the balcony that faced the beachfront. A strong wind was blowing westward, ruffling the shorter strands of his hair.

She hadn't had a chance to tell him that she liked the change—the shorter hair and clean-shaven face.

She wondered if he had done it for her, which caused a skitter in her midsection, along with warmth farther below, that he had cared enough to do it.

She had come to discover that about him. Despite all the tabloid gossip and bad-boy antics, he cared about others. Neighbors and strangers. His sister. Mother. Possibly even the father who denied his existence.

Maybe even her.

She laid her hand over her fluttering stomach and hesitated at the French doors. He seemed distant, a solitary figure looking almost lost against the vastness of the ocean before him.

Not wanting to intrude without welcome, she rapped on the glass of the door and waited for his reception.

He turned, his face grim and set in sharply chiseled lines. They relaxed somewhat as he saw her, grabbed the handle of the door, and slid it open.

She stepped out onto the balcony, and he closed the door behind them.

The wind increased the chill of a day that was quickly fading to night. Intense reds and purples painted the sky, and the ocean had darkened to slate gray with the arrival of night.

"Cold," she said and wrapped her arms around herself. Even though she still had on her winter jacket, the wind seeped beneath the wool, which made her wonder how he stood there in nothing but fleece sweats, braving the wind. Once again staring out at the ocean. The white of the bandage at his temple a glaring contrast to his skin in the dim dusk.

"Aren't you freezing?" she asked and patted her arms to try and generate some heat.

He hunched his shoulders, shot her a half glance. "I wasn't sure you'd come back."

"I said I would. I needed to see how you're doing."

He gave another shrug, seemingly indifferent, except she sensed undercurrents beneath. Dangerous ones.

"I'm here. I'm alive. Consider your obligation fulfilled."

A self-defense mechanism? she wondered. Push her away—push what he was feeling away—in order to keep from being hurt?

Only, as she had discovered after pouring her heart out to Carmen, it was no easy thing to keep him at bay. Somehow he had touched her. Infiltrated those areas she had thought safe.

Trying to shore up her defenses, she beckoned toward

the medical bag she had dropped on the coffee table on her way to see him. "I'd like to make sure you're okay. Have you had anything to eat tonight? Are you hungry?"

Some emotion finally cracked the stern lines of his face. A hint of a smile and glitter in eyes that had gone to slate gray. He took a long stride toward her, until barely inches separated them. Laying a hand at her waist, he bracketed her side with it, sending her insides quivering.

Jesse glanced down at her, sensing the tremor in her body.

She was as aware of him as he was of her. At his touch, her gaze had gone wide, revealing eyes that were nearly black with desire. When she moistened her lips, the last of his restraint disappeared.

He bent his head, whispered against her lips. "I'm hungry, but not for food."

Then he closed the distance and kissed her. Dug his hand into her hair while he held her waist with his other hand. There was a stutter, maybe a halfhearted protest against his mouth before she was answering his kiss, moving her lips against his. Slipping her arms around his back to press him tight.

Over and over, their lips met until Liliana opened her mouth and invited him in.

He went willingly, lost in his emotions, needing so much more.

He slid his one hand to the buttons on her coat, undid them, and eased beneath the wool and her suit jacket to place his hand on her side. Her body was warm, the cotton of her shirt slick beneath his palm as he trailed upward until he was cupping her breast.

She moaned into his mouth. Needy. Hungry.

Unerringly, he shifted his thumb across the tip of her hard nipple. As he took it between his thumb and forefinger, she gasped and pulled away from him.

"Jesse," she said, and disappointment arose within him.

But then she said, "The bed's inside."

Sweet Lord, he thought, swept her up into his arms, somehow one-handedly pried open the French door and closed it against the chill before stalking with her to his bed.

He released her, allowing her to slide across his body as she returned to her feet again.

So many thoughts went through his head as she pressed along the length of him and ran her hand through the strands of his hair. So many thoughts that suddenly came spewing from his mouth.

"Bruno—"

"Is downstairs eating."

"He may come up after—"

"I locked the door on the way in." She raked her fingers through his hair and gave a sexy half smile, but it turned into a frown as her fingers encountered the gauze at his temple.

"They might have killed you," she said, concern and anger warring on her features.

"They didn't, and I'm here, wanting you."

"Why me, Jesse? You must have had your share—"

He placed his index finger on her lips. "That's in the past. I'm not that man anymore. Maybe I never was."

Her gaze narrowed as she considered his statement but relaxed as she said, "Fame didn't change the real you."

"I lost the real me for a while, but I've found myself.

And I've found you," he said, bent his head, and kissed her again, only the kiss was gentler this time, not as urgent, although his need was just as great.

She opened her mouth, sampled the edges of his lips as she moved her hands to his shoulders. Shifted them across their broad width and down his arms to his hands. Taking hold of them, she brought them to her waist and murmured against his lips, "Touch me, Jesse."

This time he groaned but didn't delay. With Bruno down below, they might have little time together before he decided to come up to check things out.

Hurrying, he removed her coat and suit jacket. She was already at work on the buttons of her shirt as he undid her pants, lowered them, and she kicked them off.

As he rose, his erection bumped against her belly and she smiled, reached down, and stroked him through the fleece.

He sucked in a breath, nearly undone by the caress. She stroked him again and he realized there would be no leisure in their loving.

Her shirt was undone, revealing a gap of skin down her center and the front clasp of her bra. With a quick twist, he released it, freeing her full breasts.

He urged her toward the bed and she sat, then leaned back, the fabric parting to reveal more of her.

Easing between the V of her legs, he stripped away her bikini briefs and stepped into the gap.

She wrapped her legs around him, joining him to her center while he rolled his hips, shifting his erection against her, the fleece creating friction.

Liliana skimmed her hands across his shoulders before dropping them down to the hem of his shirt. With him helping her, he ripped off his sweatshirt, exposing his upper body.

He was beautiful, and the damage inflicted on his body failed to detract from it. Tenderly she ran her hands across the powerful muscles in his arms and shoulders. Skipped down to run the back of her hand across six-pack abs before she moved to his chest.

A broad, powerful chest. It heaved with his breath beneath her hands.

"Liliana, I can't wait anymore," he said and rocked his hips against hers, more powerfully than before, stealing her breath away. Yanking a shudder from her as his movements caressed her.

"Then don't," she answered.

He groaned once again, and the sound shook her with his need.

She loosened her hold on his hips for only a moment. Long enough for him to drag the fleece down over his erection.

She felt the tip of him, poised at her center.

Met his gaze and saw the need mingling with doubt and disbelief. Emotions she understood well, since she was experiencing them herself.

But only for a moment, as with a flex of her hips, she accepted him. With a slow shift of his body, he completed the union, burying himself in her depths. Filling her in ways that had nothing to do with the physical joining.

Above her, his body trembled as he held still, his gaze riveted to hers until he deliberately lowered his head. Paused close enough that his breath spilled against her lips. Hesitating there, he seemed about to say something but managed to only utter her name.

"Liliana."

It was enough.

She raised herself that last inch, cradled his jaw, and kissed him. Kept on kissing him, her mouth opening on his, her tongue tracing the edges of his lips until he reached down with his hand and cradled her breast. Caressed the taut tip with his fingers, then increased the pressure to tweak her nipple, eliciting a strangled cry from her.

He pulled away then, his concern evident. "Did I hurt you?"

She shook her head. "No, it felt good."

A sexy smile inched across his lips. "Maybe this will feel even better."

He dropped his head down and replaced his fingers with his mouth, sucking and biting at the hard point of her breast. Each action creating another deep inside. Down below between her legs her body responded, passion building.

She held his head to her and raised her knees, embracing his hips with her thighs. Earning a rough groan from him as that motion shifted her body around him.

Jesse stilled and sucked in a breath as the wet and warmth of her surrounded him. He needed to move. Needed to possess and be possessed, he thought, and finally rocked his hips to draw in and out of her.

A soft little cry escaped her lips, but as he peeked up at her, her enjoyment was clear.

Raising himself up on his arms so that he could watch her, he began to pump his hips, driving into her. Her body tight against his. Wet with need. Hot. *So, so hot,* he thought, watching her deep brown eyes grow even darker.

Tracking the soft bob of her breasts that matched the movement of his hips.

He bent again, licked the tips of her breasts. Suckled them as he strove to pleasure her until she whispered his name, seemingly begging him for more.

He lengthened the stroke of his hips, gritting his teeth against his desire to just bury himself deep and disappear inside her. Teething her tight nipple, he felt the first little tremor in her body that warned she was near the edge. But he also felt her resistance to allow her release.

Raising his head, he paused and stared down at her. Trembled as she lifted her hand and laid it over his heart before stroking the back of it across his chest.

"Jesse?" she asked, as if believing something was wrong.

Only everything was too right, he thought.

"Come with me, Liliana," he said, wanting to share everything about this moment together.

She brought her hand back to the center of his chest, laid her palm flat over his heart and said, "Yes, Jesse."

Lord help him, but he was lost, he thought, as he drove up into her and then retreated, building their passion until they were both shaking and a fine sheen of sweat covered their bodies. A wave of release started in his center and spread outward, like ripples on a pond, spilling over onto Liliana.

Liliana sensed it. Knew that it would be just a moment more and embraced that moment, lifting her hips up into his. Throwing her head back as the pulse at the center of her sent sensation rocketing throughout her body.

She cried out his name, and he buried his head against the side of her neck and whispered hers. Stroked his hips deep and then held them still, although his body all around her came alive with his climax. As he groaned and trembled above her.

Liliana laid her hands on his shoulders, urged him down. Embraced him and soothed with her touch.

He rolled with her, bringing her to rest on him. Cradling the small of her back to keep her close as he whispered against the side of her face, "I'm too heavy for you."

She lay there, half dressed and fully satisfied. Complete as never before and yet more confused than ever before. It was too soon for love, she thought, and yet in that moment, with him buried deep within her and surrounding her with his body, she had never been more content.

A loud noise from downstairs shattered the moment, stolen as it was.

She glanced down at Jesse, offered a smile. "Maybe we should dress?"

Reluctantly he agreed, but not before digging his hand into her hair and urging her down for another long kiss.

The noise came again downstairs, breaking them apart.

Jesse eased from her, rose, and helped her up. As she gathered her clothes, he tugged on her hand and led her to the bathroom. Whipping a hand towel off a rack, he handed it to her.

"In case you want to clean up," he said, then surprised her by tenderly brushing his fingers along her cheek before leaving her alone.

That simple touch nearly undid her again, the gesture was so pure and uncensored. Liliana gripped the towel tightly and leaned against the door, her body trembling. She could hear him outside, moving about, and then, shortly thereafter, Bruno making some kind of comment.

Jesse's response was muffled. She held her breath, expectant about what might happen next, but the sound that followed was of a door closing.

Releasing her pent-up breath, she went to the sink and ran the towel beneath the water. She washed, dressed, and dragged her hands through her hair to try and restore some semblance of order.

Satisfied that she might pass muster if Bruno returned, she exited into Jesse's bedroom and found him sitting at the sofa close to the French doors.

She approached him, and as his hungry gaze fixed on her once more, she splayed her hand across her midsection to control the nervous and needy twist of the muscles.

"What did Bruno want?" she asked.

"Whittaker called. Wanted to know if you were here," he said and rose, gallantly holding his hand out to the space beside him on the sofa.

She nodded, sat down, and laid her hands on her thighs. Rubbed them there nervously as she waited for him to make the next move.

Already unsure of what had happened between them and what it meant. Where it would lead them.

"Are you okay?" he asked, sensing the tension in her.

"I don't know. Am I?" she answered honestly.

CHAPTER 20

Whittaker paced before the assorted cages, pleased with what he was seeing. The patients seemed more responsive. Even the patient who had been nearly catatonic a few days before was alert, although still abed. His breathing was labored, and as Whittaker reached through and touched his skin, he marveled at the hardness of it and the muscle beneath.

Hard like bone. Maybe as hard as Bradford would become if his condition progressed and none of their treatments were effective.

As he strode past the patients with Shaw's gene combo, some of them changed color before his eyes. Fear or flight response still, he thought, hoping that they might be able to master control over the color change much like Shaw had.

Edwards and Morales had indicated to him that on at least two occasions Caterina had been able to blend into her environs using the skin camouflage. They had also sold another patient—or rather, it was better to say their genetically modified organism—for a hefty sum, and the GMO had performed perfectly.

Unfortunately that other GMO was now useless bits and pieces in an army morgue after her buyers had detonated the bomb-laden vest she had worn inside the Iraqi Green Zone.

The success of that particular mission had made the product Edwards and Morales had developed quite desirable in certain circles and brought it to his attention.

His black-ops group was well known in those venues, and having access to the GMOs in addition to the availability of it for his men was worth every penny he had invested.

Or should he say every million he had invested?

He walked back to where Edwards and Morales were standing beside Howard. His man was at ease, hands held before him. Body erect and mind alert in case action was needed.

The perfect soldier, still.

The perfect candidate for modification.

"The inhibitor seems to be working well," Whittaker said as he came to stand before them.

Morales nodded. "Combined with the plasmapheresis, we've satisfactorily contained the replication in most of the patients."

"It'll take some time, however, to produce enough of the inhibitor to provide the patients with another round of treatments," Edwards indicated.

"How much time?" Whittaker prompted, wondering if in the meantime he would have to secure yet another batch from the annoying Dr. Carrera.

"Possibly too long," Morales admitted.

"Thank you, Doctor. I'm grateful for your truthfulness," he said. Knowing the limits allowed him to know how much longer he had to deal with Bradford and Carrera, who were increasingly trying his patience.

"But it will take even longer to develop something to

deal with situations similar to Bradford's," Morales also confessed.

Whittaker glanced at Howard, who had been standing resolutely by the two scientists during the discussion. "You understand the consequences? Until we can find a way to control Bradford's replication—"

"I'll get stronger. Denser," Howard intoned, voice devoid of emotion.

And more able to control Bradford, Whittaker thought. Howard had not liked being overpowered by the other man earlier that night.

"It may take some time for the changes to occur. In Bradford it took several weeks for the foreign gene fragments to become sufficiently incorporated into his native DNA to make any impact," Edwards explained.

Weeks to implement, but in months the results would be amazing, Whittaker thought, recalling the force of Bradford's blow. Almost absentmindedly he ran his hands across his ribs, which still ached from the contact. It had been like being hit with a battering ram.

With a team of such men, there wouldn't be a mission they couldn't complete. All they had to do was get the changes under control.

"I understand, Dr. Edwards," Howard replied and methodically began removing his suit jacket and shirt.

Edwards gestured to the stainless steel table just a few feet away. "You'll have to remove your pants and briefs, as well."

With a slight incline of his head to note his assent, Howard stripped until he was naked, tidily folding his clothes along the way into a neat pile he placed on a chair beside the table.

Morales picked up a long, corkscrew-like probe from the surgical tray holding an assortment of gleaming steel instruments.

"If you would be so kind as to lie facedown on the table," Morales said to Howard, who immediately complied, lying on his stomach but with his face turned toward Whittaker.

Stoic, as the two doctors converged on him.

Edwards jabbed a needle into an area close to the smooth dimple in Howard's back. After he did so, he grabbed a scalpel from the surgical tray and made a small incision.

Morales approached with a test tube bearing something green and glowing. He handed it to Edwards, who sucked up a syringe full of the liquid.

Whittaker pointed to the test tube. "Is that it?"

Edwards affirmed it with a nod. "These are the DNA strands we've isolated and tagged with green fluorescent proteins. The proteins will help us gauge how well the genes are recombining with the DNA in Mr. Howard's bone marrow."

Morales inserted the corkscrew probe into the incision and pressed inward.

Barely a flinch traveled across Howard's face as Morales bored into bone. A second later Edwards was inserting the tip of the syringe into the incision and pressing inward, finding the channel between the probe and bone. Depressing the plunger to plant the GFP-laden DNA.

As soon as the syringe was emptied, both scientists retracted their instruments and closed the incision.

"Is that all?" Howard asked.

"What do you mean?" Edwards questioned as Howard rolled over onto his back and leaned on one elbow.

"If you put it somewhere else, will the change happen faster?"

An uneasy smile crept across Edwards's face, but Morales's showed no similar concern. "The long bones are excellent spots for bone marrow production."

Howard glanced toward him, as if asking permission, not that Whittaker would deny him. What did he care if Howard wanted to fuck up his body for the good of the cause?

"I'm game," Howard replied and leaned back down onto the table.

"Femur?" Morales said, arching a brow and peering at his partner.

Once again a moment of discomfort flared across Edwards's face, but then, with a nod, he reached behind him and prepared for the new procedure.

"Excellent," Whittaker said. The faster Howard developed, the sooner he could get rid of complications like Bradford and Carrera.

CHAPTER 21

Jesse turned and his knee grazed her leg. He raised his hand and brushed aside her hair. Her brown-eyed gaze flickered to his face as her hands rubbed once, then twice, across the fabric of her pants.

Everything about her communicated her nervousness, and he understood. He suspected Liliana wasn't the kind to just jump into bed with a man, much less a man who was also her patient.

And a man who was lying to her via the sin of omission.

Guilt wrenched his gut into a knot tighter than that of his earlier desire. Seeking to alleviate that guilt and her anxiety, he dug his hand beneath the thick wealth of her hair and encircled her neck with his hand. Gently, he stroked his thumb along the sensitive skin at her throat.

"It was very special for me," he said, the tones of his voice low and intimate. Even more so when he leaned a bit closer and repeated, "Very special."

Beneath his thumb came a jumpy swallow. "It was special for me, as well."

"Then let's not second-guess why it happened and be grateful that it did," he replied, wanting for the discomfort of the moment after to be gone and replaced by the earlier connection that had driven them to making love.

Making love, he thought, suddenly certain that it had been that and not just sex.

Special, he thought again, and for good measure, he bent and kissed her. Hesitantly. Tenderly. The kiss undemanding and caring.

Tension fled her body with the kiss. He eased his hand from her neck as he withdrew from the homecoming of her lips. If he lingered there too long, he might find himself picking her up and taking her back to the bed.

Instead Jesse leaned back on the arm of the sofa, dragging her against him to lie down along his length. Rubbing her back gently, he said, "You had a long day. You must be tired."

"A little," she confessed, her earlier anxiety slowly leaving her body.

"Being a doctor can be tough. Long hours. Lots of work," he said.

"I can handle it," she said, a note of defensiveness arising in her voice.

"I'm sure you can," he replied, and he cradled her chin and gently urged her face upward. "You're a very strong woman."

Before she had gotten to know him, Liliana might have said that he was putting the moves on her. Now she had little doubt about his sincerity or about his own strength of character.

"So are you. Strong, and not just physically."

He released a sigh as uncertainty flared across his face. "I wish I had been stronger. More reasonable. Then maybe I wouldn't be in this mess."

She understood, and yet...

"But then we wouldn't have met."

He brought his lips close to hers and whispered, "And that would have been the greater sin."

He kissed her, and that simple touch of lip to lip conveyed so much more than words could have alone. Love. Despair. Need. Promise. The kiss was filled with all that was and all that could be.

When they broke apart, Jesse said, "One day this will all seem unreal. Things will be back to normal. You'll be back at the hospital."

"And you'll be..." she said, anxiously waiting for his reply.

"Coaching football. Maybe in high school."

She recalled her challenge to him the other day that he stop living in the past. His answer now confirmed that maybe he had. That he was thinking for the future instead of holding on to what-might-have-beens.

"Sounds like a good plan. Would you stay here? In the area?"

"How else could we keep on seeing each other?" he teased, but she sensed it was half serious to test the waters.

Tempted to respond that she would offer his team a discount on physicals, she instead tilted her head upward until her lips were once again within kissing distance.

"I'd like to keep on seeing you. Have you meet my family," she replied.

The strong line of his smile brushed across her mouth and he murmured, "Do you think they'll approve of me?"

A loud knock came at the door, and they bolted apart as Bruno entered without warning.

"Ever hear of knocking?" Jesse asked as he rose from the sofa, hands fisted at his sides.

"It's okay." Liliana rose and covered his hand with hers. He relaxed at her touch, reassuring her that he was capable of control.

"Whittaker called. They think they found another patient," Bruno advised.

Another Wardwell escapee?

Excitement raced through Liliana at the possibility that they would soon find all of the patients and free them.

"Where is—"

"Back at your lab. Whittaker wants you to meet him there. He says it's urgent."

Liliana looked up at Jesse apologetically, regretting that she had to leave him so soon. "I'll be back in the morning."

Jesse twined his fingers with hers and squeezed gently. He had known all night that she would eventually have to go, but it didn't make the leaving any easier. Especially after the too-short encounter they had shared.

"I'll see you in the morning," he said and watched her depart. Observed Bruno eyeing her appreciatively as she walked out the door.

When Bruno returned his attention to Jesse, his guard said, "You better not get too close to the doc. Don't want to break her heart when you go."

Before Jesse could reply, Bruno exited, closing the door behind him but leaving behind the cryptic words.

When you go.

Was Whittaker planning on taking him somewhere? Had he gotten whatever he wanted from Liliana? If he had, would he keep his promise to help Jackie?

Dozens of questions raced through his brain as he paced back and forth in his room, feeling more like a caged animal than ever before. Finally it was more than he could bear.

He headed to the kitchen, where Bruno was reading the paper as usual.

He lowered it as Jesse entered, watched over the page's edge as Jesse went to the fridge. After Jesse grabbed a soda and faced him, Bruno finally brought the paper down to his lap.

"What did you mean by 'when I go'?"

Bruno shrugged. "Boss man's giving the doc another patient to work on. He got the drugs he wanted, and you're a pain in the ass."

Which meant that in Bruno's mind he was expendable, but had Whittaker reached the same conclusion?

He eyed the other man. It wouldn't take much to overpower him. Hell, he had nearly gotten past three of them earlier that night. And as sore as his body was, he wouldn't go down easy if Whittaker decided to take him out.

But there was one thing...no, make that two things that kept him from escaping Bruno right then and there.

His sister and Liliana.

Until he knew Whittaker's plans for them, he would have to sacrifice his own freedom.

Bruno must not have liked how Jesse was eyeing him, since he slipped his hand beneath his jacket, confirming his gun was in easy reach.

"No need, Bruno. I'm not going to cause any more trouble."

Not yet, anyway, he thought as he left the room.

CHAPTER 22

A cold knot of fear gripped Liliana's insides as she assessed the patient lying on the examination table.

Carmen stood across from her, face pale.

The patient was human—or at least he had been at one time. Almost his entire body was covered with what appeared to be an exoskeleton of bone. Only a few patches of human skin remained on his body and face.

The patient's breath rasped in and out of his chest, barely lifting it, as if battling a heavy weight.

Liliana wondered how far the ossification extended. Were his organs likewise being infiltrated?

She leaned over the patient and his eyes fluttered open. Still human. Pleading.

For what? she wondered. *A cure, or the peace of death?*

"Where did you find him?" She looked over her shoulder to where Whittaker stood by the door beside Howard, who seemed a little pale himself.

"Local police got a report of a body along the side of the road. Called us when they noted his condition. Haven't confirmed it yet, but I think he's one of the Wardwell patients," Whittaker lied. He was well aware that it was one of the original patients, because he and Howard had taken him from Morales's lab earlier in the day.

"It looks like what's happening with Jesse," Carmen said, sending another skitter of fear through Liliana.

As her friend noted her reaction, she quickly added, "But we've got Jesse under control. Not like this."

No, not like this, Liliana thought, slipping on her stethoscope to listen to the man's heartbeat and lungs. The heartbeat was sluggish. Labored like his breathing.

She yanked off the stethoscope. "Let's get him on oxygen. Get a blood sample."

"What about a bone marrow plug?" Carmen asked even as she was setting up the monitoring equipment.

Liliana wheeled over a respirator and eased the mask over his face. Immediately his breathing grew less stressful.

"Let's wait on the marrow until we can get him to the hospital," she said and prepped an IV. What remained of the human parts of the man's eyes, skin, and lips were showing extreme signs of dehydration.

"I'm not sure that's going to be possible," Whittaker advised, but this time Liliana wasn't going to settle for that answer.

"This man is critical," she said, motioning to the patient. "If you're worried about people nosing around, we can arrange for him to be placed in quarantine."

"If you can accomplish that, I may be amenable to moving him," Whittaker replied, surprising her. She had been expecting more of a battle. His easy surrender raised her antenna about his real agenda.

"I'll make the arrangements."

She left the room to make the necessary calls to the hospital, including an ambulance for transporting the patient. It made her wonder why he had been brought to the lab in the first place. When she had finished making all the arrangements with the hospital, she phoned her cousin Ramon.

He immediately answered. "No news yet, Lil."

"No news? As in, you haven't been able to find out anything about Whittaker and his men?"

"Nothing. None of the local branches are claiming him. Of course, he could be part of some secret unit," Ramon advised.

Liliana could picture Whittaker running some kind of clandestine operation, but it still worried her that none of the local Feds knew of him. Maybe if she had a picture of him, only...

"Wait a second, Ramon."

She raced to her desk and woke her desktop from its hibernated state. Because they had to share data in an assortment of ways, the computers had been networked to be operated remotely. Using the remote desktop connection, she accessed Carmen's laptop out on the worktable. Engaging the webcam on the unit, she was able to see to where Whittaker and Howard stood by the door.

Luckily the faces of the two men were visible to the camera, and with a few quick keystrokes, she snapped off a bunch of photos and saved them to the hard drive.

"I'm e-mailing you pictures of the agents. Maybe that will help," she said.

"Just got them. I'll use them to ask around," Ramon confirmed.

It occurred to her that while he was checking things, he could inquire about one other item. "We have another patient in the lab. Whittaker says that local law enforcement found him on the side of the road."

"If it was anywhere nearby, I should be able to check with my fellow police chiefs in the neighboring towns."

"Would you?" she pressed.

A long, drawn-out sigh followed her request before Ramon said, "You really don't trust this guy, do you?"

As she recalled the beatings Jesse had endured and all the little things that didn't seem professional, it wasn't hard to confess her misgivings.

"I don't trust him. Not at all, so anything you can get me would be truly appreciated."

"Anything for you, Lil. What about Mick?" he asked, well aware, as she was, that her older brother had the ability to access a wealth of information legally unavailable to a police chief like Ramon.

"Mick has enough on his mind right now. I'd rather he not be involved."

"Got it," Ramon said and hung up.

She closed her cell phone and slipped it into her pocket. For a moment she considered calling Mick, but he was only just getting his life back on track after the nearly fatal events of six months ago. She wouldn't rupture that peace because of her cynicism about Whittaker.

A knock came at the door and Liliana rose, opened it.

Whittaker stood there with Howard. Behind them were two paramedics she recognized from the hospital, wheeling a gurney toward the examination room.

"Good to see they got here so soon. Let me just grab my bag and I'll ride with them to the hospital."

Whittaker nodded, a chill look in his eyes almost like

that of a serpent as he examined her. "Is something wrong, Dr. Carrera?"

Liliana schooled her features, worried that they were giving away her distrust, and shook her head. "Just concerned about the patient."

A sudden commotion pulled her attention toward the examining room. She hurried there to find the two EMTs staring at the patient.

"He's going into quarantine. Is it contagious?" the one EMT asked, snapping on latex gloves.

"I'm not touching him," the other EMT advised, his eyes wide and a fine line of sweat across his upper lip.

"It's not contagious, but I understand your worry. The three of us can transfer him to the gurney."

Together with Carmen and the EMT, they lifted him from the table to the gurney, and at the last second, the fearful EMT relented and assisted them.

The EMTs wheeled the man from the room, and Liliana met Carmen's concerned gaze. "I'll keep you posted on his condition. Let me know ASAP what you get from the blood tests."

Liliana turned, pushed past Whittaker and Howard, who were still lingering by the door. Outside the lab, she climbed into the back of the ambulance and sat beside the EMT, who was wrapping a blood-pressure cuff around their patient's arm.

Liliana had opted not to try to get a reading earlier, fairly sure she would obtain an irrational result. After a few tries, the EMT gave up.

"His skin—or whatever this is—is too thick," he mumbled.

"It's compact bone, from the looks of it. I'm worried

about how much of his body has been compromised," Liliana advised as she checked the IV she had inserted earlier. It had fallen out, and the former spot for the IV had closed up with bone.

"Can you find a clear spot to re-insert the IV?" she asked the EMT who searched for a visible vein along a thin ribbon of skin at the crook of the man's elbow. The needle went in cleanly, but shortly after insertion, the area around the needle whitened as bone formed around the site.

The EMT reared back from the patient, his earlier cooperation replaced by shock and fear.

"What is this?"

"Science gone wrong."

With little left to do for the patient until they reached the hospital, she and the EMT covered him, hiding the damage to his body beneath a crisp white sheet. Within minutes, they reached their destination. Before the ambulance stopped completely, Liliana advised, "I want to get some x-rays before we get him in quarantine."

Nodding, the EMT swept into action as the vehicle stopped and his partner opened up the back doors. Liliana followed the two men as they pushed the gurney into the emergency room. The duty nurse approached and greeted Liliana.

"Good evening, Dr. Carrera."

"Hi, Maggie. Good to see you again. I need this patient taken to x-ray and then quarantined."

"You got it." Maggie handed Liliana a chart and pen, raised her hand, and waved over another nurse to take responsibility from the EMTs.

"Get this patient to radiology, stat," Maggie instructed,

and the nurse took hold of the gurney and began wheeling it down the hallway.

Liliana was about to follow when Whittaker and Howard entered the emergency room. They moved forward, clearly intending to accompany her, but she held up her hand to stop them.

"It'll be better if you wait down here until we know more."

"Don't make us wait too long," Whittaker warned and, with a jerk of his head, commanded his man to a line of hard plastic chairs in an adjacent waiting-room area.

"I understand, Special Agent," she advised, her biggest concern for the moment ascertaining what she could do about the patient being wheeled to x-ray.

Turning on her heel, she hurried down the hall and navigated the assorted twists, turns, and elevator banks to reach the radiology department. The nurse was waiting at the door for her beside one of their x-ray technicians. Peering into the room, she noted that her patient had already been transferred to the table for the procedure.

"We can't retract the IV needle," the x-ray technician advised.

"You'll have to take them with it intact. Is it all right if I watch while you complete the shots? I need you to get his entire torso."

The technician nodded and prepped shot after shot, the *kathunk* of the x-ray machine registering with each exposure until his task was completed.

"How long will it take to get the x-rays?" Liliana asked.

"Not long. It's a slow night," he said and shot an uneasy look over his shoulder at the patient.

Liliana suspected that even if it hadn't been slow, curiosity and fear would have driven the young man to develop the exposures quickly.

"Would you arrange for the patient to be transported up to his room?" She noted the room number the duty nurse had provided on a slip of paper and handed it to the technician.

"Yes, Dr. Carrera."

Liliana returned to the ER area to meet up with Whittaker and his goon. When she arrived, Whittaker stood by the chairs, pacing back and forth. Howard was seated, still pale. Beads of sweat dotted his upper lip and forehead.

As she neared, she noted a slight bulge beneath one pant leg and a darkened area on his other pant leg.

Blood? she wondered.

"Are you hurt, Special Agent Howard?" Although she didn't care for the man, she also couldn't watch him suffer before her eyes.

"He's fine," Whittaker responded curtly, and Howard didn't contradict him.

With a slow nod, Liliana provided her report. "Patient is headed to his room, and we should have the x-rays shortly. I would suggest we go there to discuss his condition."

As she turned to walk to the quarantine wing, she noted the grimace that crossed Howard's face as he rose, and his slight limp.

Howard had been roughed up during the day's earlier encounter with Jesse, but she didn't remember any kind of injury with the symptoms he now exhibited. She guessed that he could have been hurt doing some other task for Whittaker but questioned why they would be keeping it from her.

Refraining from further conjecture—she had enough to think about with her nearly ossified patient—she remained silent.

When they arrived at the quarantine wing, the patient had already been transferred to a bed, the IV had been reconnected to another bag of saline solution, and he was wired to a variety of monitors.

Liliana walked over to the monitors and reviewed the stats. All troubling: oxygen saturation down, blood pressure low, heart rate slow. Very slow, which was likely contributing to the reduced O_2 and blood pressure.

She adjusted the oxygen flow and, deciding that a more thorough physical examination was in order, eased on latex gloves. Beneath her fingers his skin and flesh were hard, even in those spots not covered by the thin layer of exoskeleton.

When the X-ray technician arrived, her worst fears were confirmed.

Thick areas of white glared at her from the x-rays, pointing to advanced levels of bone formation throughout his body.

"Well?" Whittaker prompted, his tone irate.

"There's little I can do for this patient. The damage is extensive, and his major organs have been compromised."

"What about the inhibitor? Can't that help?" Whittaker once again pressed, triggering even stronger distrust in Liliana. But she needed to play it carefully until she knew more.

"As soon as I get some additional information, I can decide how to treat him."

Her acquiescence mollified Whittaker, and he left the room but instructed Howard to stand guard.

The special agent did so inside the room, hands crossed before him as he silently stood by the door while Liliana noted the patient's vitals on the chart. As she was finishing, she shot a fleeting look at Howard.

Sweat marked his face, and his pristine white shirt was damp in spots. His skin was as white as chalk against the black of his suit.

"I'm assuming our patient is a John Doe?" she asked and Howard nodded, but not without some apparent discomfort.

She dropped the metal chart into the holder at the foot of the bed and approached Whittaker's man.

"Are you feeling all right, Special Agent?" she asked, eyeing him up close for any additional symptoms.

"I'm fine, ma'am," he answered woodenly.

"Right," Liliana replied and eased a chair to where Howard was standing.

"Why don't you take your jacket off and rest a bit."

That he didn't argue was a testament to how badly he must have been feeling. When Liliana returned to the patient's bedside, she caught a glimpse of Howard as he removed his jacket. His shirt was totally soaked in spots. Beneath the fabric near the small of his back, she detected what looked like a bandage and a trivial spot of blood staining the fabric.

Trivial, except for the location of the apparent wounds.

His femurs and the area right above his ilium. Perfect spots for the sampling of bone marrow.

"You didn't care for Bradford beating the crap out of you, did you, Special Agent?" she asked, hoping to elicit a response.

"Bradford's a loose cannon. Has been ever since his

playing days," Howard replied, calmly and with no hint of malice.

"Still, it must have pissed you off," she continued while easing her hand into their John Doe's to test one of the reflex points there.

No reaction came from either man.

She shot a look at Howard, who remained impassive as he sat on the chair, some color restored to his face.

"Well, Special Agent? Did it make you angry?" she pressed.

A deadly smile spread across his features, creating a chill in her as he said, "I don't get angry. I get even."

She was spared from answering as her cell phone chirped—Carmen calling.

"What do you have for me?" she asked.

CHAPTER 23

The lab results Carmen had provided had been bad, but not as bad as the call that had come from Ramon in the wee morning hours.

Whittaker was not an FBI agent. At least not anymore. He had been forced into retirement after a mission had gone wrong thanks to a serious error in judgment on his part.

The current information on Whittaker, provided to Ramon by another FBI agent who happened to be a friend of her cousin's, was that Whittaker headed a private security group known to engage in an assortment of activities, some of them not so legal. Unfortunately, neither the FBI nor any of the other organizations supposedly keeping track of Whittaker and his men had been able to find sufficient evidence to charge them with any wrongdoing.

As for Howard and Bruno, more bad news.

Howard had been dishonorably discharged from the military. Bruno had spent substantial time behind bars due to his participation in organized crime.

Ramon had wanted to act immediately to round them up, but Liliana had asked him to wait, needing to know what they were doing and why. More importantly, desperate to know why Jesse had thrown his lot in with men like these.

Sleep was impossible after getting Ramon's news. Every time she closed her eyes, the image of her nearly skeletal patient replayed itself, and each time, his face had been replaced by Jesse's.

With sleep evading her, she had slipped on jeans, a sweatshirt, and a thick jacket and had gone for a walk along the boardwalk. It was dark, but the streetlamps along the walk cast a weak light. She paused in the dim circle of light, reached up, and took hold of the crucifix she wore.

Closing her eyes, she said a prayer for guidance.

How he could be lying to me even as he made love to me?

It hadn't been just sex, as rushed as it had been. They had made love, because she had no doubt they both had feelings for each other.

But her judgment of men was suspect, she reminded herself again. Look at how horribly it had turned out with her ex-fiancé. And Jesse's reputation with women was far worse.

Which had her wondering how she could have developed feelings for him.

Opening her eyes, she noticed the dawn inching up past the horizon. Crimson trails spread upward into the pitch-black morning sky, bringing to mind an old saying.

Red sky at morning, sailors take warning.

She had to maintain a sense of caution, she realized, even while acknowledging that she had to confront Jesse about his lies. Her one hope was that he would have a plausible explanation for why he was helping a man like Whittaker.

Shoving away from the boardwalk railing, she walked toward the center of town, needing to work off the nervous energy that had kept her awake for the better part of the early morning.

A lone jogger approached her, a mutt on a leash attached to the fluorescent safety vest he wore. He ran right past her, dipping his head in a breathless greeting.

She returned the welcome and pressed onward on the empty boardwalk. In the summer there would be dozens of people along the beachfront, even at such an early hour. Surfers, joggers, and bicycle riders mostly, trying to get in their activities before it got too crowded.

On Main Avenue, she turned westward and strolled past the still-closed shops. It was barely past six, and the seasonal stores would not open even later in the day.

The bakery, however, was already active as people dropped by for breakfast rolls and pastries. When she walked in, one of the young women behind the counter tossed out a greeting.

"Morning, Lil. The usual?" she said, and Liliana confirmed it with a smile. She was a creature of habit, which made her wonder why she had deviated from such routines with Jesse or even Whittaker. Her normal inclination would have been to refuse a request to leave the safety of what was familiar—the hospital. But then again, she would have done anything to extend her brother Mick's happiness and help Caterina return to normal.

And now there was Jesse to think about.

And the John Doe in the hospital.

And the nearly half-a-dozen missing gene-therapy patients from Wardwell.

A bushel of reasons for why she had strayed from her

comfort zone, but she had never expected that such a journey would risk the safety of her heart.

As the young woman behind the counter handed her a cup of coffee and a buttered roll, Liliana thanked her, paid for the food, and then hurried from the shop. She turned up Pilgrim's Pathway, opting to return to her condo through town rather than back along the beachfront.

As she sipped her coffee and nibbled on the roll, she considered her plan of action for the day, deciding on what she would say to Jesse. Trying to determine what, if anything, she was going to do about Whittaker and his men.

She hastened toward her condo, past the ochre and brown auditorium with the large white cross smack in the middle of the structure facing the ocean. Nearby, small sheds and wooden tent frames stood empty. The tents dated back to the days of religious revival meetings but now sat empty, waiting for when the residents would return and pitch the tents in which they would live for the summer.

For nearly a hundred years the tents had routinely been going up and down. Liliana suspected that a hundred years from now, the routine would be the same.

Routine was important it reminded her as she sped the final few blocks to the street of her condo. As she entered her building, she had already decided what she would do. How she would restore order and protect all those who needed her.

She only had one hope for herself for the day—that Jesse would not fail her.

CHAPTER 24

Jesse paced back and forth along the balcony of his home, staring out at the ocean.

Angry red streaks colored the morning sky.

Angry being an apt description of how he was feeling.

He was angry at Morales and his partners for lying to him about the gene therapies.

Angry at Whittaker and his thugs for threatening his sister and Liliana.

But more than anything else, he was furious with himself.

Once again he had failed to do what was right.

God might forgive him for the sins of lust and greed when he had lost his way during his football career.

God might even forgive him for the pride that had made him bribe his way into the Wardwell experiments.

But he was certain God was never ever going to forgive him for making love to Liliana while he was living a lie.

Jesse wasn't even sure that he could forgive himself, much less hope that Liliana might absolve him.

Not even the chill wind blowing off the ocean could cool the rage churning inside him, creating dangerous heat at his core that needed relief.

He entered his bedroom and tore off the sweatshirt and pants he had worn to sleep.

They smelled of her. Womanly, with the faintest whiff of some kind of flowery fragrance. He hadn't noticed that aroma at first. Only when he had buried his face in the side of her neck had the slightest hint of perfume teased him.

He brought the shirt up to his face and inhaled deeply, imprinting her scent in his mind. Safeguarding it and the associated memories.

Dressing in fresh fleece, he nearly skipped down the stairs in his haste to reach the gym and work out his anger and frustration.

It was dark downstairs still, but at the sound of his footsteps, a light snapped on in the guest bedroom, where Whittaker's men took turns sleeping.

Howard stumbled to the door. His sandy blond hair was disheveled, sticking up in spots but matted in others as if drenched with sweat. The white T-shirt he wore was stained with light and dark spots that looked wet, and at midthigh, a rusty red blotch marred the leg of his gray sweatpants.

He looked like shit, Jesse thought.

And pissed off.

Howard's hazel-colored eyes glittered with an unusual light that penetrated the dimness in the hallway.

"Mornin'," Jesse said, trying to avoid a confrontation.

Howard grunted and staggered back into the room.

Jesse paused in the doorway as Howard fell onto the bed. The linens were in disarray, half off and on and twisted, as if he'd had a rough night. Judging from the way Howard lay staring up at the ceiling, almost distractedly, Jesse guessed this morning was not much better.

Jesse sought out Bruno to tell him about Howard's condition.

He found the man in the kitchen, half asleep in one of the kitchen chairs. His eyes opened sluggishly at Jesse's entry.

"Dontcha ever sleep?" Bruno asked, annoyance in every syllable.

"Howard is looking kinda punk." Jesse jerked his hand, thumb extended, in the direction of the guest bedroom.

"Boss man said not to worry. Thinks Howard caught some kind of bug at the hospital last night. That's why I'm still on duty," Bruno advised. He rose from his chair to switch from the dim cabinet accent lights that were on to the overhead spotlights, bathing the room in brightness.

Jesse doubted it was just a simple bug but needed more to confirm his suspicions. Maybe when Liliana arrived...

When Liliana arrived he intended to come clean, he thought, leaning his hand on the frame of the door as he wavered, exhausted both physically and emotionally.

Bruno immediately jumped on it.

"Are *you* okay?"

Jesse shook his head to clear the slight wave of dizziness that had hit him. "Fine. Just a little woozy after last night."

Bruno rolled his eyes and pointed to his swollen nose. "I get it."

Jesse doubted Bruno understood but didn't say. He headed toward the gym, where, with a measured pace, he did a circuit with the free weights, working past the pain in his side. When he was done, he jumped on the AMT machine, pushing on the pedals and arms in alternating paces, from a stair climb to a long running stride. He kept at it until heavy sweat rolled from his body and the pool of angry heat at his center had dissipated.

Snagging a towel from a pile by the door, he dried his face and returned to his room for a shower, feeling energized but also in control.

He knew he would need to keep in check when Liliana returned.

In the shower, he ran soapy hands across his skin, recalling the feel of her touch. Flinching as he ran one hand over the bruised spot on his ribs where Howard had beaten him. Despite the pain, the bruise was a good sign. It was still tender and purplish. No sign of bone formation. Yet.

He was hopeful that bone would not develop. With his other injuries, his body's response had been almost immediate.

Since the treatments of the other day, that had all changed. For how long he didn't know, but he was grateful for even a short reprieve from the destruction being wrought on his body.

He rinsed off, stepped out, and dried himself. Strode to the sink, where he checked the gash on his head. Beneath the butterfly bandages Liliana had applied, the injury was only just starting to knit.

With a thankful sigh, he left the bathroom, but as he did so, Liliana walked into his room.

He knew immediately from her face that trouble had arrived.

CHAPTER 25

Liliana had a stranglehold on the handle of her physician's bag. Dark circles marred the skin beneath her eyes, as if she hadn't slept well.

He understood.

The winter chill had brought pink spots to her cheeks, but under that spot of color, her olive-toned skin was pale.

All was not right.

"Mornin'," he said lamely, unsure of just how to start the day with her.

Liliana was obviously not as unsure.

"Is there something you want to tell me, Jesse?" She arched a brow for emphasis, reminding him of his mother when she had been about to punish him for being bad.

And he had been bad with Liliana. Horrible, in fact. There was only one way to make it right.

"I haven't been totally honest with you," he said and approached her, but she stepped back toward the closed door.

"I would never hurt you," he reminded, only she let out a harsh sigh and shook her head.

"You already did."

She knew, he realized. There was no hiding the deception any longer. Which meant that more than their relationship was at stake. Her life was at risk if Whittaker found out.

"You can't even begin to understand what's going on," he said, hands outspread as he pled his case.

"Try me, and while you're at it, put on some clothes."

She flicked her hand at his nakedness, clearly disturbed by it. Or maybe she was distracted by it, a good thing to remember for the future.

For right now he wanted her focused on what he would say.

Snagging the sweatpants tossed on his bed, he jerked them on, then stood before her, hands on his hips as he fumbled for how to start. Raking his hand through his hair, he finally dragged the words from inside him.

"I'd do anything for the people I care about," he confessed.

She swung her bag back and forth before she said, "If you care for me, how about starting with the truth?"

Starting with the truth? He wasn't even sure where to begin, much less where honesty came into the picture. So he just started at the beginning.

"I didn't plan on becoming a guinea pig when I signed up for the Wardwell treatments. I thought they would make my life better. Let me go back to playing football."

He blew out a harsh sigh and dug both his hands through his hair, dragging back the shorter strands and releasing them before returning his hands to his hips. Looking away from her condemning gaze, he continued.

"For the past year I've been poked and prodded. Tortured. I would have done anything to be free, only . . ."

Only he wouldn't have traded his freedom for hurting someone he loved. But he hadn't been given a choice.

"Whittaker came into the picture about a month ago. Maybe he was involved all along, but I only found out about him recently," he explained.

"Whittaker freed you?" Liliana prompted.

Jesse laughed harshly and shook his head. Held up his hands and motioned to everything around him. "If you can call being a captive in my own home free."

"But it's better than being in a lab, isn't it?" she challenged.

"Yes, but being in a lab didn't risk others. Didn't risk my sister's life. Or yours."

Liliana shook her head forcefully and her hair shifted violently with the motion. "I don't get it."

Jesse spread his hands wide again, awkwardly circled them in the air as he tried to explain. "When Whittaker arrived, he told me my sister was sick with a more aggressive form of what I have. He said that if I helped them, they would help cure her."

"But look at you," Liliana said, gesturing to the ruined portions of his body.

"They said you might have the way to control this."

She tapped her chest, her eyes wide with disbelief. "Me? I'm a novice at this. A rank amateur."

"But you had something they wanted—a new inhibitor. And they told me that might stop the damage," he said and ran his hand down the large exoskeleton of bone on his ribs.

Liliana tossed her bag onto the bed and strode away from him, pacing as she considered his words. Clearly upset. She finally faced him and once again pointed to herself. "What I know can't help you, as much as I want it to. That inhibitor could kill you if it's administered."

He didn't doubt her.

It hit him hard, as if he had been punched in the solar plexus. His knees wobbled and he sucked in a rough breath, took a step back, and sat on the bed as he considered her words.

He had risked his life, his sister's, and Liliana's for nothing. Shaking his head, he mumbled, "I didn't do it for myself. I did it for Jackie."

"How do you even know Whittaker is telling the truth about your sister? How could he know if she's sick?"

"I don't know if he's telling the truth, but if he was...Could I risk not helping her? I wanted for her to be well."

Liliana didn't doubt that, but nothing that she did could help. She approached him, wanting to hold him, but she held back. "I wish there was something I could do, but the inhibitor isn't the answer."

He nodded but averted his gaze, looking downward. "He said he would kill Jackie if I didn't help. If I told anyone what was happening." His head shot up, fear in his eyes. "Whittaker isn't FBI, Liliana."

"I know, Jesse. My cousin is a police chief. I asked him to investigate Whittaker."

Jesse shook his head vehemently. "You can't let him know that. You can't tell Whittaker the inhibitor won't work—"

"It won't work on *you*, Jesse. But it'll work on other patients."

Relief washed over him. "That's good. Some of them were in pretty tough shape."

"How many?" she asked, wondering at the number of Wardwell patients who were still alive.

"Over a dozen," he replied, surprising her.

"A dozen? But there were only eight original—"

"They started grabbing homeless people off the street. There were at least a dozen at my lab location," he advised.

"Your location? There's more than one?" she asked, pacing before him as she considered his revelations.

Jesse laid his hand on her hip to stop her nervous motion. "You can't let Whittaker know. He'll kill you and everyone in your lab."

She faced him, her features intense as she examined his face. "Is that why you lied to me?"

"I had no choice, Liliana. I had to protect you and Jackie," he pleaded and squeezed her hip tenderly, urging her closer.

"I'm sorry," he said and leaned his head against her midsection, submitting himself to her judgment.

She had hoped he would have a reasonable explanation to justify his lies. His behavior was so humbling and his actions so selfless, they didn't fail to touch her heart.

Wanting to comfort him, she wrapped her arms around his shoulders and dipped her head to rest along the top of his. "Don't ever lie to me again."

His body shuddered against her with a massive release of emotion. "Never again. I promise."

Maybe it was foolish to rely on that vow, but sometimes risk was warranted due to the possible rewards.

Jesse's freedom.

A cure for Jackie if she was in fact sick.

Safety for herself, Carmen, and the others in the lab.

Kneeling, she cupped his face in her hands and dropped a quick kiss on his cheek.

"We need to plan, Jesse. We need to figure out what to do."

Jesse laid his hand on the side of her neck and rubbed his thumb along the line of her jaw. "We'll do it together."

"Together," Liliana said and sitting side by side, they formulated their strategy.

CHAPTER 26

The plan took on a life that neither of them expected.

"Are you sure about this?" Jesse caressed the line of her jaw repeatedly as if to reassure himself she was still with him.

"No, but I can't think of any other way to keep everyone safe."

Everyone except the two of them.

If they embarked on this course of action, they risked themselves, but as their gazes locked, Liliana knew he was set to act and so was she.

"I'll have your back, Liliana," he reassured and teasingly added, "And maybe your front, as well."

She smiled as he had intended. "You're incorrigible."

He grinned. "It's why you love me."

Her smile wavered a bit, and he understood, even though it created a well of pain in the area of his heart. It was too soon to speak about love, especially when that fragile emotion had been birthed in a sea of lies.

"It's okay, Liliana. I won't pressure you."

She nodded, and a watery glint collected in her eyes. "I care for you, but..."

"I'm fine with whatever you want," he urged again, and

to silence any further protest, he kissed her. She was stiff at first but soon responded, her kiss confessing what she couldn't with words.

Liliana battled him. Battled herself, but it was a lost cause. She cared for him more than was possibly good.

He had lied to her.

But for good reasons, the voice inside her head countered. He was only trying to protect his sister. Watch over her, too. Except Liliana didn't need his protection. She was perfectly capable of taking care of herself, she thought, and withdrew from the kiss.

"Liliana?" He ran his fingers down her cheek, almost pleading.

"Not yet, Jesse."

With a slight nod of his head, he released her, earning her respect by honoring her wish.

She rose and waved for him to stand. "I want to take a look at your injuries."

He did as she asked, held his arms up, which caused a slight hitch in his side.

"Still sore?" She ran her hand across the bruise, palpating it gently as she did so.

"Still sore, but that's a good thing," he said, peering downward to where her hand rested at his side.

"A good thing," she repeated, her mind clearly on something else for a moment before she tardily retreated her hand.

"Something wrong?" He bent slightly so he could better read her face and what she was thinking.

"The patient they supposedly found yesterday is like you."

Jesse recalled another bone patient in the lab. Like him, but not, since the man's disease had been far more advanced. He understood then Liliana's distraction.

"He's dying, isn't he? Frank is dying," he said, the man's name suddenly popping into his brain.

"Frank? Dark-haired. In his early fifties?"

It fit the description of the other patient, so he nodded. "Frank Lambert. I think that was his name."

"He's not dead yet," Liliana said, although she was uncertain how much longer they could sustain his life. The fever was not a good sign, and she feared that the possible use of an inhibitor complex might have compromised his bone marrow. She had delayed in taking a specimen because of his weakened condition, but if they couldn't control the fever, she might not have any choice.

Which made her think about someone else who seemed to be exhibiting signs of a fever.

"Have you seen Howard this morning?"

Jesse nodded and rubbed his hands along the tops of his thighs. "He doesn't seem to be doing well."

She recalled the blood on his pants leg. The patch and bit of blood at his back. There was only one conclusion she could reach.

"I think they injected him with the same genes they used on you." She looked away from him, plucked at the sheets on his bed.

He covered her hand with his, attempting to calm her. Offering comfort as he slipped his hand into hers.

"If they did that, he may become dangerous. Quickly."

Her hand trembled slightly, arousing his need to protect, but also to understand more about her.

"There's more to it, isn't there? When we first met, you were already afraid of the violence. Why?"

She evaded him, but he placed his thumb and forefinger at her chin and gently insisted that she face not only him, but his query.

"Doesn't violence frighten you?" she dissembled.

With a harsh chuckle, he replied, "I was a professional football player. I saw violence of one kind or another every day, but I suspect you've witnessed more than you care to."

Liliana could have continued to hide but unexpectedly realized that to do so was akin to the lying of which she had accused him.

"My ex-fiancé abused me. Mentally. Physically," she confessed and met his gaze, wanting to reveal all that was in her heart.

Jesse shook his head, confused. "Why did you become engaged to him?"

She shrugged. "He wasn't like that at first. Something happened. Whatever it was, he wouldn't share it with me. As time passed, he got more and more reclusive. Abusive."

Narrowing his gaze, Jesse considered her carefully, and his scrutiny drove her to reveal more.

"Last year one of Morales's patients kidnapped me. Santiago. He nearly killed my brother."

"But you survived," he said and eased his hand into her hair, tenderly cradling the back of her head. Massaging it gently, he continued. "You survived, and you're stronger for it."

"But maybe not smarter."

Although she didn't withdraw from him physically, she did retreat emotionally. He understood. She had placed herself in danger again, not only by agreeing to their plan, but by caring for him.

"We'll survive this together. And we'll be stronger for it," he exhorted, and a weak smile came to her lips.

With that, he provided his concerns about Howard.

"I don't know why, but when they first injected me, something went crazy inside. You can call it anger. Rage."

The scientist in Liliana kicked in. "You're introducing a foreign substance into one of the body's key systems. If you don't suppress the immune system beforehand, your body is going to war against the invader."

"Maybe that invasion is what causes the reaction, but it lasted for a while. I can't say how long, because they pumped me up with drugs right after," Jesse admitted, struggling to recall the specifics of those early days in the lab but unable to do so.

"Whatever it is, we'll need to stay clear of Howard until our plan is under way."

Their strategy. A risky and dangerous endeavor. But there was no other way to safeguard all the innocents who might suffer if Whittaker, Morales, and their associates continued their illegal enterprise.

"Be safe, Liliana. Don't take any unnecessary risks," he said and kissed her yet again.

The kiss was one filled with hope, and as she responded, it became one of possibilities.

His mind let go of all the danger. Filled with the taste of her. The scent of her, that flowery tone over the more womanly aroma.

They would survive this. *Together,* he thought, lost in the promise of the kiss.

*   *   *

Frank Lambert, if that was really her John Doe's name, worsened within half an hour of her early morning arrival at the hospital.

The fever they had been trying to contain throughout the night spiked, driving his temperature up to a perilous 104 degrees.

Liliana, Carmen, and an assortment of nurses worked like demons, getting him into an ice bath and pumping him full of antipyretics, but to no avail. His fever continued to climb until his body erupted into violent convulsions.

Nothing they did controlled the seizures or rising temperatures.

Shortly before noon, Frank Lambert passed away.

Liliana and Carmen shut down all the monitors and covered Frank's body with a sheet.

"I'm assuming you want me to do the autopsy," Carmen said as she handed Liliana the chart so she could sign off on the cause and time of the patient's death.

Hands shaking, Liliana accepted the chart. Pulled the pen out of her lab jacket pocket and scrawled the list of the actions they had taken and the factors leading up to the patient's demise. With each word, a sick feeling grew in her stomach until the pain was so intense, she had to stop writing, sit down, and double over.

Immediately Carmen was at her side, patting her back. "It's not your fault. You did all you could."

How many times had she heard those words? Liliana thought.

Too many.

And if they couldn't figure out how to stop the proliferation of the proteins in Jesse's body, he might one day be just like Frank.

"Lil?" Carmen pressed and leaned forward until she was almost level with Liliana's downturned face.

"Can you take a bone marrow sample when you do the autopsy? Make sure to take plugs from both his hip and femur."

She met Carmen's anxious gaze. As her friend stared at her, worry apparent in the deep ridge across her forehead, Liliana peered past Carmen to Frank's now still body.

"Why a fever?" she wondered aloud and dredged up the thoughts she'd had earlier that morning as she and Jesse had discussed Howard.

Carmen shrugged. "We'll know once we do the autopsy."

"I suspect someone dosed him with an inhibitor complex, even though we were worried that might kill off his bone marrow."

Looking back toward their dead patient, Carmen seemed to understand where she was going.

"If the inhibitor worked too efficiently and he lost all his bone marrow, he'd be immuno-depressed—"

"And subject to all kinds of infection, hence a fever," Liliana finished for her, then surged up out of her chair and snapped the chart shut.

"We can't use an inhibitor if it will kill off all his bone marrow."

"You're talking about Jesse. About what to do to stop *that* from happening if we treat him," Carmen said and swung her hand back toward Frank.

Liliana nodded, strode toward the door, and paused with her hand on the knob. "Let me know what you find out from the autopsy."

Carmen eyeballed her again. "Is something wrong? Something you're not telling me?"

With a quick jerk of her head, Liliana confirmed it. "I can't say until I know more."

And because Carmen trusted her friend without hesitation, she didn't ask Liliana for anything else.

When Liliana was ready, she would fill Carmen in on whatever she should know.

CHAPTER 27

It always seemed so much more clandestine in the movies. Secret meetings tucked away in the corner of a coffee shop somewhere. Furtive glances to make sure they weren't being observed.

Instead, Ramon sat across the kitchen table in the late afternoon, passing over copies of photos of Whittaker, Howard, and Bruno along with their rap sheets.

Liliana shuffled through them, reviewing the information on their assorted felonies and misdemeanors. While Bruno's was colorful and Howard's worrisome, Whittaker's was infinitely deadly.

Assassination, sabotage, extortion, spying, kidnapping, torture, fraud, gun smuggling, and now, human experimentation.

Liliana rubbed a hand across the back of her neck to quiet the fearful hackles there and tossed the materials on the tabletop. "Quite a background."

"He's a dangerous man, Lil. You don't want to mess with him," her cousin said and gathered up the papers.

"I have no choice. There are too many people to protect."

Ramon leaned back in his chair and shoved his hands into his pockets. "It's risky, but—"

"You'll get together everyone you need to in order to protect us, my family, Carmen—"

"And Jesse. He's a big part of the reason why you're doing this, isn't he?" Ramon pressed, cocking his head to one side in a gesture she assumed he often did. Usually in an interrogation room.

She splayed her fingers against the oak surface of her kitchen table. Pressed down until her knuckles were white as she held back all she wanted to say.

That she was confused.

That she was possibly in love with Jesse.

That she was afraid he would die and nothing she could do would save him.

"Yes." She glanced at him directly, daring him not to ask more. Begging him not to further question her.

With a quick nod of his head, he acknowledged her plea. Reaching into his pocket, he pulled out a pen and passed it to her.

She picked it up and, arching her brows, examined it.

Ramon made a rotating motion with his hands. "Twist the barrel to activate the GPS device in the pen. Whittaker will be sure to snag your cell phones to keep us from tracking you."

Wagging her head, she gingerly laid the pen back down on the tabletop. "I understand."

"He'll be watching you the moment you start this, so..." He rose, walked over to her, and wrapped his arms around her.

"Be safe, *prima*," he said and kissed the top of her head.

"You, too, Ramoncito," she replied, embracing him also and squeezing tightly. Certain she could trust her cousin to keep them safe.

Not so sure she would have the bravado to carry out the plan.

Ramon must have sensed her hesitation. He pulled away and said, "It's not too late to back out. We already have enough to round up Whittaker and his goons."

"But not enough to find the missing patients or Morales and Edwards."

Ramon's lips tightened with displeasure. "Not enough."

"Then let's do this. Before I chicken out." She patted his hand, trying to reassure him almost as much as she was herself.

She could do this, she thought.

She had to do this.

Jesse heard the thump and clank from up in his bedroom.

Loud and repetitive. Almost insistent.

He hurried down the stairs and to the gym.

Howard was there, lying on the bench and doing a press. His body bathed in sweat. Ripped muscles strained with each press and release of the weights. A lot of weights. Well over two hundred pounds, Jesse guessed.

With a final clang, Howard dropped the weight stack and sat up, clapping his hands like an Olympic weight-lifter who had just completed a world-record lift.

The man contained his enthusiasm as he realized Jesse stood there.

With reason.

Although Howard had been strong before, he seemed more defined now. His muscles larger, almost bulging.

Could it happen so fast? Jesse thought, trying to drag

up memories of when he had first been injected, but it was still all a haze. Morales had wasted little time in pumping him full of drugs so that he could be controlled after the introduction of the genes.

Had he been like Howard? he wondered, taking in the man's almost feral gaze and flushed features. Sweat rolled down Howard's hairline and along the side of his face, gathered at his chin before dripping onto his soaked muscle shirt.

"What're you looking at, Bradford?" Howard challenged with a jerk of his head.

Jesse raised his hands in a sign of surrender. "No problem, dude. Just wanted to make sure everything's okay."

"Dude," Howard mimicked and laughed, almost maniacally. "I'm just fine, *dude*."

The other man was bucking for a fight. In another life, Jesse would have willingly engaged him, uncaring of the end result.

But not today.

Too much was at stake for him to risk a beatdown of Howard for the sake of male vanity.

With a submissive pump of his hands, he stepped away from the other man but didn't turn his back on him. He didn't trust Howard for a moment in his current state.

The man was a loose cannon, which only made the plan he and Liliana had worked out even riskier.

And made Jesse reconsider their strategy.

He continued retreating, focused on Howard until he was in the hallway and heard the creak of the front door opening.

"Howya doin' Dr. Carrera?" Bruno said.

"Okay, Bruno. Is Jesse around?"

Jesse rushed down the hallway but paused to appreciate her as she waited in the foyer.

"Liliana," he said, leaning against the wall and laying his arms across his chest to contain the jump in his heartbeat at the sight of her.

A guarded smile came to her face. "Jesse. You're looking well."

He held his hands wide and sauntered toward her. "Feeling great, Doc. You look good also."

Her smile brightened until Bruno ribbed, "Can we take this mutual-admiration society to the kitchen. Boss man called to say he was on the way."

"Because I called him, Bruno," she said and, brushing past him, strode to the kitchen, Jesse close behind.

He leaned toward her and whispered, "I need you to take a look at something."

"Are you okay?" she asked, worry coloring her tones.

Because Bruno was near enough to hear them, he lied. "My ribs are still a little sore. Could you see what's up?"

"Let's go to the gym—"

"No, not the gym. Howard is in there… working out. My room would be better."

Liliana nodded but spoke to Bruno over her shoulder. "We'll be back as soon as I examine Jesse."

Bruno grunted his assent, and Liliana and Jesse rushed upstairs. After they entered his bedroom, Jesse closed the door and leaned on it.

"Howard is in the gym pumping over two hundred pounds of iron like it was a feather pillow."

Liliana's eyebrows shot up. "I didn't think it could happen that fast."

With a shrug, Jesse said, "We need to reconsider what we're doing. Howard could be a major problem."

Liliana laced her fingers together and shook her head. "I'm not sure we can. Ramon is already working on it."

Jesse pushed off the door and walked to her. He laid his hand on her shoulder. So small beneath his palm. So fragile.

"I don't want you hurt."

She smiled and covered his hand with hers. "You won't let that happen, and I won't fail you."

He shook his head. "I know you mean that—"

"I won't fail you," she urged, rose up on tiptoe, and kissed him. Pressed close, sealing her promise with her lips and body.

"Yo, can I get this kind of exam?"

Jesse and Liliana jerked apart and faced the door where Bruno stood, mouth agape. Eyes wide as his mouth flopped up and down while he struggled for what else to say.

"Whittaker here?" Jesse asked while at the same time wrapping his arm around her shoulders, presenting a calm and unified front.

Liliana wasn't feeling so peaceful. Her stomach was alive with nervous flutters, but she knew she had to tame them to handle Whittaker.

"Yes, has Whittaker arrived? I've got news for him," she said, hating the slight quaver in her voice.

"He's here, and yeah, I can see you've got something to tell him," Bruno advised cynically and left.

Jesse patted her arm. "You did fine, Lil."

The shakes she had been controlling intensified, so much so that Jesse must have felt them.

He embraced her tightly, steadying her. She wrapped her arms around him, used him as her anchor, and peace flooded her body.

"Ready?" he asked.

"Ready."

CHAPTER 28

Whittaker waited in the middle of the kitchen, arms across his chest. Bruno and Howard flanking him.

Bruno had a goofy look on his face. Howard had a towel around his neck, hands wrapped around the ends of it. The pose made his muscles look even larger and more menacing.

"You wanted to see me," Whittaker said, his composure even although she could sense the annoyance beneath the seeming calm.

"She wants to tell you she and Bradford are an item, boss," Bruno said, earning an elbow from Howard and a rebuke.

"Shut your mouth, you baboon."

Whittaker arched a brow. "Is that true, Dr. Carrera?"

"Frank Lambert died several hours ago."

"Since you found out his name, I guess you can notify his family," Whittaker replied with a careless shrug.

Liliana continued, but beside her Jesse's body tensed with anger.

She covered his hand with hers, and Whittaker's gaze flickered down for a moment, then returned to her face.

"I believe Lambert died as a result of the administration of an inhibitor complex."

Another cavalier shrug preceded his reply. "Wardwell has had that medication for some time."

Liliana advanced on him and pointed at his chest. "It wasn't Wardwell's formula that destroyed a substantial portion of Lambert's bone marrow cells."

"What are you suggesting, Dr. Carrera?" Whittaker asked, as calm as could be.

"I'm suggesting you administered *our* version of the medication. Lambert's dead cells, together with his depressed immune system, resulted in a systemwide septicemia that killed him."

"Shame, don't you think, Mr. Bradford?" Whittaker replied and peered past her to Jesse.

"Lambert was no longer valuable, but you need Liliana to help with the remaining patients," Jesse said and twined his fingers with hers in a show of support.

Whittaker narrowed his eyes and considered them. "So you're a team now? And you think I need you?"

Howard chuckled ruthlessly, until Liliana said, "Howard needs us unless you want him to end up like Lambert."

Whittaker smiled, but it didn't register in his flat, cold eyes. "So you think you know?"

"I know you're felons and not the FBI. I know you need me and my team to help you."

His smile flickered, and Howard took a step toward them, but Whittaker snapped up his arm to hold back his associate.

"How can you help?" Whittaker asked with a desultory jerk of his head.

Liliana glanced upward at Jesse from the corner of her eye. There was no going back now. No retreat.

She plowed forward, nearly strangling Jesse's hand with the force of her grip.

"We've got the capabilities to adapt the inhibitor. Develop different strategies to control the gene replication."

Whittaker jammed his hands into his pants pockets and jingled the change there. "And you'd help me? Fully aware of what I am? What I do?"

She nodded and waited for him to continue.

The change jingling stopped while Whittaker shot a sidewise glance at Howard. "And in exchange? What do you want, because no one ever does anything for free."

"Jesse leaves with me. Right now. You stay away from Jesse's family and mine. My lab people. And you provide me whatever information I need about the genes implanted in Jesse."

The words left her mouth in a rush, and Jesse's hand tightened on hers, urging caution and restraint.

She paused after the stream of words, waiting for a read on Whittaker.

"That's not all you want, though, is it?" he said, obviously sure of her intentions.

He wasn't wrong. "I want you to let me treat the Wardwell patients and the others you've taken."

Whittaker laughed out loud, the sound booming across the tiles in the kitchen. Then he began that maddening jingle of the change again.

"You think that's funny?" Jesse confronted, pushing her back toward the man.

Liliana restrained him, then turned and cupped his

cheek. "It's what we have to do, Jesse. I hate it as much as you do, but it's what we have to do."

Facing Whittaker again, he was examining her freshly, as if ready to believe her offer. When he gave a controlled, almost methodical bob of his head, she realized he had accepted it.

But before she could react, he raised his forefinger. "Understand this, Dr. Carrera. *No one* fucks with me. Break the deal and you'll all be slowly and painfully dead."

She didn't doubt he'd make good on his threat. Which only strengthened her resolve that they would not fail.

"Jesse is leaving with me. *Now,*" she repeated, and although Howard made another threatening move in their direction, Whittaker restrained him.

"Bradford is free to go. I know where to find you."

And your loved ones.

He didn't say it, maybe because he didn't need to. Both she and Jesse understood the stakes of this game, as did the others helping them with their plan.

"I'll wait to hear when we can treat the other patients," she said, and Whittaker confirmed her request with a sharp nod.

Her one hope as she tugged on Jesse's hand and led him toward the front door was that the players on their team would be stronger. Faster. Wiser.

The lives of so many depended on them.

And on her and Jesse, she thought, braving a smile as she looked over her shoulder at him.

"It'll be okay," he urged, a determined look on his face. His blue gaze bright with hope and love.

She wanted to believe. Wanted to hope as he hoped but

averted her gaze so he wouldn't see the doubt there. The fear that whatever emotion they shared could not survive this challenge.

Instead, she tightened her grasp on his hand. When he asked where they were going, she said, "Somewhere safe."

CHAPTER 29

Some sought refuge in church.

Others with friends.

Still others found it in a bottle or drugs.

To Liliana, her refuge was her home and family.

Home first, she thought as she unlocked the door to her condo and ushered Jesse inside.

"This is nice," he said as he entered and strolled to the sliding glass doors.

She met him there, staring out at the views of Asbury Park and the crosses along the beach in Ocean Grove.

"Not quite like your home—"

"Home isn't about the size or location." Jesse clasped her to him and brought his forehead to hers. "It's about the heart in the home. The love."

Liliana moved, brushing her cheek along his. The rasp of his early evening beard chafed her skin, yet she welcomed it. "Love makes all things possible," she whispered close to the shell of his ear.

The movement of his smile caressed her cheek a second before his lips covered hers.

She welcomed his kiss. Welcomed him into her home and heart as she deepened the intimacy, opening her mouth to his. Pressing her body tight until they were almost melded into one.

An unexpected knock at the door, loud and relentless, tore them apart.

Shooting him a quizzical glance, she grasped his hand and led him to the door. With a deep breath, she called out, "Who is it?"

"*Mi'ja.* We wanted to surprise you," her mother said past the boundary of the door.

"I'll say it's a surprise," she muttered before opening the door.

As soon as she did so, her family plowed through. Mother, father, and brother trudged in, arms filled with bags that soon flavored the air with enticing aromas.

Tony was the first to react to Jesse's presence. He stopped before him awkwardly and said, "It's really you. I mean, you're—"

"Jesse Bradford," he said and held out his hand.

Tony took it in his, pumping it up and down enthusiastically.

"You'll have to pardon, Tony. He's a big fan," Liliana explained, failing to contain the smile on her face at her brother's exuberance.

"And you're not?" Jesse teased, enjoying the immediate calm he had felt wash over her as soon as her family had entered her condo.

Tony guffawed. "Liliana? She can barely tell a football from a hockey puck."

A becoming flush spread over Liliana's face. She stammered, obviously embarrassed. "You're exaggerating, *hermanito.*"

Luckily her parents approached, sparing Liliana from

further sibling commentary. "*Mi'ja.* We're so glad you're safe," her mother said.

Or at least Jesse assumed it was her mother, since there was no mistaking the obvious resemblance between the two, although her mother was a bit shorter and plumper. Before he could react, her mother's doughy arms were around him, hugging him tight.

"*Mi'jo. Bienvenido,*" she said.

His college Spanish was rusty, but he gave it a try anyway. "*Muchas gracias, Señora Carrera.*"

Liliana's mother stepped back and raked him with a motherly eyeball as she said, "*Hablas español?*"

He raised his hand, gestured with his thumb and forefinger. "*Muy poquito.*"

The older man that Jesse assumed was Liliana's dad, because they shared eyes of a similar color and shape, stuck out his hand, his demeanor entirely serious. "Mr. Bradford."

"*Señor Carrera.* I wish we were meeting under different circumstances," he said as he shook the man's hand and shot an uneasy glance at Liliana.

"As do I," the man replied but then swept his arm wide in the direction of the table. The bags with the intriguing smells sat on its surface.

"Sit. Eat. It has been a difficult day," her father said.

"My family's solution to everything—food," Liliana explained, but there was no condemnation in her tones. Just love and possibly pride.

"We'll go now so that the two of you..." Her mother didn't finish, clearly at a loss as she glanced from one to the other, obviously aware that danger was close.

"It'll be okay, *Mami.* Would you like to join us?"

Liliana said, although for safety's sake she wished they would go.

Her family seemed to comprehend the situation.

"We should leave, *mi'ja*. I'm sure you and your young man have a lot to discuss," her father said in a peaceful tone.

"*Gracias, Señor Carrera*," Jesse responded and once again shook his hand and Tony's, returned her mother's almost tearful embrace.

As her family walked to the door, her mother handed Liliana another bag.

"Your brother Mick wanted to be here, only . . . He sent this. He thought it might help," her *mami* said and pressed the bundle into her hands.

Once they had departed, Liliana leaned against the door and faced him. "I think you just survived the first challenge. My parents."

"What's the second challenge?" he asked, and she glanced down at the package in her hands.

"*Mi hermano,* Mick," she said, but as she opened the parcel, she smiled and passed it over to Jesse.

"You're about the same size. He must have suspected that we would have to leave your house in a hurry."

Jesse peered inside, and when he looked up, she detected the glint in his eyes.

Walking up to him, she laid her hand on his cheek, aware of where his thoughts were traveling. "You're family now. You won't ever be alone again."

The groan that erupted from his body shook her to the core. She stepped into his arms and grabbed him tight, rocking to and fro with him as he bent his head and pressed it to the top of hers.

"I don't deserve this. I don't deserve you," he muttered, his voice thick with emotion.

She raised her head until her lips were barely an inch from his. "Why don't you let me be the judge of that?"

His groan rumbled through her body this time, close as they were. Pressing herself to him, she made their embrace even more intimate until she knew she had to break away or take it to the next level.

Slightly breathless as she stood before him, she said, "Let's eat, then get some rest. What we have to do will be difficult, and we'll need to be strong."

Jesse agreed, and together they emptied the takeout dishes from the bags and sat down at the table.

As he sat beside Liliana, eating and discussing their plans, Jesse wondered if it had only been one night since they had come together. Was it possible to feel this way in so short a time? So part of another human being?

While he ate, the aromas of the meal enveloped him, as did the lingering warmth of her family's visit. As he picked up his fork and took a bite of the shredded meat swimming in a tasty tomato sauce, he recalled Liliana's story. Imagined her and her mother sitting together, talking and shredding the meat. Sharing as families should do.

Unlike his family had done.

"It will be okay, won't it?" Liliana asked from across the narrow width of the table, almost seemingly picking up on his disquiet.

He hadn't realized that he had stopped with the fork halfway to his mouth, prompting her attention. Finishing the motion, he forked up some more and, as he chewed, said, "It has to be."

She leaned close and squeezed his hand and resumed eating, although her bites were delicate compared to his.

Silence reigned as they finished the early evening meal and cleaned up the table. Working together in the kitchen to load the dishwasher, acting as if it was just another ordinary day.

As Liliana dried her hands on a kitchen towel, she turned and faced him. Her gaze was filled with such a mix of conflicting emotions.

He grabbed hold of the ends of the towel she held and drew her near, embracing her. "It *is* going to work out."

"How can you be so sure?" she asked, finally giving in to the doubt that had been plaguing her since they had agreed to the plan.

He bent his head to hers, nuzzled her nose with his as he said, "Because I've waited too long to meet someone like you. I'm not going to let anything screw this up."

"Me neither," she admitted, and he tightened his hold on her.

She inched up on her tiptoes, brushed her lips along his. Opened her mouth to invite him in. To show him his place in her heart and seal the promise that there would be more tomorrows together. When she finally stepped away, it was only long enough to take his hand and guide him to her bedroom.

He didn't stop to ask this time if she was sure.

Maybe because he no longer had any doubts, either.

Hand in hand they walked to the side of her bed and faced each other. Before he could act, she was slipping her suit jacket off her shoulders and tossing it onto a chair by her bed.

"No need to rush," he said as she reached for the first button on her blouse.

"Really?" she asked when he brushed aside her hands and replaced them with his.

"Really," he replied and skimmed the back of his forefinger along the V of skin exposed by the open collar of her blouse.

She peered downward for only a moment, raising her gaze to watch his face as he leisurely reached beneath the edge of her shirt with his thumb and traced the swells of her breasts.

Her nipples tightened in reaction, wanting his touch, but he continued to delay, slowly building her need.

She was trembling by the time he finally undid the buttons. Parting the fabric, he exposed her breasts in the pale pink bra, and the soft flesh of her midsection. Leisurely he skimmed the back of his hand across that skin, inching upward until he bared her breasts.

"You're so beautiful," he said with a sigh, cupping her breasts and strumming his thumbs across the tips, bringing them to ever tighter peaks. Initiating a corresponding pull between her legs that wanted assuagement.

As he butted his hips against hers, his erection pushed against her abdomen.

She wanted to feel him beside her. Feel the warmth of his skin.

She displaced his hands only long enough to yank off his sweatshirt, pants, and underwear, leaving him beautifully naked.

As he returned his attention to her breasts, she encircled his erection in her hand, exploring the length and width of him. The responsive head that made him jump in her hand as with one finger she traced the edge of it and then the sensitive underside. The bead of moisture as he sucked in a breath and covered her hand with his to still her caress.

"No rush, love. I want to sample all of you first," he said and she acquiesced, sitting on the edge of the bed and opening her arms in welcome.

"I'm yours," she said.

CHAPTER 30

The night was young, and it might be their final one together. The last thing he wanted was to disappoint. They'd had little tenderness the other night in their rush to satisfaction. Jesse wanted this time to be different.

He stepped close until his erection nestled at her center, and the warmth and wet of her teased him. She raised her legs, grasping him with her thighs, but he placed his hands on her shoulders and gently urged her onto her back.

At her confused look, he said, "I want to make love to you all night long. Until I don't have the strength to stand. Until I have no breath left in my body."

"*Mi amor,*" exploded from her lips and he pinned her hands above her head, covered her body with his.

"I *am* your love, Liliana."

She smiled, but her eyes were heavy with sadness he understood.

"We're stronger together." He brushed his lips across hers, once again offering her promise and hope in his kiss.

"Powerful, *querido,*" she murmured beneath his lips and opened her mouth, accepting the thrust of his tongue.

Raised her legs to cradle his hips with her thighs and rock her center along the length of him, yanking a strangled moan from him.

Jesse answered the call of her invitation, trailing his lips down the side of her neck to the sensitive crook of her shoulder. Moving his hands down to her breasts to caress the sensitive tips until Liliana wanted more. Needed more.

"*Por favor, Jesse,*" she pleaded and he responded, lowering his head to suck her nipples, tugging and pulling them into the warm moistness of his mouth. Swirling the dampness left behind by his mouth with his fingers.

Between her legs the heat built. Intensifying her desire to be one with him.

Reaching between their bodies, she covered him with her hand and held him to the softness of her belly. Stroked him and shifted her hips to mimic what would soon follow.

"Liliana, love. I want you so badly—"

"Then have me," she said and, exerting gentle pressure on his shoulder, she changed their positions, urging him to his back.

Copying his earlier actions, she pinned his hands above his head as she draped her body along his side. Lowered her head and teethed his dark brown nipple while she encircled him with her hand. Slowly stroked up and down as she bit down gently, and he cradled her head, urging her to continue.

A plea she was not going to ignore.

She shifted, laying her body along the length of his. Straddling his hips, she reached beneath her, guided him to her center. She paused with his tip just breaching her core, but then his hands came to her hips, nearly spanning the width of them with their large size.

"Love me, Liliana." To leave no doubt about what he wanted, he guided her down. Held her still as her body acclimated to the length and width of him.

Liliana bit her lower lip, fighting the desire to moan from the pleasure of his filling her. Sucking in a broken breath as he cradled her breast, teased the tip with his fingers, and then surged upward, kissing her nipple. Tugging on it, encouraging her to move with the subtle upward press of his hips.

She rocked her hips, drawing him in and out. Creating friction and heat throughout her body as he loosely wrapped an arm around her waist, bringing her near. Her breasts rubbed along his chest, teased by the soft hair there and by his touch and kisses.

Inside her, pressure built until she had to close her eyes and focus on the motion of her hips. On the wet of his mouth at her breasts. At one rough tug, she finally cried out, but in pleasure as that caress nearly pulled her over the edge.

Jesse knew she was near her release. He was almost there himself. Just another stroke of her hips. Another brush of her gorgeous breasts against his chest.

Just another, he kept on repeating in his brain, fighting his climax. Wanting to fall over the edge with her, but above him she was tiring.

"Let me, love," he said and she understood, falling to her side as he rolled and trapped her beneath him.

He stopped, wanting to memorize her features. Wanting to savor the look on her face. One of wonder. One of love.

He bent and kissed her. She whispered against his lips, "*Te quiero.*"

"I love you, too," he said and began to move. Pumping his hips. The force so strong that it drove her up along the bed.

That pushed them both to a climax that left them shaking as they cried out their completion.

It took long minutes for their breathing to return to normal and for the tremors of satisfaction to subside. But even then Jesse couldn't leave her. The physical union of their bodies was so much more than that. And being within her...

Peace such as none he had ever experienced before filled his soul. Calmed his heart.

As he moved only far enough to give her some breathing room, he stayed tucked within her, his erection ebbing slowly. Moving his hands along her side, he savored the softness and warmth of her skin.

When she shifted her hand to his ribs, he stiffened, but she dropped a kiss on the side of his face and whispered, "I wish I could take away your pain."

"But you have, love" he said, trapping her hand beneath his and sliding their joined hands to a spot over his chest.

Beneath her palm his heart beat strong. Sure.

Liliana propped her elbow on the mattress and leaned her head on her hand, allowing her to see his face. She rubbed the spot above his heart, deep in thought.

When she was with him like this, it all seemed right to Liliana.

But it wasn't.

He had lied to her, although she had forgiven him due to the reasons behind the untruth.

He was her patient, something more difficult to handle. Ethically she had crossed a line, but had ethics ever considered a situation like this one? she wondered.

"I'd say, 'A penny for your thoughts,' but I'm afraid to know what you're thinking," he said and ran his index finger along her forehead, smoothing a furrow of worry.

"There's just so much to contemplate," she confessed and inched up to see his face more clearly, but as she did so, he slipped out of her.

His absence was immediate, but he was quick to remedy that by flipping onto his side and bringing every inch of them into contact.

"There's only one thing to think about—how right this feels," he said, stroking his hand down the length of her back.

But as right as it seemed, she had to unburden herself of her concerns.

"This started in a lie, justifiable as it was."

"It won't happen again," he said, bending his head down to rest his forehead against hers.

"You're my patient, and—"

"I guess I have to fire you," he teased and brushed a kiss on the tip of her nose.

Despite the seriousness of the discussion, his playfulness lightened the severity. "You can't fire me. I'm the one who is going to cure you."

His breath caught in his chest, and beneath the hand now sandwiched between them, she thought his heart skipped a beat.

A little more earnestly he said, "I've told myself not to hope for that or for a cure for my sister. That it was impossible."

She brought her lips to his and whispered, "Is it any more impossible than finding your true love?"

His breath exploded against her mouth. "God, no."

"Believe, then," she said and opened her mouth on his once more, urging him to love her yet again.

CHAPTER 31

Liliana awoke to a pleasant tenderness between her legs and the heat of Jesse's body plastered along her back. One arm was tossed over her waist, and his big hand was resting casually against her belly. He stirred, drawing in a long breath that he held for a moment before relaxing again.

"Good morning," he whispered sleepily along the side of her face.

She rubbed her hand across his, smiled, and repeated the greeting. Along the small of her back, something else was awakening with the morning.

"Ah, Jesse," she said as he moved his hand downward and brushed his fingers along her center before parting her and finding the nub hidden within.

Her body immediately came to life, sensitive as she was from the many times they had made love last night. It was almost a painful desire that he must have sensed, since he whispered in her ear, "Let me kiss it and make it better."

Before she could protest, she was on her back and he was between her legs, whispering kisses along all that aching sensitivity. Pulling from her a hard, fast climax that had her arching off the bed and nearly screaming his name in the quiet of the morning.

Her body was trembling as he worked his way back up, teasing her with kisses along the center of her body until he was back at her mouth, kissing her once more.

In between their bodies, his erection jutted into the softness of her belly, reminding her of his need. Pleading for her to offer him the kind of pleasure with which he had just gifted her.

She gave it to him. She kissed the side of his mouth, dropped down to the hard line of his collarbone, running the tip of her tongue along his skin, then continued farther down, leaving a trail of kisses along his midsection. Swirling her tongue around his navel before going lower. She took him into her mouth, moving her tongue all along the tip of him as she stroked him with her hand.

Jesse called out her name, raised his hips ever higher, and she slipped between his legs, continued kissing him until, with a tremendous jolt, he climaxed.

His breathing was rough as she gave him one final kiss and pulled her body up to blanket his. He kissed her, bracing his hands on her hips to keep her close. Between their bodies, his erection slowly faded, and Liliana tucked her head beneath his, totally satisfied and completely tired.

She could have drifted off to sleep again, but on the nightstand her phone began to vibrate angrily. She reached over, dreading that it would be Whittaker so soon.

It wasn't.

"Good morning, Carmen," she said, and it *was* a good morning for the moment. Jesse was moving those big hands up and down her back in a lazy caress, and she allowed herself to imagine other mornings just like this in the future.

"His sister is a match," Carmen replied excitedly.

A match?

Liliana shot up, easing from Jesse's body to a spot beside him on the bed. Sitting there, she dragged her hair back off her face as she asked, "Are you sure?"

"Jesse's sister must have had her DNA sampled to make a possible donation to someone. You see them asking for donors on the news all the time."

"And she was in the donor database," Liliana added.

"I started thinking some more about what we discussed the other day. How we could treat Jesse's problem like leukemia. Kill off all the hybrid marrow and implant new cells to replace them," Carmen advised.

"So you checked to see if we could find a donor if we did that, only . . . Whittaker told Jesse that his sister had an aggressive bone disease."

Beside her, Jesse nodded to confirm her statement.

"There are no unusual markers on either of their DNA samples. Just the typical patterns you would expect in siblings."

Liliana considered Carmen's report. If there were no out-of-the-ordinary results showing up on their DNA tests, it was possible that Jesse's disease wasn't hereditary and that his sister wasn't ill.

"See if you can get any information on Jesse's sister. She's an athlete. Maybe she had a sprain or something where they might have done an x-ray," Liliana instructed.

"You think Whittaker is lying about this also?" Carmen replied, totally in sync with her friend.

"He's lied about everything else. What better way to get

Jesse to help him?" she said, and as Carmen confirmed Liliana's instructions, she hung up and faced Jesse.

His features were rigid, set in unforgiving lines. The muscles of his arms were bunched, his fists clenched, warning her that anger simmered beneath, held on a short leash.

Laying her hand on the taut muscles of his chest, she ran her hand across the hard width of it and urged calm.

"Take a breath, *mi amor*. Whittaker will get the punishment he deserves, but not by your hand."

"My sister isn't sick? You know this for sure?" he questioned, his voice tight with barely suppressed emotion.

"Not for sure. Not yet. But by comparing your two DNA samples, we could see that whatever caused your initial bone loss might not be genetic."

"How is that possible? So many doctors, and none of them could figure it out. So they assumed it had to be some kind of genetic disorder," he said and beneath her hand, the tension fled from his body.

There were so many possible explanations for bone loss, but sometimes the most obvious ones were overlooked.

"Your mother said you were a healthy boy. No sicknesses—"

"Nothing," he immediately confirmed.

"No serious injuries during high school or college?" she pressed.

"Nothing," he verified, and then, for a moment, it seemed as if he reconsidered that answer, since he looked away, almost hesitant in his actions.

"Jesse?" she asked, cradling the strong line of his jaw and applying pressure to shift his face upward.

"I was out for a couple of games in my senior year at

college. Got hit in the middle of the back. Doctor said it was a deep muscle bruise. Possibly some minor injury to my kidney, since I urinated blood for a day or two."

Rickets, she thought instantly. *Renal rickets.*

"If your kidney was compromised, you could possibly not be getting enough vitamin D. We can do some tests to confirm that."

He tightened his jaw as the implications of her comment registered. Sweeping one hand down his body, he said, "All this pain and damage, and you're telling me it could be something as simple as a vitamin deficiency?"

"I'm sorry, Jesse. But if that's what it is, we can treat it. We can kill off the hybrid bone marrow—"

"How?" he asked, bitterness in his voice.

"Radiation is the most likely way, only..."

"Only what, Liliana? Only if we survive the next few days?"

She slipped her hand over his lips, tracing the grim line of them. "We will survive, and after, I will be by your side to decide what treatment is best."

She didn't know what kind of reaction she had expected from him. Certainly not the cold and almost distant glare on his face that was so far removed from how he had been just moments before Carmen's call.

She tried to put herself in his place. Tried to imagine what it might be like to lose everything. To sacrifice as much as he had for something as simple as a vitamin deficiency.

She struggled to imagine but failed. So instead, she attempted to distract him from such thoughts, because she feared where they would lead.

"Let's take a bath. It'll ease all those sore spots," she

offered, and while he didn't immediately jump at her suggestion, he also didn't object.

Brushing a fleeting kiss on his lips, she left the room to prepare the bath.

Jesse remained in bed, watching her go. When she was out of sight, he grabbed hold of one of the pillows and squeezed it in his muscled arms, imagining that it was Whittaker. Or Howard or Bruno, or the doctors who had treated him and possibly missed something as simple as what Liliana had suggested.

How different would his life have been?

He could have avoided becoming some kind of scientific freak.

He could have gone back to playing football.

He could have been alone again. Without his family and without Liliana.

He relaxed his crushing grip on the pillow and tossed it aside. Jumped to his feet and took a step or two, the heat of anger still swimming dangerously close to the surface, ready to explode.

Liliana feared that anger, he knew. She was scared of the violence lying just beneath his skin, but despite that, she was here for him.

With him, he thought.

Inhaling a few slow, deep breaths, he marshaled the rage. There was no place for it here now with her.

The only thing there was room for was love.

He strode to the door of the bathroom, somehow contained the desire to rip it open so he could be closer to her faster. Guardedly he opened it.

She was by the bath, spilling something powdery into the swirling waters of a Jacuzzi.

"Please tell me I won't smell like petunias," he said, dragging a smile from her.

"I'm not sure petunias have much smell," she teased and ran her hand through the water. Cupped a handful of it and brought it to her nose.

"More like eucalyptus and citrus. It'll destress us," she replied, opened her hands to let the water cascade back into the bath.

Rising, she held her hand out to him, her beautiful body naked. Welcoming. Her face peaceful and with a slight flush at his prolonged perusal.

He stepped toward her, took her hand, but brought his other up to trail it across the rosiness on her cheek. "You're not embarrassed, are you? Because you're lovely."

She dipped her head down and mumbled, *"Gracias."*

Something new he was learning about her. She occasionally slipped into Spanish when she was discomfited.

Or when she made love.

To ease her apparent shyness, he stepped into the water and then sat down. With a tug on her hand, he asked her to join him, but she shook her head.

"Just relax for a bit. I'm going to bathe you," she said, reaching past him, those enticing breasts just grazing his chest as she grabbed a pale pink shower puff and a bottle of bathing gel.

She squirted the gel onto the puff and lathered it up. Smiled as she leaned toward him and said, "Now, this *will* make you smell like roses."

The light scent he had detected on her. Not perfume, but a remnant of her bath.

Liliana brought the puff to his chest and ran it across the muscles there. Then to his shoulders and arms, spreading the slick lather across his upper body. After, she cupped her hands and washed it off, running her hands over the spots where the suds clung to his skin. So smooth beneath her fingers.

Her gaze skipped to his to see his reaction to her touch, because need was rising in her despite her wish that this would be about comfort and not sex.

If he was feeling anything, he was a master at hiding it, she thought.

Grabbing the shower puff once again, she reached beneath the surface of the water, passing it along his center before easing toward his side.

He snagged her hand then, obviously uncomfortable with her touching him there. Where he was broken. Only she needed for him to understand.

"You're beautiful to me. This," she said, pushing past his resistance to spread her hand over the bone on his side, "proves the strength of your love. For your sister. For me."

He literally melted before her eyes, losing all of the stiffness she had first experienced in him.

With a tug on her hand, he said, "Join me."

She didn't hesitate.

Slipping into the tub, she lay across his body and he cuddled her to him. The moment one of tenderness. Desire banked as the need for understanding took the forefront.

The Jacuzzi kept the water heated nicely, but eventually they both recognized it was time to leave their cocoon.

As they stepped out onto the bath mat and snared some

towels to dry off, Liliana heard the insistent buzz of her phone.

She raced from the bedroom and grabbed it from the nightstand.

Whittaker.

Their short-lived interlude was over, she thought as she answered.

CHAPTER 32

Liliana scooped up all the tubes of inhibitor complex Carmen had prepared over the course of the last few days. Then she handed one back to her friend.

"Caterina isn't due for a treatment soon, but keep this just in case."

"You won't be gone long, right?" Carmen asked, and her worried gaze skipped over Liliana's shoulder to where Jesse stood.

"You're going to make sure she's okay, right?" Carmen pressed, the hint of challenge in her voice making it clear she would hold him responsible if anything happened.

Jesse stepped up to Liliana and laid his hand on her shoulder. "I'll take care of her."

With a curt nod, Carmen moved to another part of the lab and grabbed a handful of syringes. She handed them to Liliana.

"You'll probably need these to dose the patients."

Liliana nodded, took the syringes, and arranged them in her bag. Beside the test tubes and other supplies sat her scrip pad and the pen Ramon had given her, clipped onto the pad as if it was just another pen.

When the door to the lab opened, she quickly reached

in and was about to twist the pen but then reconsidered activating the GPS.

Closing the bag, she turned to find Whittaker standing there with Bruno and Howard.

"Howard, check them out," Whittaker said and jerked his head in their direction.

As Howard approached, Jesse stepped into his path. "Don't lay a hand on her."

"It's okay," she said and sidestepped her lover. Raising her arms, she advised, "Check whatever you want."

Howard's grin was part leer, but he merely pulled out a small wand from his inside jacket pocket and waved it across her arms, legs, and torso. The wand beeped as it passed over her suit jacket pocket.

He waggled his fingers, palm upward.

She reached into her pocket, withdrew her cell phone, and handed it to him. He laid it on the workbench and then gestured to her bag.

"What's in there?" he asked.

"Medicine, syringes. Routine treatment items," she advised, but he urged her to open it with a wave of his hand.

She did, holding her breath as Howard passed the wand over the bag and then into the open interior where the GPS pen sat in a side pocket. She dared not look upward at Jesse to see his reaction and tried to school hers to be as neutral as possible.

It must have worked.

"She's clean, boss. Now it's your turn, Bradford."

Jesse assumed a position similar to the one she had adopted earlier, arms up and legs spread wide. Howard quickly ran the wand across Jesse's body, but not a chirp registered from the machine.

"Also clean."

"Very good. Then we're ready to go," Whittaker said and swept his arm forward.

Bruno immediately jumped to do his silent bidding, approaching them with two long black strips of cloth while Howard put away the wand and returned to Whittaker's side.

Blindfolds, Liliana realized. She also realized she had to activate the GPS device so that Ramon and his team would be able to track them.

She held up her index finger. "One second."

Opening her bag, she removed the scrip pad and the pen. She twisted it to activate the device and reveal the point of the pen but also took a moment to jot down an order as a ruse to cover her actions. She handed the scrip to Carmen and advised, "You'll need this to get the supplies from the hospital."

Before Carmen could grab the slip of paper, Whittaker snapped his fingers and Bruno snared the scrip. He handed it to Whittaker, who perused the note.

"It's a prescription for the citrate we need for the plasmapheresis treatments," she explained.

Whittaker peered at the prescription more closely, then muttered, "Damn chicken scratch."

He handed the paper to Bruno, who passed it to Carmen.

With a sigh of relief, Liliana clipped the pen back onto her scrip pad and dropped it into her bag.

Jesse had to admire her calm and foresight. She had managed to engage the GPS device and cover her tracks like an expert. But as her gaze flipped to his for the briefest of moments, there was no denying the apprehension there. He wished he could reassure her somehow, but a second later, Bruno was slipping the blindfold over her eyes.

Several seconds passed before Bruno came to his side, and from the corner of his eye, he caught Carmen's concern. "Don't worry, Carmen. We'll be back for dinner and margaritas."

The barest hint of a smile passed over Carmen's lips before the blackness of the fabric blinded him. He reached out and encountered the warmth of Liliana's arm. Followed the line of it down to her hand, where he twined his fingers with hers and squeezed gently.

She returned the caress, but a second later Bruno's rough shove at his back pulled them apart.

"Get going," the other man said and applied pressure on Jesse's back to guide him forward.

He stumbled against a chair leg. Bumped his knee sharply along the edge of a cabinet. As he hesitated, Bruno shoved him hard once more.

"Get a move on, Jesse," Bruno advised.

He took a larger step, found himself up against Liliana's back. He wrapped an arm around her midsection, and they step-stumbled their way blindly out of the lab and to a car that was apparently waiting outside. In front of Jesse came the motion of Liliana stepping upward, and he followed, plopped down next to her in the seat.

Something landed in his lap. As he laid his hands on it, the shape and texture were familiar—Liliana's medical bag. The one with the pen.

He fumbled along the edge of her bag until he found her hand. Her relieved sigh sounded beside him and he twined his fingers with hers, hoping to provide comfort with that touch. Hoping that in just a few more hours, the nightmare he'd created with his own foolish pride and selfishness would soon be over.

Somehow Jesse fell asleep in the SUV.

It had been deliciously warm in the car. That warmth, combined with the darkness from the blindfold and the road noise, had lulled him to sleep.

It probably shouldn't have been a surprise, considering how little rest they had gotten the night before.

As he stirred, the weight of Liliana's hand in his brought contentment. Peace. Desire.

Jesse doubted that he would ever think of Liliana and not want her.

He bent toward her. Smelled her scent, which had become imprinted on his brain. Bumped his nose against the side of her face.

She turned, and even with the blindfold, he discovered her lips and kissed her. Shifted back toward her ear and whispered, "It'll be okay."

"*Yo se,*" she confirmed, and with a squeeze of his hand, they slipped back into silence.

He didn't know how much time passed before the car decelerated and inched down a bumpy road. No more than fifteen minutes, if he was a good guess of time. Of course he couldn't tell how long they had been traveling, since he had fallen asleep.

If his rest had been no more than a power nap, he suspected the trip had taken a little over an hour. Enough time to move them into South Jersey and closer to Camden and Philadelphia. Remembering that Morales and his assistant Jack had mentioned grabbing people from those two cities, he suspected that they had arrived at the location where he had been kept.

A few minutes later, the SUV came to an abrupt stop. Doors opened and slammed before someone roughly grabbed his arm and yanked him from his seat.

He lurched from the car, struggled for footing on the uneven ground. A smaller body plowed into his, and he steadied Liliana as she tumbled from the SUV.

"Get a move on," Bruno said, applying pressure on his arm to turn him around, Liliana behind him, her hand on his side as she used him for a guide.

His foot kicked a metal threshold, rattling it and stubbing his toe. He stepped over the threshold and continued walking forward. Liliana's body was tucked tight to his.

Finally Bruno yanked off his blindfold and then Liliana's.

As his eyes adjusted to the brighter light, he confirmed where he was.

Back in his prison.

His body tensed, and it took all of his willpower to not let anger and fear overwhelm him. Especially as from the shadows of the large warehouse, Morales approached with Jack beside him.

Frankenstein and his faithful servant, Jesse thought.

Beside him, Liliana stiffened, and he remembered that she, too, had a history with the scientist.

Morales smiled as he neared. An unctuous smile that left Jesse feeling covered in slime.

"Mr. Bradford. Dr. Carrera. What a pleasure to see you two again," Morales said.

Whittaker stepped forward, hands in his pockets,

change jingling. "The good doctor here has offered her assistance. She has more of the inhibitor complex and will help us out with the patients."

Morales arched a thin brow, apparently dubious. "Really? Out of the goodness of her heart?"

"In exchange for me. For my freedom," Jesse admitted, knowing that Morales could never comprehend doing something for nothing.

Morales screwed his eyes almost shut as he peered at the two of them and then smacked his lips, as if savoring something delicious. "Ah, I understand. Mr. Bradford is quite well endowed."

Liliana trembled beside him, but with fear.

"I know you could never understand, but I want to help Jesse get better. I want to make sure your patients are also well," Liliana countered.

"We'll see about that," Morales said and cocked a finger in Jack's direction.

"Get them set up at the worktable while I speak with our friends," he instructed.

Jack was about to take Liliana's arm, but when Jesse almost growled at him, he reconsidered and instead just held his arm out in the direction of the far side of the lab.

As they moved away, Whittaker said, "We need to transfer two of the patients. Have a buyer for them."

"But they're all unstable," Morales whined, sounding like a child being deprived of a favorite toy.

Whittaker was not about to relent. "Edwards will get them ready for the sale at the other location."

Despite Morales's continued protests, Whittaker and his men pulled two of the patients from their cages.

Liliana watched from across the room as they half

carried, half dragged the patients out the door, but Jack prodded her in the ribs.

"Mind your own business," the little man warned, but Jesse made another threatening motion and the scary man backed away, clearly afraid.

"Not nice, Jesse," Dr. Morales advised as he neared, a long rod in his hand.

Beside her, all color slid away from Jesse's face, but he remained steadfast by her side.

As she took a longer look, she realized why her lover had gone pale. The rod in Morales' hand was a cattle prod. The instrument with which the scientist had goaded Jesse, creating the damage that had produced the bony exoskeleton along his ribs.

"You won't need that," she said and pointed to the weapon.

Morales grinned and held up the prod. "I see Jesse has told you about our little games. They were quite amusing."

About amusing as baiting bears, she thought but kept her cool despite her disgust with the man and her anger at how he had abused Jesse.

"If you have charts on the patients, I'd like to review them. Take some blood samples so we can decide on a course of treatment for each of them," she said, her voice clinically professional.

Morales snickered and tapped the prod against the palm of one hand. "You may have fooled them, Dr. Carrera, but you can't fool me."

"The charts, please," she urged yet again and held out her hand.

Morales jerked his head in the direction of the more

than half a dozen cages holding an assortment of individuals. "Charts are by each door. You may want to be careful with some of the patients. They might bite."

Turning his attention to his assistant, Morales said, "Keep an eye on them, Jack."

Jack bowed and rubbed his hands together, eying her in a way that gave her the creepy-crawlies.

Morales then walked away to a far corner of the large space, where temporary walls had been erected to create an office. The two walls that faced the laboratory were half glass, allowing him to observe whatever was happening in the area.

With Morales gone, Liliana set up a small space on the top of the worktable, laying out the test tubes with the inhibitor complex in one rack, the syringes along the surface, as well as her scrip pad with the pen. No sense not making things appear normal, she thought and faced Jesse.

He had been standing by her side, vigilantly watching her and Jack, who hovered nearby, doing as his master had bidden—keeping an eye on them.

Realizing she hadn't brought extra test tubes for taking the blood samples, she said to Jack, "Do you think you could get me some more test tubes and another rack?"

With a shrug, he replied, "I guess I could."

He scurried off to a locker beside Morales's office and, as he did so, she looked up at Jesse. "Come with me to check the first patient."

Jesse followed her to one of the cages holding a frightened and naked young woman who pulled up the sheets and blanket on her cot to hide herself as they neared. As she did so, she immediately turned the drab olive-green of the army blanket.

Liliana raised her hand in a gesture meant to console. "Don't be afraid. We're here to help," she said, but the woman remained huddled beneath the sheets, cowering in fear.

Liliana was about to grab the chart when she noticed Jack at the worktable with the equipment she had requested. But as he placed it down, he glanced around furtively and picked up her pad with the pen.

"No," she muttered, drawing Jesse's attention to Jack's actions.

"Fuck. I forgot he's a klepto," he said and raced toward Jack, but not in time.

Jack twisted the pen, then pulled the cap off, exposing the GPS device within. He stared at it for a moment, confused, but then, as realization set in, he raced for Morales's office, screaming the doctor's name.

"You've got to go, Liliana. Now, before it's too late," Jesse said and ran after the man, his long strides eating up the distance between them and catching up to the smaller man.

Jesse tackled Jack to the ground, but by then Morales was on his way out of his office and running toward them.

Liliana knew she should run. That escaping was what Jesse wanted her to do, and yet she couldn't, afraid of what the men would do to her lover. Unable to move closer because fear was rooting her to the ground.

As Morales dropped the pen to the ground and stomped on it several times with the heel of his foot, Jack elbowed Jesse in the ribs, attempting to get free, not that the puny man could really inflict much punishment.

With a rabbit punch to the back of Jack's head,

Jesse knocked him unconscious and approached Morales, hands fisted at his sides. A mix of desperation and hope forcing him to act. Making him pray that Liliana would heed his plea and escape before Morales could neutralize him.

"You're not being a good boy again," Morales said and turned his attention to Jesse, the cattle prod held before him defensively.

"She's leaving," he said and expectantly held his breath as Liliana slowly moved toward the door of the warehouse, finally doing as he asked.

"You know I can't let her do that, Jesse," Morales said, his voice deceptively calm. Seemingly unconcerned with Liliana as she inched ever closer to freedom.

"You're not going to stop her," Jesse warned and took a step toward Morales, hiding his fear at what the prod would do to him. Planning for how to get Morales to strike him where it would do the least damage—in the bony area Morales's previous attacks had created.

Morales raised the prod and jabbed it in Jesse's direction like a fencer executing a lunge.

Jesse avoided the dangerous tip, feinting to one side. Dodging it as Morales attacked again.

Behind the scientist, Jesse could see that Liliana was already at the exit to the warehouse.

Jesse's moment of joy was short-lived, as the tip of the prod grazed his upper bicep, unleashing a torrent of pain when the electrical shock traveled across his nerve endings.

He called out in agony and crumpled to one knee. As Morales prodded him again, the rage the scientist had somehow created with his virulent combination of genes awoke, creating a burning pit in his gut. Sending adrenaline racing through his body.

"Stop it!" he screamed, so long and so hard that Liliana paused in her flight and turned wary eyes in his direction.

"Run!" he hollered, wanting her to keep on going. Wanting her to escape, but then Morales jabbed the prod toward him again.

Jesse managed to turn. Absorbed the blow against the deadness at his rib cage.

The pause in the pain provided the opportunity he needed.

He snatched the offensive device from Morales's hands. Smiled at the look of fear that crept onto the doctor's face.

Liliana was at the door, but she hesitated, looking back toward him. Her eyes pleading with him to come along, as well. But he couldn't and safeguard her freedom.

"Go, Liliana!" he called out, urging her on. Praying for her success.

The pain of the barbs in his side registered only a second before another jolt of electricity surged through him.

His body jerked, dancing on the ends of the wires connected to the Taser that Jack held. Long moments passed before Jesse could no longer bear the pain and crumpled to his knees.

As he fell, he realized Liliana had stopped and closed the door to the warehouse.

Dizzying circles of black danced before his eyes and the smell of his burning flesh reached his nostrils, but Jesse exhorted her once again. "Run."

CHAPTER 33

The signal from the GPS device disappeared from the computer screen.

"What the fuck? Try to get that signal back up," Ramon instructed his computer tech, but the FBI agent beside him just shook his head.

"Someone shut off the signal. Maybe they've been found out," Special Agent Rafael Sanchez advised.

Ramon shot an angry glare at the man, at the same time hoping Sanchez was wrong. With the kind of people with whom his cousin was dealing, being discovered meant certain death.

"Pull up the last location for the signal. Maybe they had already reached their destination."

"It seemed that way, Chief. The signal was stationary for a good half an hour or more," his technician advised.

With a number of keystrokes, the young man opened the GPS tracking log and displayed the last destination before the signal had been lost.

Agent Sanchez tapped on the edge of the monitor. "Can you get us a map or photo images for the location?"

"How about both?" the technician said. Within seconds, the technician brought up satellite images of the area, overlaid with a map showing the various roads nearby.

Ramon motioned to one main drag close to the last location. "This is a small county road, but it gets a lot of traffic from people heading to Atlantic City who want to avoid the Parkway."

Sanchez made a circular motion around the fairly empty area surrounding the possible location. "Seems like a lot of open space."

His tech Manny piped up. "There are lots of small towns with fairly spread-out homes. Most of the space you see is probably part of either Fort Dix or Fort Maguire."

"Are you saying the military is involved in this?" Sanchez challenged.

Ramon was quick to clarify. "What he's saying is that the two bases take up a great deal of area in that part of South Jersey. In between them are the towns and lots of green acres."

Sanchez bent and peered at the monitor once again. "According to this satellite photo, there are no buildings in the area."

Manny tapped away on the keys and then said, "Satellite photo is nearly two years old."

"The Wardwell scientists and their patients went missing just over a year ago. Someone could have built a facility there in the meantime," Ramon offered for consideration.

Sanchez pulled back his suit jacket and placed his hands on his hips. With a nod, he said, "I'll call and try to get us an updated satellite image."

Ramon straightened from the monitor and faced Sanchez. "Can I call the local police? Ask them to check out the area and report back to us?"

The FBI agent hesitated but then nodded. Almost immediately thereafter, he held up his forefinger and said, "But make it clear they are not to engage. We're dealing with a dangerous crowd who they are not equipped to handle."

"Confirmed," Ramon said and went to make the call.

Jesse's unnatural roar, so much like Santiago's lunatic howling when she had been held captive, stopped Liliana as she went to exit.

She turned and watched as Morales jabbed Jesse with the cattle prod again.

"Run!" Jesse shouted and then grunted with pain as he dropped to his knees.

Morales stuck Jesse again, but this time her lover ripped the rod from Morales's hands.

As Jesse rose, his sheer size and muscular physique intimidating on their own, Liliana noted the wicked gleam on Jesse's face. She'd seen that kind of emotion before—on Santiago as he killed the psycho mercenary who had been holding her captive. On her ex-fiancé as he had pummeled her one night in a rage.

Debilitating fear gripped her, making her hesitate.

"Go, Liliana," Jesse called out and she finally moved, dragging open the heavy warehouse door.

"Run," she heard Jesse say once more, weaker this time. Then the howling began again. A strange, desperate howl filled with pain and frustration.

Turning, she saw that Morales was on the floor but slowly rising. Before him, Jesse jerked and staggered as Jack laughed with glee.

"Hit me, will you?" the man said, his hands wrapped around a small box. Wires led from the box to Jesse, who was still howling, although not as strongly as before. His body twitching as he crumpled to his knees.

It took Liliana a moment to register that Jack had Tasered Jesse. That Jack was continuing to pump electricity into him, heedless of the fact that it might be fatal.

Jesse was enduring the torture so that she might escape. All she had to do was step out the door, only something had her turning back to the tableau before her.

Morales, cattle prod back in hand.

Jesse falling to the floor, his body still reacting to the flow of electricity.

They were going to kill him, she thought. They were going to kill Jesse because of her.

Liliana couldn't allow that.

"I'm pretty sure there's a warehouse up a ways from the road," the sheriff said in response to the address Ramon had given him.

"Is there any way you can send a man to the area to confirm that?" Ramon said, and the FBI agent beside him nodded in agreement with his request, listening to the exchange over the speakerphone.

"Possibly. I think I have an officer who passes by there toward the end of his shift." A muffled sound came across the phone line, as if the sheriff had covered the mouthpiece while he was asking something, but then he came back on the line, loud and clear. "Make that a definite. Should be able to swing by in no more than five minutes."

"Make sure your man understands he's not to be seen and not to engage. These are dangerous individuals with whom we're dealing," Special Agent Sanchez advised.

"Ten-four. I'll make sure he understands."

Ramon met Sanchez's gaze as they stood there, hunched over the speakerphone. He understood what the other man wanted. "We're on our way down, Sheriff. We could use backup if we need to enter the premises."

A long pause was followed by a loud, uncomfortable sigh. "We're a small force, Chief. Only four of us, and two are already on patrol."

"Roger that. I'll see if I can't muster up another man or two here," Ramon said and then provided the sheriff with his cell phone number so he could keep them advised of developments.

Ramon straightened and looked around his squad room. His department was bigger, but not by much. Besides his computer technician, there was a desk sergeant and a community-relations officer. All were trained officers and certified to use a handgun, but none had the experience necessary for any kind of raid.

His four other officers were out on patrol.

"Wintertime is quiet around here. I have two officers I can pull off patrol," he advised and for a moment considered phoning Mick but then remembered his promise to Liliana.

Sanchez was already dialing his cell phone. As it rang, he said, "I can roust two agents from the Philadelphia branch that are working with me on this case."

Ramon did the math. Six of them against Whittaker and at least two others. Two-to-one odds being generally good until he recollected the information he had gotten on Whittaker and his men, plus the 411 that Sanchez had provided.

"We could call in the state troopers," he said, worried for his men and for Liliana and Jesse.

Sanchez nodded. "Once we confirm the existence of the warehouse, I'll make the call."

Which seemed logical. No sense pulling in a dozen officers only to find nothing of value, although with every second that passed, Ramon worried about what was happening with his cousin and Jesse.

"I'll yank my men from patrol. It shouldn't take all that long," he said, hoping their delay would not cost someone their life.

Liliana took a deep, steadying breath, rallying her courage. Then she charged back toward the trio of men, setting her sights exclusively on Jack, who was so gleefully electrocuting Jesse.

The little man clearly hadn't been expecting her.

He cried out in surprise as she barreled into him, knocking him to the ground but failing to dislodge the Taser from his hand. It was jabbing her in the midsection, since she had landed on top of the slight man, driving the air from his body.

She reached beneath her and pulled it from his grasp. For good measure, she yanked loose the wires from the machine.

From behind her came a footstep.

She knew what was coming and rolled off Jack, avoiding the first blast from the cattle prod.

She rose, but as she scrambled to get away, her feet got

tangled up in the loose wires from the Taser. She fell hard, scarcely a foot away from Jesse. He was lying facedown on the ground, eyes open but barely focusing.

As Morales grabbed her, Jesse surged up off the floor and captured the scientist, freeing her. Jesse fell and hauled Morales down with him, urging Liliana, "If you love me, you'll go."

Her heart broke with his words, but she understood.

She scrambled for the door, Jack just a few feet behind her. He caught up to her as she struggled to open the heavy door, but she knew the only way to now save Jesse was to get free.

With strength she didn't know she possessed, she jabbed the man in the solar plexus, driving the air from his body. When he doubled up, she turned and drove upward with her knee. A sickening crunch told her she had connected successfully and Jack stumbled back, hands to his face, blood leaking from between his fingers.

She dashed out the door and into the woods, searching for some way to hide. The pines here were thin and provided little cover, but she ducked down, dodging from one large bit of underbrush to another. Trying to keep her steps quiet to avoid detection.

Finding one large pine overgrown with trailing vines, she hid beneath it and waited. Held her breath as from a distance came pounding footsteps and the crunch and rattle of leaves and debris.

"Bitch, I'm going to kill you," Jack called out and continued mumbling over and over as he traipsed through the woods, attempting to locate her.

His noisiness was good, she thought, huddling in the protection of the foliage. She could tell that he was heading away from her, searching closer to the road she had noticed on her dash from the warehouse. She had to get to that road and follow it to what she hoped would be a main thoroughfare. For now, though, she just had to sit tight and stay free.

She didn't know how long she hid there, waiting for Jack to finish his search. She didn't dare move and possibly alert him to where she was concealed.

The groan of metal filtered through the afternoon air, followed by the sounds of screams. Multiple voices, and in that cacophony she searched for Jesse's but couldn't discern it.

Then came the heavy thud of a door closing, shutting off the cries of the patients.

Had they been screaming all during the melee to escape? she wondered. She had been so focused on Jesse and securing their freedom that she hadn't noticed. But now those cries, along with Jesse's unnatural howl, whipped at her soul, forcing her to act.

Cautiously she moved the first inch, holding her breath to listen for any sounds that might give her away.

Nothing.

She shifted another inch, finally poking her head from the protective cover of the vines and evergreen.

Nothing again.

As she peered back toward the warehouse, she noted the door was closed. No sign of Jack anywhere, not that she could rely on that.

Carefully, keeping her head down, she moved from her sanctuary and out into the woods. Cautiously considering each step to remain undetected. Pausing every few feet to wait and see if someone was still trying to locate her.

A loud snap came from up the road, followed by the sounds of tires crunching along the uneven ground of the dirt-and-stone path.

Someone was coming.

She crouched low to the ground, held her breath as the noise grew louder, signaling the approach of the vehicle. As she waited, she prayed it would not be Whittaker returning with his men.

Instead, as the car passed by, she noticed its two-tone paint—dark blue and white—with some kind of emblem on the side.

Police? she thought and gingerly inched a bit higher, confirming that it was a police car heading toward the warehouse.

Joy surged through her, but she tamped it down.

She had to warn the police officers.

Risking discovery, she hurried after the cruiser.

CHAPTER 34

Morales jabbed Jesse with the cattle prod, but the only response he received was a reflexive jerk to the electric shocks. He would have kept on electrocuting Jesse as punishment for his helping Dr. Carrera escape, except Whittaker would be angry if Bradford ended up dead.

The warehouse door slammed shut and Jack rushed in, bits of branches and leaves sticking to the blood that had streamed down his face and onto the front of his shirt. His nose was swollen, and the skin beneath his eyes was already turning black from the female physician's blow.

Unfortunately, Jack was alone.

Not a good thing. It wouldn't take Carrera long to make it up to the highway and flag a car to a local police department. They didn't have much time left before discovery, especially if whoever had been monitoring the GPS signal had gotten a good read before he had destroyed it.

As Jack approached, hunched over and eyes averted like a whipped dog, Morales pointed to Jesse with the prod.

"Get him back in his cage. I've got to contact Whittaker and advise him of what's happened."

Morales hurried to his office and slammed the door, dialed Whittaker while he watched Jack dragging Jesse's body across the warehouse and into the cage.

He waited while the phone rang and rang, then went to voice mail.

Weird, he thought. Whittaker never failed to take a call.

Trying his partner Edwards, he had a similar result.

Unsure of why they were unavailable, Morales was certain of one thing—he had to clear out before any law enforcement types arrived. As for Jack, there was no reason to bring him along for the ride. He needed someone to watch the patients until he could decide what to do. If the police did arrive before that...

Jack had always been an expendable part of the operation.

Opening his drawer, he removed two handguns and laid them on his desktop. Grabbing his coat from a nearby rack, he slipped it on and then tucked one of the guns into his coat pocket.

Walking to the far wall where Jack was busy cleaning himself at one of the slop sinks, he laid the second gun on the edge of the sink.

"I'm not expecting trouble anytime soon, but just in case."

Jack's gaze jerked down to the gun, but he didn't hesitate to tuck the weapon into the gap between his jeans and stomach.

"What do you want me to do with them?" Jack jerked his thumb in the direction of the cages, where the patients had finally quieted down.

"Same as always. Keep an eye on them. I'm going to

meet Whittaker at the other location. I'll call you with instructions."

With that, Morales walked out, only to find a police cruiser pulling up in front of the warehouse.

Fuck, he thought but planted a bright smile on his face and strolled to the clearing in front of the building.

Liliana was halfway back to the warehouse, keeping hidden along the underbrush, when the building door opened and Morales exited.

He had that smile—the dangerous one. Only you had to have experienced the sting of that smile to understand that.

She ducked lower but continued pressing forward. She had to warn the officers.

As the car door opened, a dark blue uniformed leg became visible before the officer stepped from the cruiser. Only one officer, she realized.

"Good afternoon, sir," the officer said. He stood behind the open door, one hand on the roof of the car. The other on his holstered gun.

Morales's smile broadened and he took another step forward. Put his hand in his coat pocket.

"Can I help you, Officer?" Morales said.

The officer closed the door, and as soon as the officer was clear, Morales moved in a flurry of action.

He pulled a gun from his pocket and fired.

Liliana gasped as the officer stumbled back a step before his knees crumpled, his one hand on the cruiser, struggling for purchase.

Morales fired again.

The barest recoil of the officer's body indicated Morales had not missed. Then the officer slowly fell back, his knees still bent as he collapsed into an unnatural heap.

Liliana held her breath as Morales walked toward the fallen man, his gun upraised.

She couldn't see clearly enough to determine whether or not the officer was dead, but if he wasn't, she feared Morales would finish him.

Pressing forward, she tried to think of what she could do to distract Morales. How she could stop him, but before she reacted, Morales reached the officer.

He pointed the gun at the man.

Only a slight twitch came from the officer. A death twitch? she wondered as Morales lowered the weapon and then tucked it back into his coat pocket.

With a careless shrug, Morales pivoted on one heel and walked away.

Liliana continued moving forward, but the sudden roar of an engine made her pause again. Seconds later, a black SUV came around from the side of the building and plowed down the road, passing the fallen officer and his cruiser. Continuing with the crunch of tires on the hard, frozen dirt until the sound faded into the cold of the late autumn day.

Jumping out of the underbrush, Liliana hurried to the officer, praying that he was alive and that she could help him.

But before she could reach him, the door to the warehouse opened again and Jack stepped out.

Liliana ducked back into the foliage along the edge of the road.

Jack scurried toward the car, and his eyes opened wide as he noted the officer slumped on the ground.

"Fuck me," he said and raced back into the warehouse.

Liliana cursed beneath her breath. How long did she have before Jack did something drastic?

How long did she have to do something—anything—to help Jesse?

Not long, she thought and pressed forward toward the police officer.

CHAPTER 35

The cold of the floor registered first against the side of his face.

Chilly. Hard. Wet.

As he rolled onto his back and stared at the metal struts of the warehouse ceiling, Jesse realized he had been drooling. His entire body seemed disconnected from his brain. Not under his control.

He attempted to rise but couldn't.

He decided to do something less strenuous and focused on moving a finger.

His pinky twitched. The pinky he had broken during the Rose Bowl in the last quarter of his senior year. He had hit a linebacker's helmet as the man had charged at him during a blitz. He'd had the trainer wrap the pinky and finished the game.

He focused again, managed to move his entire hand this time.

The hand Liliana had touched just earlier that day. Closing his eyes, he remembered the warmth of her skin. The feel of it, so soft and smooth.

Jesse wondered if he was dying. If this was what people

saw when they said that their lives flashed in front of their eyes.

If so, he wanted to hold on to the picture of her, smiling at him. Her dark eyes welcoming and promising so much love.

A loud bang intruded.

The door to the warehouse slamming shut followed by Jack's mumbled and repetitive, "Fuck me."

He wasn't dead. At least not yet, Jesse thought.

Forcing himself to concentrate, other things slowly registered, and he wished that they hadn't.

His head was pounding and his body felt on fire. The combination of numbness and ache in his right side was a testament to where Morales and Jack had managed to shock him. Somehow he rolled onto his side and, using his arms, managed to finally get upright.

Jack was pacing back and forth in the center of the lab. He was pulling at his hair, clearly distraught. Mumbling under his breath as he walked to and fro in the empty space.

Jesse wanted to stand, but his body was still not cooperating. A hangover-like haze lingered in his brain, possibly from the electric shocks he had endured. Pulling in a deep breath through his nose, he held it, then released it. Repeated the action until his mind cleared a bit.

Reaching up, he wiped the drool from his face and got to his knees by holding on to the bars of the cage.

His action drew Jack's attention.

The man stalked over and, as he neared, Jesse realized Jack had a gun tucked into his waistband.

When Jack reached the cage, he kicked out at Jesse's hands, landing an awkward blow above them, making Jesse yank his hands back.

"Fuckin' bitch. Bastard. It's your fault this is happening," Jack said and kicked at the bar again, his actions clumsy.

"She got away, didn't she? The police are coming," Jesse said, feeling energized at the thought that Liliana was safe. That they might all soon be safe.

Jack stepped away from the cage and whipped out his gun, aimed it at him. "Bastard. The police are here, but he's dead. Shot."

Jack's obvious agitation and the brandishing of the gun awakened the attention of the other patients. They streamed to fronts of their cages, saw what was happening, and then erupted in a cacophony as their drug-addled minds reacted to the menace.

"Shut your fuckin' mouths," Jack said and spun around, gun raised high, which dimmed the noise, but only a little.

Jesse laid his hands on his thighs and glanced up at Jack. "It's not too late to do the right thing."

Jack whirled to aim the gun at him. "Right thing? I'm in this too deep, Bradford."

"It's not too late," Jesse said again, containing his fear as he stared down the barrel of the gun.

Before Jack could respond, the loud chirp of a cell phone penetrated the air. Jack reached into his pocket, whipped out his phone, and put it to his ear.

All Jack did was listen as the voice on the other end of the line droned on, punctuated by an occasional barked comment. When the caller stopped, Jack whined, "I didn't sign up for this. This wasn't part of the deal."

The barking grew stronger across the line, more insistent. Brooking no disagreement.

"This'll cost you," Jack said, snapped the phone shut, and tossed it aside.

Facing Jesse once again, Jack raised the gun, pointed it at Jesse's head. "You're dead meat."

Ramon sat in the back of their police van along with Sanchez and two other officers. Another of his men drove while the last one sat shotgun as the van sped the final few miles down the parkway, siren blaring.

Ramon's cell phone chirped and he answered.

"Gonzalez here."

"Our officer finished his shift nearly ten minutes ago but hasn't reported back. He's not at home, and he's not answering his radio," said the sheriff from the small local town they had nearly reached via the parkway.

"He was advised not to—"

"Engage. Yes, he was advised. We have a squad car sitting at the entrance to the road," the sheriff confirmed.

Ramon stood and moved to peer out the windshield. Based on the mile marker, they would be at the exit soon.

"We should be at the scene within a few minutes. Tell your men—"

"Man. Our cars are only manned by one officer."

Ramon moved back to his seat in the van. "Roger. We have two FBI agents joining us at the scene, as well."

"Keep me posted, Chief. I need to know what happened to my officer."

"Roger."

Ramon turned his attention to Special Agent Sanchez. "How close are your people?"

"Should be arriving at the same time as we are," Sanchez advised.

The van shifted to the right and slowed. The man riding

shotgun killed the siren. Based on their investigations, the dirt road leading to the warehouse was only five minutes up ahead. The newer satellite photos obtained by Sanchez had confirmed the location of the building, and minutes later, the van pulled up to the left and stopped.

"Suit up," Ramon instructed, and the men in the van donned their protective gear and checked their weapons while Ramon and Special Agent Sanchez stepped outside.

A cruiser sat along the side of the road, an officer leaning against its bumper.

"Police Chief Gonzalez. Special Agent," the officer said in greeting and stood, easing from the side of the cruiser.

"Do you have anything?" Special Agent Sanchez asked as Ramon's men piled out of the car.

"I was told not to engage, only . . ." The officer jerked his hand in the direction of a small home across the highway.

"Witness came over. Said they had seen another cruiser head down the road and then a black SUV speeding away shortly after. They also think they heard gunshots."

After he finished, a loud *pop* sounded in the cold air, but the officer didn't react.

"Like that?" Ramon asked, arching a brow.

The officer shrugged. "People hunt in the woods nearby at this time of year. It could be hunters."

"Except that sounded like a handgun," Sanchez said and stared down the road.

"Are you sure?" Ramon asked, placing his hands on his hips and gazing into the woods.

"Can we take a chance that I'm right?" Sanchez replied and tracked Ramon's line of sight.

"No, we can't," Ramon advised and then said to the officer, "Can you stay here? We're waiting for two other FBI agents to join us."

"I'll check with you before sending them in." The officer shot them a small salute.

His face grim, Ramon faced Sanchez and then his men.

"Ready?" he asked.

They all nodded.

CHAPTER 36

Jesse grabbed the bars and pulled himself to his feet.

If he was going to die, he was going to die like a man.

Jack's hand wavered, the tip of the gun bobbing before he whipped the gun down. "You know what. I'm going to save the best for last."

He spun around and hurried to the cage farthest away— the young camouflaged woman Liliana and he had been about to examine less than an hour earlier.

As she had done with their approach, she huddled in a corner and pulled the sheets up to hide her body when Jack came close. But as he raised the gun and took aim, she started screaming.

The other patients, sensing her agitation, responded, chiming in with an assortment of cries and yelling. Some ran to the walls of their cages to watch. Grabbed hold of the bars and rattled them, slowly increasing the noise level until Jack fired.

Silence immediately took hold as the young woman in the cage collapsed onto her bed and then rolled to the floor.

For good measure, Jack strode to the cage, stuck the gun through the bars, and fired into her head, delivering the coup de grâce.

Jack walked to the next cage and took aim but then seemed to have a moment of conscience. He strode away, back into the center of the room, and paced again, mumbling to himself.

Jesse heard only part of those mumbled words.

"Didn't sign up for this," Jack seemed to be saying. Jesse hoped that meant Jack was reconsidering his obvious instructions—to eliminate everyone in the lab.

"You don't have to do what they say, Jack. You can be your own man," Jesse called out, and Jack whirled in his direction.

Pointing the gun at him, Jack strode over, screaming as he did so. "Shut the fuck up, Bradford. *I* say what I do. Just me."

With another abrupt whirl, Jack stalked to another cage.

Again the noise built, this time to almost deafening levels as the inhabitants of the various cages understood what he planned to do.

As Jack raised the gun and took aim, the building nearly shook from the volume of the noise.

But it wasn't loud enough to silence the unforgiving burst of sound from the gun as Jack fired.

As before, Jack walked to the cage, jammed his hand between the bars, and discharged a follow-up shot.

That was enough to quiet the other patients, who either shifted to the farthest corners of their cages or tried to hide beneath their cots.

It was also enough for Jesse, especially as Jack walked back to his desk and reloaded the weapon.

He wasn't going to let Jack shoot him down like a dog, and he wasn't going to let Jack shoot anyone else, either.

*   *   *

A faint pulse registered beneath her fingers as Liliana pressed them to the officer's neck.

She laid him out on the ground, tore open his coat and shirt, then located the bullet wounds.

One high up on his shoulder, bleeding more profusely than the one in his chest.

The officer had a small knife on his gun belt. She pulled it out of its sheath and used it to cut off a large piece of his shirt and make a few strips. Wadding a piece against his shoulder, she applied pressure and then bound the wound with the makeshift bandages.

She was about to treat the chest injury when she heard the noise leaking out of the warehouse.

She stared at the building, wondering what was going on inside when a loud *bang* brought silence and made her jump.

A gunshot? she worried. Anxious about Jesse.

Hurrying to finish caring for the officer's injuries, she was about to head back to the warehouse when she spotted Ramon hurrying down the road, flanked by several other officers carrying weapons and wearing bulletproof vests.

In a half crouch, Ramon rushed to her with another man right next to him. He held up a closed fist to stop his men.

Hugging her hard, he said, "This is Special Agent Sanchez."

She shook the man's hand and he glanced down at the officer. "How is he?"

"Alive, but you need to get him to a hospital quickly," she advised.

Ramon inclined his head in the direction of the warehouse. "Do you know what we're facing in there?"

"Morales shot the officer and left, so there's just one man. Guy named Jack. About eight to ten patients, but they're caged. Jesse's in there," she said, laying her hand on Ramon's arm.

"Don't worry. We'll make sure he's safe," he said and, with a few hand signals, called over his men.

"Do you know where Morales went?" the FBI agent asked.

Liliana shrugged and shook her head. "Whittaker and his men were headed to a second location, but I don't know if he was going there."

Ramon's men surrounded them, crouching behind the safety of the police cruiser.

"You two take the back of the building. Jenkins, you provide cover for the special agent and me. We're going in," Ramon instructed, motioning to the various locations with his hand.

"What about me, Chief?" asked the last officer, a young man who barely looked twenty.

"Call for an ambulance and stay with Dr. Carrera—"

"I'm going with you. I need to know Jesse is okay," Liliana said, and as she met Ramon's gaze, he realized she wasn't going to back down.

"Stay with the officer until the ambulance arrives," Ramon instructed the young-looking officer and then jabbed a finger almost in Liliana's face.

"And you stay behind Special Agent Sanchez and me at all times. Get it?"

"Got it," she confirmed. When Ramon and the FBI agent hurried toward the warehouse, she followed.

•

*   *   *

For so long Jesse had struggled to control the anger created in him by whatever Wardwell had decided to put in his body.

Now he called it forth, feeling the burn in his gut sizzle along his nerve endings. Experiencing the rush of power that came with it, surging through his bones and muscle.

The weakness in his body disappeared.

He tightened his grip on the bars of his cage, but not to stand up.

With his hands on the bars, he pulled on the door while pressing on the frame. Straining until his muscles were nearly rock hard from the force he was exerting.

The thick steel bars held.

Jesse redoubled his efforts, driven by the screams of his fellow patients and another *pop* as Jack executed a third prisoner.

Putting one foot on the crossbar of the frame, Jesse jerked again. This time the steel gave beneath his hands.

Satisfaction energized him.

He yanked and pressed repeatedly, and with a sudden, loud snap, the door flew open.

He lurched forward with the release of the lock but then righted himself and rushed into the center of the warehouse.

Jack spun around and his eyes went wide as he realized Jesse was free. But that surprise lasted only a moment.

Jack raced toward him, lifting his gun as he did so.

Aiming it at Jesse's head.

Jesse had no flight response in his body. He had never run from anything in his life.

It only made the gene-amplified fight reaction even stronger. More dangerous as every bone and muscle in his body answered his call to battle.

He leapt at Jack, flying across the floor of the warehouse so quickly that Jack didn't have time to fire.

As they hit the ground, the impact jarred the gun loose from Jack's hand. It skittered a few feet away, but Jack was slimier than he had counted on.

He somehow escaped Jesse's grasp and half crawled the few feet, snagged the gun, and rose.

Jesse likewise came to his feet and opened his arms wide, inviting Jack's violence.

"I'm not caged like the others. Are you man enough to do it now?" Jesse taunted.

If he could distract Jack, keep him occupied long enough, the others would be safe for a little longer.

Just a little longer, he thought as Jack aimed at him.

There were no images of his life running through his brain this time.

Only one thought: *Survive.*

He had too much to live for now.

He had Liliana.

As Jack pulled the trigger, Jesse dodged to his right, but the bullet smashed into his side.

The impact stole the breath from his body, driving him to one knee.

Jesse covered his side with his hand, the pain intense.

"Son of a bitch," Jack said and took a step closer, gun still held high, only this time Jesse's head was his target.

Jesse braced for the kill shot, certain that at this range Jack would not miss again. Preparing to attack the moment Jack was near enough.

"Drop the weapon," someone shouted from the side of the warehouse.

Jack pivoted in that direction, weapon raised, and fired toward the sound of the voice.

A duo of gunshots rang out in response.

Jack fell to the ground beside him, eyes open in death. Crimson blotches visible against the white of the lab jacket.

Jesse came to his feet gingerly, pain still radiating from his side. As he pulled his hand away, there was minimal blood, but he cradled his arm close, finding that it eased the discomfort.

Pounding footsteps approached, and he smiled as he realized it was Liliana leading the charge.

But he held up his hand to stop her as she neared.

"You're hurt," she said, seeing how he was favoring his side.

"He shot me." He moved his arm away and looked down, revealing the blood along his ribs.

Liliana sprang into action, shifting to his side and raising his shirt to expose the damage.

"We need to get you to the hospital," she said. There was a break at the lowest end of the exoskeleton layer, and blood leaked from a small graze nearby.

"I'd rather you treat me at home if it's not serious," he replied, tired of hospitals and confinement.

Liliana examined the wound once again and met his gaze, a guarded smile on her face. "It's not serious."

"Good," he said and drew her against his good side.

She willingly welcomed his embrace, hugging him with great care.

"Jesse Bradford. I saw you play in the Rose Bowl," the

one man said as he tucked his gun into his holster. "I'm Special Agent Rafael Sanchez."

"Nice to meet you. I hope you have some news on Whittaker and the rest," Jesse said, fearful that once the fake FBI agent found out that they had broken their promise, he would exact revenge.

"Nothing, but I've got several agents on this case. Two just arrived from Philly, and we'll establish protective details on your families," Sanchez advised.

"What about them?" Liliana asked, glancing at the patients in the cages.

Sanchez studied the scene, taking note of the situation. "Looks like we have six live patients. If you don't mind temporarily assuming their care, I can have them transferred to your hospital. Then we can ID them and notify their families."

Liliana answered without hesitation, "Anything I can do to help, but first, I'd like to get Jesse home."

"If you don't need me and my men, I'll get them home also," Ramon advised, and Sanchez nodded his assent. "I've got the other agents here and the local sheriff."

"Then we'll be on our way," Liliana said, weaving her fingers with Jesse's and gazing up at him.

"Let's go home," he repeated and smiled, finally feeling free.

It didn't take long for her to treat the wound in Jesse's side when they had returned to his home. After cleaning and bandaging the slight graze from the bullet, she was able to pull away the cracked portion of the exoskeleton as if it was the shell on a hard-boiled egg. That lowest part of the bony casing had yet to fuse with the flesh under it to become permanent. The rib beneath the shell, while bruised from the impact of the bullet, was intact, requiring no further treatment. With the extra bone proteins filtered from Jesse's blood, no new bone was forming at the site of the injury.

"It looks good," she said, smoothing the simple bandage in place.

"Hurts like a bitch," he replied and grimaced as he rose from the bed.

"Let me kiss it and make it better," Liliana teased, bending to brush a kiss close to the site but then trailing a line of kisses up to the middle of his chest, where she placed another one directly over his heart.

Jesse groaned and cradled her head to him. "Is it too much to believe that this might be over? That we can live our lives free of fear?"

"Ramon said everything was under control. That he had news for us," she reminded him, repeating what her cousin had called to say shortly after dropping them off at Jesse's home.

As if on cue, the front doorbell rang. Jesse grabbed a clean T-shirt and pulled it on before they walked down the stairs to answer the door.

When he yanked it open, Ramon was there beside Bruno. Jesse immediately shifted in front of Liliana to protect her, only Ramon raised his hand to stop him and said, "No need, Jesse."

Bruno smiled at him, the easygoing smile of a friend. He pulled a badge from his pocket. "I'm sorry I couldn't tell you sooner. CIA. I've been working deep undercover to catch Whittaker and his men for gunrunning and an assortment of other activities."

Liliana stepped from behind Jesse's protection. "So you were able to catch him? How about Morales and Edwards?"

"Morales, Howard, and Whittaker are dead. They tried to shoot it out with the team I called in to apprehend them," Bruno advised as he tucked his badge back into his pocket.

"What about Edwards?" Jesse questioned.

"In custody. He's got a great deal to answer for," Bruno advised, and neither Jesse nor Liliana could argue. Besides the various dead and altered patients, Santiago had killed a park ranger, she had been kidnapped, and a police officer had been shot.

Too many bodies for there not to be some kind of punishment, Liliana thought.

Jesse asked, "So we're safe? Our families—"

"Are fine. Whittaker was the head of the snake, and with him gone..."

Bruno didn't need to finish.

"Thank you for that," Liliana said and offered her hand to Bruno.

He shook it and then held his hand out to Jesse. "I'm sorry for anything I did."

Jesse hesitated, but then he shook Bruno's hand. "Not sorry about the nose. It'll add character to your face."

Bruno chuckled but then winced and touched the tip of his injured nose. "Still sore," he advised.

Ramon grinned. "I guess we can go. I'm sure the two of you would like some privacy."

"I'm sure we would," Jesse said, and, with a final wave at the two men, he closed the door and then leaned on it, facing Liliana.

"Is there something you can think of that requires privacy?"

She hunched her shoulders, playing it coy, and sauntered up to him, sexily rolling her hips. When she reached him, she eased her hands beneath the hem of his T-shirt and laid her hands on his bare skin. Rubbing them up and across his midsection, she said, "I can think of one thing."

"Really? Just one?" he teased and ran his hand over her hair and down to rest on her shoulder.

"Just one, but there's a little problem," she teased and took hold of the hem of the shirt.

"And what's that?" he asked, shifting his hand to her face to run his thumb along the edges of her lips.

"You've got way too many clothes on," she said and yanked the shirt over his head.

Jesse chuckled and pulled her into his arms but then turned serious.

"Tell me this isn't a dream. That this nightmare is over—"

She laid her index finger on his lips. "This is for real, Jesse. The bad stuff is over. Now it's time for us to explore what we're feeling. To find out if it's real."

He kissed the pad of her finger. "It's real for me, Liliana. I love you."

As she glanced up at him, the truth of it was clear on his face. In his eyes—those beautiful blue eyes that reminded her of the ocean on a summer day. The doubt she'd had in her heart evaporated with the love pouring from him.

"I love you, too. I know we can make this work."

He bent and she rose on tiptoe, met his lips in a kiss to seal that promise.

CHAPTER 37

Four months later

Jesse ran his hand over the soft swell of her belly, and Liliana covered his hand with hers and brushed a kiss across his lips.

He returned her kiss hungrily, but then a soft, amused laugh broke them apart.

"Get a room, bro," his sister Jackie said and walked up to the table in the radiation-therapy room.

"Already did, sis," he said and once again ran his hand along Liliana's burgeoning belly.

Jackie chuckled, took a position on the opposite side of the bed, and grabbed hold of Jesse's hand. "I know you'll make a good dad."

Liliana glanced at her new sister-in-law fondly. "And how do you know that?" she asked.

Jackie smiled and playfully shook her brother's hand. "'Cuz he was a great big brother."

"I wish you didn't have to do this," Jesse said, all traces of lightheartedness gone from his demeanor.

Liliana knew that it weighed on him to have to rely on his sister for a transplant, but the plasmapheresis treatments had lost their efficacy. If they didn't undertake the radiation treatment to kill off his bone marrow and reintroduce untainted cells, she feared what the implanted genes would do to his body.

"It's nothing, Jesse. Not when you were willing to risk your life for me," Jackie said, bent, and dropped a kiss on his cheek. "Just get better," she whispered and, with a final playful tug on his arm, left the room.

Liliana stared at him and pressed his hand tighter to her belly. "You're going to be fine. I need someone around to chase after this baby."

A glimmer of joy crept back into his gaze at the mention of their child.

Their baby.

It had taken some discussion to go ahead with having a child, but both of them had known it was the right decision. Samples of Jesse's sperm had not shown contamination by the Wardwell DNA strains, but with the prospect of radiation therapy, sterility was a risk.

Becoming pregnant hadn't taken long, much to Jesse's regret. She imagined that he wouldn't have minded keeping her in bed for far longer, not that she would have complained. Being with Jesse was . . . well, just amazing. Emotionally and physically.

And because they wanted to possibly have more children, they had stored away more of Jesse's sperm for the future.

The future.

She had hopes it would be a long and happy one.

Bending, she kissed Jesse and whispered, "We will grow old together, *mi amor*."

Beneath her lips she could feel his smile as he said, "Just as long as you never stop loving me."

"Never," she said and, with another kiss, left him alone in the treatment room.

In the viewing area, Carmen came over with a heavy lead apron and handed it to her. "No sense taking any chances," she said, and, together with Jackie, they stood at the window to watch as the tech began the series of irradiations to kill off the hybrid bone marrow.

The apron dragged on her shoulders, much like the fear that despite all the favorable prognoses, Jesse's condition would get worse.

Sucking in a breath, she bit her lower lip as the *kathunk-kathunk* of the radiation unit signaled that it was working.

A moment later, Jackie and Carmen bracketed her and slipped their arms through hers, offering their support.

"It's going to be okay," Carmen said, and Jackie echoed the sentiment.

Their faith bolstered her sagging optimism, reminding her that she wasn't alone. Outside in the hallway, the rest of her family waited, along with Jesse's mother.

Their family, she thought and reached beneath the heavy lead apron. She placed her hand over their baby. A child conceived by their love, and inside of her hope chased away her fears.

They would grow old together, she repeated, certain in their love.

Certain that it was stronger than anything that would come their way.

CHAPTER 38

Men like Morales and Edwards possessed incredible vision, Bruno thought as he stared at the reports sitting on his desk.

But it took more than mere vision to change the world.

It took genius.

Many had possessed such genius in the past, he thought and flipped open the first report. Men like the Roman Caesars, Alexander the Great, and Napoleon. Even those society looked upon as murderers—Hitler, Stalin, and Mao—had defied their own limits to envision a different world created by their hand.

Bruno considered himself such a man, and so did the CIA.

It was why he was involved in the most delicate and complex of matters. The ones where either failure or success meant a possible change in the way most people lived their lives.

Bruno grabbed the second and third reports and laid them out next to the first.

Each report contained information on a case solved and information acquired by the Firm. Separately they were interesting in and of themselves, but put them together...

World-changing.

Edwards and Morales's magnificent genetic engineering and mind control had been revolutionary.

Hiroto's nanotechnology was cunning.

And then there was the adopted son he had called Adam. Nearly twenty years had gone by since he discovered Adam and his people. Learned about all they could do. Coveted their abilities.

Bruno faced his computer and began melding the information from all three reports, preparing the documents necessary to create the special project that would incorporate the most viable elements from all three into something amazing.

He worked through the night and into the morning, so caught up in his zeal that neither hunger nor fatigue registered.

And when Bruno was done, he gave it a name.

Genesis.

He already had Adam. He needed to find an Eve.

Once he did, a new race would arise and change the course of mankind.

THE DISH

Where authors give you the inside scoop!

♥ ♥ ♥ ♥ ♥ ♥ ♥ ♥ ♥ ♥ ♥ ♥ ♥ ♥ ♥ ♥

From the desk of Roxanne St. Claire

Dear Reader,

I'm the youngest of five, a position of little power but great benefits. Yes, it meant I got the car floor on road trips (seriously, the floor!) but that position also allowed me to reap the rewards of parental guilt for sometimes treating #5 as an afterthought. On my tenth birthday, that meant the ultimate gift for a budding writer: a typewriter. I think I've had my fingers on a keyboard ever since.

So when I decided to launch a new romantic suspense series, I knew I wanted to anchor the stories around a big family. I hoped to translate the always-fascinating sibling dynamics into complex relationships and unforgettable characters. Since I married into an Italian family, I'd been given a window into one of the most colorful of all cultures, and choosing that background for my characters was a natural move. But this couldn't be an ordinary Italian family, since I like extraordinary characters. To work in my stories, they'd have to be fearless, protective, risk-taking, rule-breaking, wave-making heroes and heroines, willing to take chances to save lives. Oh, and the guys must be blistering hot, and the ladies? Well, we like them a little on the feisty side.

Thus, the Guardian Angelinos were born. They are the five siblings of the Boston-based Rossi family and their two Italian-born cousins, Vivi and Zach Angelino. The security and investigation firm these two blended families form is

created in the first book, EDGE OF SIGHT. When soon-
to-be law student Samantha Fairchild witnesses a murder in
the wine cellar of the restaurant where she works and the
professional hit man has her face on tape, she seeks help
from her friend, investigative reporter Vivi Angelino. Sam
gets the protection she needs, only it comes in the form of
big, bad, sexy Army Ranger Zach Angelino...who stole her
heart during a lusty interlude three years earlier, then went
off to war and never contacted her again.

I had fun with Zach and Sam, and just as much fun with
the extended family of renegade crime-fighters. One of my
favorite characters is eighty-year-old Uncle Nino, who is
grandfather to the Rossi kids and great-uncle to the Angelinos. He joins the Guardian Angelinos with typical Italian
passion and gusto, carrying a spatula instead of a Glock, and
keeping them all in ziti and good spirits. Oh, and Uncle Nino
is a mean puzzle solver, a trait that comes in handy on some
special investigations. But what he does best is Sunday
Gravy, a delicious, hearty meat dinner in mouthwatering red
sauce that the family gathers to enjoy at the end of a hard
week of saving lives and solving crimes. He's agreed to share
his secret recipe, just for my readers...

Uncle Nino's Sunday Gravy

Ingredients

- 1–2 pound piece of lean beef (eye of round)
- 1–2 pounds of lean pork (spare ribs)
- 2 pounds of hot or sweet Italian sausages
- 4 tbs. olive oil
- 4–5 garlic cloves, sliced
- 1–2 Spanish onions, chopped
- Pinch of dried chili flakes (optional)

- Pinch of sugar
- 1 can tomato paste
- 2 26 oz cans whole, peeled San Marzano tomatoes
- 2 cups dry red wine
- 1 tsp dried thyme
- 1 tsp dried oregano
- ½ cup torn fresh basil leaves
- Salt and pepper to taste

Instructions

1. Cut and trim the meats into smaller pieces; halve the sausages, cut eye of round in four sections
2. Heat olive oil in large pan or Dutch oven (deep, heavy casserole) over medium heat
3. Sear meats in hot olive oil until golden brown; may be done in batches and removed from pan, set aside
4. Sauté onions in same the same pan until translucent
5. Add garlic and continue to sauté until garlic turns golden (spicy Italians—and these guys are—add the chili flakes here)
6. Add tomato paste and constantly stir until paste reaches rich, rusty color
7. Add thyme and oregano and stir
8. Deglaze the pan with red wine, using spatula to scrape all bits of charred meat (Uncle Nino says this is the key to success) until reduced by half
9. Crush whole, peeled tomatoes (by hand!), then add to sauce
10. Season sauce with salt and pepper and—this one from Grandma Rossi in the old country—a pinch or two sugar to balance the acidity of the tomatoes
11. Add seared meat into the sauce and simmer for two hours, stirring occasionally

12. Serve over pasta (Uncle Nino recommends rigatoni)
13. Sprinkle fresh basil on top just before serving

(Note: with one pound of pasta, this recipe serves six. Hungry heroes may want more to keep up their stamina, so feel free to add homemade meatballs. Sorry, but Nino's recipe for meatballs remains a family secret. Stay tuned for future books to unlock that and many more mysteries.)

Mangia!

Roxanne St. Claire

www.roxannestclaire.com

♥ ♥ ♥ ♥ ♥ ♥ ♥ ♥ ♥ ♥ ♥ ♥ ♥ ♥ ♥ ♥

From the desk of Caridad Pineiro

Dear Friends,

I want to thank you for the marvelous reception you gave to SINS OF THE FLESH! Your many letters and reviews were truly appreciated and I hope you will enjoy this next book in the Sins series—STRONGER THAN SIN—even more.

From the moment that Mick's sister, Dr. Liliana Carrera, walked onto the scene in the first book, I knew she had to get her own story. I fell in love with her caring nature, her loyalty to her brother and her inner strength. There was no doubt in my mind that any story where she was the heroine would be emotionally compelling and filled with passion.

Of course, such an intense and determined heroine demanded not only a sexy hero, but a strong one. A man capable of great love, but who needs to rediscover the hero within himself.

Jesse Bradford immediately came to mind. Inspired by the many sexy surfer types I encounter on my walks along the beach, Jesse was born and bred on the Jersey Shore. A former football player who had to leave the game he loves due to a crippling bone disease, he is a man who has lost his way, but is honorable, caring and loyal. Jesse just needs to meet the right woman to guide him back to the right path in his life.

Together Jesse and Liliana will face great danger from a group of scientists who have genetically engineered Jesse, as well as the FBI Agents entrusted with his care. The action is fast-paced and will keep you turning the pages as you root for these two to find a way to be together!

If you want to find out more about the real life Jersey Shore locations in STRONGER THAN SIN, please visit my website at www.caridad.com where you can check out my photo gallery or my Facebook page at www.facebook.com/caridad.pineiro.author@Caridad Pineiro!

Wishing you all the best!

♥ ♥ ♥ ♥ ♥ ♥ ♥ ♥ ♥ ♥ ♥ ♥ ♥ ♥ ♥ ♥ ♥

From the desk of R.C. Ryan

Dear Reader,

My family and friends know that I'm obsessively neat and organized. I work best when my desk is clean, my office tidied, my mind clear of all the distracting bits and pieces that go into being part of a large and busy family.

And so it is with my manuscripts. When I created the McCord family and started them on their hunt for their ancestors' lost fortune, I had to find a satisfying ending to each cousin's story, while still keeping a few tantalizing threads aside, to tempt my readers to persevere through this series until the very end.

My editor remarked that, until reading MONTANA GLORY, she hadn't even been aware that the family needed the balance of another generation. Cal and Cora provided the narration for much of the family's history, and a steady anchor for these three very different cousins. Jesse, Wyatt and Zane provided enough rugged male charm to stir the hearts of even the most unflappable female. The women they love brought excitement and fresh flavor into the family dynamic. But it was four-year-old Summer who changed each member of this fascinating household in some way. It is the ultimate gift of a child. They touch our lives, and we are forever changed.

In MONTANA GLORY, I was free to delve even deeper into the McCord family's history to reveal long-held secrets. I made a point to reveal a bit more about Cal, Cora, and the things that shaped them and the other members of this family. And, I hope, we learn things about ourselves in the process.

I hope you fell in love with this diverse, fascinating family as much as I did while writing their stories. And I hope you're as satisfied with the ending as I am. Like I said, tidy, organized, with all the loose ends neatly tied up. I'm a sucker for a happy ending.

Happy Reading!

R. C. Ryan

www.ryanlangan.com

Want to know more about romances at Grand Central Publishing and Forever? Get the scoop online!

GRAND CENTRAL PUBLISHING'S ROMANCE HOMEPAGE

Visit us at www.hachettebookgroup.com/romance for all the latest news, reviews, and chapter excerpts!

NEW AND UPCOMING TITLES

Each month we feature our new titles and reader favorites.

CONTESTS AND GIVEAWAYS

We give away galleys, autographed copies, and all kinds of fun stuff.

AUTHOR INFO

You'll find bios, articles, and links to personal websites for all your favorite authors—and so much more!

THE BUZZ

Sign up for our monthly romance newsletter, and be the first to read all about it!